# Sam 'n' Ella 'n' Wullie too

To

My editor and pal —
PAM

Love Norrie
29ᵗʰ oct. 2010

# Sam 'n' Ella 'n' Wullie too

"Happy days are here again,
Tra – la – la – la..."

Norrie McKinlay

Spiderwize

# Sam 'n' Ella 'n' Wullie too

Spiderwize
3 The Causeway
Kennoway
Kingdom of Fife
KY8 5JU
Scotland  UK

www.spiderwize.com

This is a work of fiction. Names, characters and incidents are products of the author's imagination. Any resemblance to persons living or dead is entirely coincidental.

The views expressed in this work are solely those of the author and do not necessarily reflect the views of the publisher, and the publisher hereby disclaims any responsibility for them.

ISBN: 978-1-907294-76-1

To my long-suffering wife – Pam

# *Table of Contents*

# CHAPTER ONE

## THE FLITTING

The day outside is blearily overcast, blearily oppressive and blearily hung with bleary gloom, the gloom adding another dimension to my already depressed mood as I stand here looking out my lounge window at the living theatre I've enjoyed for the last fifteen years; now for the very last time. A sad, doom-laden moment in my ever increasing turbulent life. I've been posted lookout for the removal vans. Yes vans. We're flitting.

Moving house - to those unfamiliar with the local Glasgow vernacular. Not my decision. You'll soon find out whose.

On reflection I'm going to miss old Senga across the street, totally balootered, pole dancing every pension day round the lamppost outside her house having spent the best part of her day, not to mention the best part of her pension, in the Drookit Duck. Then there was Davie, regularly hanging upside down entangled in his TV aerial; yet another of his hang-gliding practice manoeuvres gone wrong. And of course Les who, late in life, having decided to adopt the female side of his name now struts his stuff in designer stubble, tattoos, and three inch stilettos. Finally, but by no means least the voluptuous mini skirted Betty "Boobs", my next door neighbour, bending from the waist down weeding the lawn showing off her - gardening prowess. Whoops! I almost forgot Big Derek – But hold on a

1

sec, I think we're about to witness a live happening. I've just spotted the self same Big Derek turning into the road at high speed on two wheels, tyres screeching in protest. I have to close my eyes as he just misses Nan the lollipop lady, whose deadly swipe at Dek with the lollipop misses causing old Archie, the streets octogenarian, to do a miraculous "Fosby flop" over a garden wall to save his head being cleft from its body. Brakes protest in agony, rubber burns twin furrows in the tarmac as Big Dek brings the four wheel drive to a stop on its nose. No sooner have the back wheels re-entered earth's gravity than the big man's out the door. His cat, Tiger, sunning itself atop the gate post, realising from several previous experiences the danger it's in, takes off into the hinterland. This can only mean one thing, a bad day at the golf and I can tell by the body language it's going to be celebrated in grand style. He slams the driver's door leaving the vehicle shuddering like a well skelpt jelly. Next the tailgate is violently ripped nearly off its hinges. Out comes the golf bag. One, two, three deadly kicks to its solar plexus then, wait for it, this is the good bit guessing what club is going to get its comeuppance. Dek's hand hovers over the bag - yes, yes it's going to be the old favourite - the putter. Ripping it out of the bag he lofts it high and with his usual diabolical swing, based on the twirling rotor blades of a geriatric helicopter, brings it earthwards to shatter against the pavement edge. The poor putter's head twirls and finally hangs its head in shame. The final coup de grace is Big Dek's twenty stone stomp on it. That's Dek destroyed at least a dozen putters that I know of this year. Punching the air with his mighty fist, you would've thought he'd just won the Open Golf Championship, he continues into his house in total vindicated tranquillity. What did I think of it all? Well I'm no expert but personally I thought Dek's hands were too high at the top of his backswing.

You couldn't make it all up could you? All sadly about to be past memories.

I've digressed a bit. How did I get into this situation? It's not going to be easy to explain but I'll try my best. We'll start with a bit of background. My name is Sammy Robb, married to wife Ella for twenty of my forty three years. She's still a very attractive looking woman, currently a brunette at last sighting. This could of course change as I speak. At present we live in a bungalow in Bishopbriggs, on the outskirts of Glasgow, but this, as you will now have gathered, is about to change imminently.

Oh yes, I almost forgot, as you would too if she was yours, we have an offspring - the dreaded Karen. According to her mother she's in Afghanistan doing charity work in her gap year from university. Personally I think she's more likely to have joined the Taliban in their fight against Western Imperialist regression - her words not mine. I base this on the fact, gleaned from one of her tutors, that she tried unsuccessfully to resurrect the Baader Meinhof gang in her first year at university. It goes without saying that Ella holds me responsible for Karen's rebellious bent on account of my failure to pay the TV licence - more on that one later.

For all this the marriage is still sound - the sound of Ella's voice. However, to get to the nub of the matter, Ella's worst attribute, in my humble opinion, apart from her vicious temper and total failure to be reasonable, is her inability to be content with her lot.

I understand it's called social climbing but whatever it's called, it's responsible for my present predicament. To explain, Charlie, her brother, my slimey low life brother- in- law, is coming back to Scotland after a period of twenty five years - permanently.

Now this replaces my previous worst nightmare - the resurrection of Ella's mother.

Why, you might be wondering, do I not like him. All will be revealed later.

It would appear that Charlie is an investment banker, a bastion in Uncle Sam's financial world. I got Ella to confirm the word "banker" for when I knew him he certainly was something very similar sounding. Incidentally, could that be the same financial world, complete with its bankrupt institutions, that introduced the rest of the world to "toxic mortgages and credit crunch" et al and landed us all in the shit with *their* debts?  Call me cynical, or what, but with Charlie as one of their leading investment bankers it comes as no surprise. Putting my own prejudices aside, the skinny weed, an apology for manhood, is apparently so stinking rich he's just rolling in greenbacks. So nothing new there then, just another thieving financial asshole retiring, in this case, to his homeland to spend all his mugs' hard earned cash.

Nothing earth shattering so far. That is, in so far as if you were dealing with a sane person. But, in my humble opinion yet again and with deep regret, I have to inform you that Ella should have been sectioned years ago. I still can't understand how my anonymous letters throughout the years to the Mental Health Board, have been ignored.

There I go digressing again - but what follows is good reason to doubt her sanity. A few months ago, prior to my learning of Charlie's return, I was out in the back garden picking up empty lager and beer cans and various left over evidence – including a bra, from the previous evening's barbeque garden party. I'm reflecting on the ample size of the bra and who might just have removed it when the genteel summons of Ella's voice comes floating through the airwaves inviting me to have a tete-a-tete.

'Sammy! Get yerself in here.' She has such a poetic way with words.

'Yes, Ella dear, how may I be of assistance?' I reply, having the satisfaction of giving her the finger, out of sight of course, as I enter the kitchen.

'You can start wie cutting out your usual sarcasm,' she growls.

I'm about to exert my masculinity but before I can - I'm ordered,

'Sit!' A finger being violently pointed to the kitchen stool. I should at this stage point out that this finger which I have christened Kung Foo carries a dangerous weapon classification and is to be avoided at all costs.

'Yes?' I query, perching nonchalantly on the stool, pretending not to be worried, but only because I'm within easy escape of the open back door .

'We're moving.'

'Grrreat. Is that as in moving - *the furniture, the bowels* or...' Too late, I realise that's not the right thing to say as she moves in a swift pincer movement to cut off my escape.

'We're moving house. H-O-U-S-E. Got that, knobhead?'

'Why?' I manfully reply, whilst looking for another escape route.

'Why? Why? he asks. Because my brother Charles is coming home from America tae stay.'

'You didn't tell me that,' I manage to croak, totally dumfounded and now sinking fast into a complete state of shock. All my nightmares rolled into one.

'Aye, I did. I'm telling you now.' Ella logic.

'So what if he is coming home. Why do we have to move?' I sullenly reply, still reeling from the shock.

'So what if he is,' she mimics, 'I'll - tell - you - why. Because he's no coming all that distance tae live in - a - rabbit - hutch.'

'Well, he used tae live in worse.'

I refer to when Ella and Charlie were brought up in a tenement with no wally close. Not like me. I came from a wally close. You were somebody if you lived in a wally close. To the uninitiated a wally close, in the Glasgow vernacular, is the tiled wall entrance to a tenement dwelling. Depending on your circumstances in the city these could be, and many still are, works of art. My close was plain white tiles but with a fancy dado tile. Ella's and Charlie's - plain cement render. No tiles. Mind you there's more to it than that. I have to admit I'm not from Maryhill like them or Wullie, who you have as yet to meet, I'm from the the posher North Kelvinside (North Kelly) neighbouring district. There I go digressing again. Where were we? Yes.

'Then's then. Now's now.' More Ella logic, snarled at me through gritted teeth.

Right! Enough of this nonsense. Time to assert my masculine authority. With my hand raised high in protest and in my best authoritative voice I cut her short, 'Now look here, Ella. Charlie's not likely to be living with us for ever, is he? Surely with his dough he can go and live in the Hilton until he finds a place of his own. So I ask you again. Why do *we* have to move house to suit him?'

As she advances towards me with that vicious look of intent that I recognise from a thousand previous encounters I realise once again my masculinity might not be all I thought it was.

'Don't you ever, "now look here Ella" me… you nyaff,' she spits out with her customary venom as the Kung Foo finger thrusts out with the sole aim to maim.

It's fractionally too late as with nimble dexterity I didn't know I possessed, I manage to get the kitchen table between us. I remember the days when we used this table for other more pleasurable purposes. I wonder if I suggested a table-edger… Dream on Sammy.

'Who me?' I reply, coming out of my daydream.

'Aye. You. I've had enough of you talking back, ya scunner.' Her thrusting deadly digit just out of reach of my nose. 'First things first. His name's Charles, not Charlie. Got that. Secondly he's my big brother, my only living relative and if he wants tae live with us that's all right with me. And *you* as well - Sammy boy. So we're moving…. Finito.'

Thankfully, the finger retracts as I was getting cross-eyed staring at it. So there you are, I'm moving just to put on a show for bloody Charlie. To be fair to her, she's grudgingly informed me that my new stomping ground is going to be the very posh and pleasant suburb of Bearsden, just outside the city boundary. How did this happen without my knowledge? Truthfully, I haven't a clue. Nobody tells me anything.

After all *it's only a mansion* she's bought. However, if I was to hazard a guess I would suspect that my slimeball brother-in-law Charlie would be involved in it right up to his oxters. Frankly, Bearsden needs Ella like a hole in the head.

With that I'm rudely awakened from my reverie.  KER-UMP! The lounge door bounces off the wall surviving another Ella'va attack on it.

'Sammy!' she roars. 'Get your arse into gear. The vans are turning into the road.'

'Yes, dear,' I reply tugging my forelock and at the same time giving her the finger. All as usual behind her back as I move into the hall to open the door.

'Robb?' enquires the removal man, with a fag dangling out his mouth.

'Aye. That's me.'

'Good. Widnae like to be "robb-in" the wrong house.'

Everyone wants to be a comedian these days but in this jokers case it's about to be short lived. Ella has just burst into the hall. She hasn't as yet, quite mastered the art of arriving. She's got to burst into or explode into places. Elbowing me aside, she starts into him.

'You. Fag out. Nae smoking in my house.' The dreaded finger stabbing under the poor sod's nose. 'Aye, you,' as he looks around in panic for matey help.' In there. NOW! - I want tae personally supervise the packing of my Lladro.'

'I don't do the packing I'm the drive.....' He's no chance. She's in full flow.

'NOW,' roars Ella pointing to the room. With shoulders slouched and with the hands that are about to pack Lladro trembling, he looks towards me for help. I ignore him. It's every - man - for - himself day in this house.

On Ella's instructions two enormous pantechnicon behemoths are sitting outside. We'll be lucky to fill one. After all, as I've said before, we only live in a bungalow. However, I'm on to her little game. The arrival of these two giants, at our new abode, will make it look good to her posh new nosey neighbours. More importantly I've managed to rescue Seamus, my garden gnome, from the bin. He's been classified as socially undesirable for Bearsden. Lucky him. Wish I had.

The vans are packed and ready to go. Ella signals the off, as with a, "Forward ho, the wagons" hand action from her car she leads the cavalcade into the promised land. I will follow eventually when I've done my sad farewells

Well, with a heavy heart, I've now said my fond farewells to my neighbours. Senga has promised me she'll come to see me and do a pole dance. That should liven things up a bit in Bearsden but I know it won't happen - sad to say. Dec says we must have a game of golf again. I said yes, but that won't happen either, I'm glad to say. My nerves couldn't stand it. Nan, the lollipop lady, says I can lick her lollipops anytime. Now she tells me. Davie says the next time he's up in the Campsies hang-gliding he'll drop in to see me. I've asked him to give me prior warning so I can remove the TV aerial. Les cooed "what a darling I was" and wanted to kiss me goodbye. I had to decline; no way I was getting beardy. Betty "Boobs" says she'll come and see me. 'Anytime,' I reply, returning her ample sized bra. I'm really going to miss those barbies. They were fun.

Nothing left now except to bid the whole street a fond adieu with a blown kiss. Call me cissy, I don't care. I love you street; always will. That's it I'm off. Don't look back.

All this and Blair still in Downing Street. How bad can life get? Little was I to know.

# CHAPTER TWO

## THE NEW PLACE

The removal, some two weeks ago now, went reasonably smoothly by our standards. The bloke assigned to the Lladro packing, if you remember, under Ella's supervision, is being treated for extreme post traumatic stress disorder. Of the remaining crew, after minor skirmishes with Ella, one appeared to sport a swollen multi-coloured eye socket, whilst another ended up walking in a crab like gait. The remainder have signed on the sick. I received a letter from the removal firm thanking me for my custom and wishing me a very, very, long tenure at my new address. That was a nice gesture.

As I get ready for work, I find myself looking out my new bedroom window. I can tell from previous years of experience, there's not going to be a "theatre of life" out this window – "morgue" would be more appropriate as our arrival in the avenue has reduced the average age of the residents to a mere eighty odd. The bedroom is part of a massive stone built Victorian detached villa with umpteen rooms and an enormous garage all set in gardens the size of Hampden Park. It must have cost Ella and Charlie a fortune.

How has this affected Ella? Well I can tell you that there's never been a more enthusiastic prospective member of, "To – the – manor – born" brigade than Ella. She's joined every known association and charity in the Bearsden area other than the Happy Widows. I suspect she can't wait to join that as well. Baking cakes and making jam seems to have become a cottage industry out of the kitchen. Apparently that's what associations and charities do. I should mention that everything has been sweetness and light for these last two weeks. That translates into there only being four attempted brutal attacks on my personage. Further, we've only moved two miles from Bishopbriggs and it appears to have affected her accent. It's now like living with a BBC news reader. Well that is before the present crop with all their regional accents that "naebody can understaund". I've given up paying the licence fee in protest at these regional assaults on my eardrums. As I told that last bloke from the TV detector van, I've gone for the Freeview option. He tried to tell me it's not free. Who's he kidding? I told him in no uncertain terms, free's free in my book. That gave him something to think about. It would appear I'm due in court next week to sort out this little misunderstanding. This minor hiccup, according to Ella, is where Karen gets her rebellious trait. Little does Ella know that the BBC is high on Karen's hit list, being classified as the mouthpiece of the Establishment and an enemy of the oppressed. At the price they're asking for a licence tae hear them espouse the constant virtues of New Labour I couldn't agree more with her.

Well that's me ready for work. Looking at my watch I discover I can squeeze in a quick practice session in the back garden trying out my new golf swing before breakfast. I'm excited as I've just read in this months, "Golf for Duffers," about the bionic thumb method. This, after all these years of fruitless endeavour is definitely it - *"The Secret"*. I've just got to the top of my new bionic thumb backswing, which might take a bit of getting used to since I appear to be strangling myself, when the peaceful tranquillity of the morning is shattered by the dulcet tones of Ella.

'SAMMY!' My whole body shakes and quivers. It's like being trapped inside Big Ben, as her command summons me to the kitchen. I enter via the back door making sure to leave it wide open. Always plan your escape

'Sammy, have you given any thought to upgrading your car?' conveyed in her new Bearsden posh accent. No surprise here, I've been expecting this.

'Not as yet, Ella'

'Don't you think it's time you did?'

'Why?'

Taking her usual umbrage to my use of the innocuous query, she snarls, 'Because that load of junk out in the drive, is a disgrace tae the street.'

With her demure posh accent gone, a war-footing now exists.

'That load of junk as you call it happens to be this week's star buy, a five year old, top of the range, Ford Focus GTI.'

'Sammy-I-don't-think-you're-listening-to-me,' said with an emphatic threat in each word.

'Yes I am Ella, honest - hanging on your every word.'

'Don't get me started, you nyaff.  Now pin back your lugs and listen tae me real good. All the cars in the neighbours' drives have quality wheels ….'

I interrupt her. On a war-footing this is perfectly allowable. 'The Focus *does* have quality wheels. They're "Smarty" alloys - you cannae get smarter than that.'

'Don't try to get smarty wie me, smart arse. You know what I mean. The word here is *quality*, not wheels. Not as if you'd know the meaning of quality.'

'Ah! But that's where you're wrong Ella, my dear. I do…. I married you.'

'Right, that does it. I've had enough of your facetious crap.'

I instantly recognise the strike pose. A nimble pirouette points me in the direction of the open door. What did I tell you about forward planning? I'm through it and going like the clappers towards the garage. Following me, comes the booming sonic waves of Ella,

*'I'm not picking Charles up in that load of scrap. You've until Friday tae get it sorted out, dae you hear me?'* This was followed by the kitchen door getting a brutal Ella'va attack on it. I'll say one thing for those Victorians; they knew how to make hinges.

On reaching the relative safety of the garage but with all senses still on red alert, I bring my escape to a juddering halt. There, with its feet sticking out the rubbish bin is, Seamus, my gnome. I suspected Seamus was a casualty, as he, along with the plastic wishing-well, had gone missing from where I'd located them - in the middle of the front lawn. Apparently plastic wishing-wells and gnomes are gnot de riguer in Bearsden.

So far I haven't mentioned what I do for a living, have I? Well, I own a second hand car business in the Maryhill area of Glasgow - home of the mighty Partick Thistle F.C. or "The Jags" as they are affectionately known. I'm, so to speak, tied up with them – I sponsor their boot laces.

Right, enough of this frivolity. Down to business.

I trade as Sammy Robb Motors - Maryhill, *"The name you can trust."* Nobody can dispute this fact since Mary Hill's been dead for yonks. My niche market is your average family car, popular makes, quick sell, no- guarantee - out - the - door vehicles, a formula that has seen me build the business into a nice wee earner.

I don't, however, deal in rich boys toys, like Mercs, Jags or Beamers. So unfortunately, it looks like I'll need to go to the trade to get something of quality to keep Ella quiet.

I hate dealing with the trade, they're such a dishonest bunch of rogues and charlatans; they'd shaft their granny for a groat.

'Right, Seamus, let's hit the road tae gnomeland,' I say, lobbing him into the passenger seat. I suddenly jolt ridged, Ella's last words have just sunk in to my befuddled brain, *"I'm not picking Charles up in that load of scrap."*

It can only mean one thing, Charlie's on his way. With a handbrake start, tyres burning and screeching in protest, I zoom out of the driveway scaring literally the crap out of Benjie, old Mrs Watson's dog from across the road, as it is about to leave its calling card on the lawn. Serves it right, it's a pal of Ella.

It's no wonder people leave their clothes on the beach and pretend to disappear.

Pulling into my business premises, a gap site between the grey tenement buildings just off Maryhill Road, I park the Focus in the forecourt. Sitting back, lighting a cigar, an ethereal calm descends over me. This is my, virtually, Ella proof sanctuary. The name, Ella, is forbidden on the premises by order of the management. Finishing the cigar, I pick up Seamus and head for my office. I'm met at the door with a light sensuous kiss by the lovely, delectable, gorgeous Vera. I don't know how it happened but I seem to have acquired her on my travels. She's my secretary, my confidante, my lifeline to sanity, my, my......well you know.

'Good morning, Sammy. How are you this fine morning?' delivered in that husky, smoldering, well educated voice that sends shivers down my spine.

'All the better for seeing you, Vera, my dear.'

'Who's your little friend?'

'This, Vera, is Seamus, a victim of Ella-ethnic cleansing'

'What a lovely little chap. Shall we get him a fairy for company?'

'I'll ask Waldo – the next time I see him,' I say with an affected limp wrist.

'Oh! You are hilarious, Sammy. Absolutely hilarious.'

I'm never quite sure whether she's taking the mickey but with her looks who cares?

'Where's Eck?' My gormless young salesman.

'He took a trade-in to the market, Sammy.'

'How long ago?'

'Five mins max.' That I'm pleased to hear, as a slight surge in my lower DNA is happening, as is usual on seeing her. She hands me the morning mail then glides lithely, oozing sex, into her office. The mail is surprisingly light, no writs, no threats, no glossy windows from HMG's offices of torture: just bills to add to the monthly raffle.

As I set off towards the garage to see Hughie, my long suffering mechanic, Vera enters, 'Nice cup of tea for you, Sammy. Helps get the day started. What say you?'

'Just seeing you, gets me started.' I can feel those DNA dots starting their discs-a-go-go dance.

'Oh!' Sammy, you say the sweetest things,' purred as she puts down the tea and uplifts the mail from the out tray. In doing so a letter floats to the floor. In her effort to pick it up, her skirt or what there is of it, rides up her shapely leg exposing the giggly band on her sheer black seamed stockings. You know the old adage, once past the giggly you're laughing. Old but true. By this time my DNA dots have gone into complete meltdown.

'Time for a little dictation, Miss Richards'

'You know me, Mister Robb, I love taking things down,' purrs my ever accommodating secretary.

I turn Seamus, who has taken up residency on my window cill, to face outwards into the forecourt and my hung photo of Mrs Thatcher to face the wall. Decency now prevails.

Ten minutes later, straightening my tie, I set off for the workshop.

'Hughie!' I shout, on entering the workshop.

'Over here, Sammy.' The voice echoing from under the hoist. Hughie, ducks out from under the hoist, presses the button and the hoist starts its downward motion.

Emerging into view is a Jaguar car. This one's the real deal, finished in British racing green with cream leather interior. A beauty, absolutely minted, and winking at me.

Sex on alloys.

'Morning, Sammy, how's you?'

'Just grrrreat.'

'I'll bet,' says Hughie, with a hint of, "I - know - what - you're – up – to" playing around his mouth.

'Where's Rab?' Hughie's apprentice.

'Sent him down to Nutters scrap yard, for a spare part.'

'Not for the Jag?'

'No way, Sammy. It's absolutely minted.' Hughie has just confirmed my visual.

'Well what's wrong with it then?'

'It was brought in with a rattle. Turns out it's just a loose exhaust. It's going to be a cracking buy for the next owner.'

'Who owns it?'

'Dugald.'

'Dugald, four eyes?'

'The self same one, Sammy.'

Dugald drinks in our local, Rileys, up on the main road - a mere stone's throw away. He's as blind as a bat and shouldn't really be driving.

'Is it up for grabs?'

'Yeah, I think so. He tells me his trouble and strife wants him to get rid of it because he cannae see beyond the bonnet any more.' My early warning system has kicked in and is twitching violently. It never fails.

'When's he coming to pick it up?'

'Don't know, Sammy, but I do know he's up in Rileys playing doms.'

'Now that's put a notion into my head.'

'I'll bet it has, Sammy.'

'Hughie, I'm surprised at you. Would I take advantage of an auld guy like Dugald?'

'Nah, not your style, Sammy,' said with what I suspect to be more than just a tinge of sarcasm, concluding, 'By the way, dae yourself a favour an get rid of that egg on your chin.' This said with a chortle as he disappears under a car.

I shoot my hand downwards to my flies and sure enough they're wide open. Bugger.

# CHAPTER THREE

## THE NEW LANDLADY

As I walk up the street and turn the corner heading for Riley's I bump into Glasgow's favourite Eyetie - Toni. The nearest he's been to Italy is Giovanni's fish and chip shop across the road. He is dressed in his usual garb of pacific blue teddy-boy suit resplendent with black velvet collar, black shirt with white tie, black hat with white band, black suede brothel creepers on his feet, and dark sunglasses or, as he refers to them, "shades".

'How's ita going, Sammy boy?'

'Ita going OK tilla met you, Toni boy.'

'I knowa you no meana that, Sammy. For you, Iva great opportunity.' He stops, looks around furtively, then continues, 'Pst! Sammy, over here.'

I notice for the first time a sandwich board set against Riley's wall with a menu on it. That's funny Riley's don't do meals, I'm thinking. Then Toni reveals all. Another furtive look around, a quick flip of the wrist sees the menu sheet fold over to reveal another sheet underneath. On it are squares forming a pyramid. The squares are advertised at a quid a go. Each square is numbered in its corner, but empty, awaiting the name of some poor gullible mug. After another furtive look around, it's catching this furtive looking as I find myself furtively looking around with him, he whispers conspiratorially, 'Did you clocka that, Sammy?'

'Aye.'

'Whata you think, Sammy?'

'I think - that's known as pyramid selling, Toni, and that's illegal.' What a stupid thing to say. Everything Toni does is illegal.

'That only applya tae them financial scams. They geta us real pyramid sellers a bad name.'

'And this isn't a financial scam?' Another stupid question.

'No, Sammy, I'ma raffling the real McCoy – a chance tae owna a real pyramid.'

'A real pyramid? In Egypt?'

'No Sammy. In Scotland.'

'*In Scotland?*'

'Aye, Sammy, Alexandria.'

'The Alexandria near Loch Lomond?'

'Aye. Sammy, aye.'

'And how'd that happen?'

'Well, thisa pharaoh bloke - Tooty Cameroon - he meeta this Glesca girl at the sand dancing....'

'Wait a minute, Toni. When was this?'

'Thousands of years ago.'

'Thousands of years ago in Glasgow?' I wonder if the tourist board knows about this.

'Aye, Sammy, aye. You gona listen an stopa interrupting me.Thisa pharaoh bloke, he falla in love wie the girl. She die. He builda pyramid ina her memory.'

'How did this pharaoh bloke, Tooty whats-his-name, end up in Glasgow?'

'Sammy, Sammy,' shaking his head in bewilderment, '......where your Scottish history? When the Egyptians invada Scotland, ofa course.'

'Ofa course. Stupid me, Toni, fancy forgetting a thing like that. Here's your quid.'

'Grassy mila, Sammy.'

'A very detchy, Toni.'

Another one of his hare-brained ideas doomed to failure. Who in their right mind would buy into such an obvious scam? Mind you, as I've oft commented on mugs, there's one born every minute. So why did I buy one, if I'm so smart? Because I love a trier and, in Toni's case, there's nobody more trying than him. Apart from that, I thought the story, in itself, was well worth the quid. Who knows, I might end up being the new pharaoh of Alexandria. As I enter Riley's, Toni's voice drifts over my shoulder.

'Whata number dae you wanta, Sammy?'

'Any one, but the winner, Toni.' Now that *is* a racing certainty.

I enter Riley's through its magnificent oak swing doors with their etched glass logo of a long gone brewer. It's a grand old pub, a total rarity, still in brewer's control, but never been altered, or by the looks of it, decorated since its establishment. The paintwork is faded and peeling, the wallpaper varnished, at least I think it's varnished, you can't tell for the layers of nicotine.

Nicotine - now that was in the good old days, when you went to the pub for your smoke with your pint before the present bunch of maladjusted, arrogant, incompetents forced through an ill-thought out ban on smoking, allegedly on behalf of the BMA (British Medical Association to some - Bloody Meddling Assholes, to others). I mean, for god's sake, a pub's a pub - yes? Logic or what? Calm down, Sammy, calm down, watch that high blood pressure, you're only a voter after all. Voters don't get votes on trivialities like this, or hanging or European interference in our affairs or immigration or..... We know what's best for you, and in any case it's all in the interest of National Security. Just like the non disclosure of their expenses.

Sorry, I've digressed big time, but be honest, is there anything left we can do without them sticking their self - righteous nose in it? Bring back Maggie, she'll sort them out.

Pass me my "Elf and Safety" helmet. I'm off for a game of dangerous dominoes.

Right, got that out my system. As you enter the main body of the pub, you are confronted with a superbly ornate carved mahogany bar topped by a marble counter. Brass footrails, no stools, standing only allowed on the polished oak floor. Circular cast iron columns hold up three storeys of tenement above. I love it. It reminds me of one of those posh London clubs but without the poncey members. Forget that bit about a posh club, I've just had a reality check by way of grievous bodily harm to my earhole.

'Aye, whit dae you want?' This from a harridan, hands on hip, standing behind the bar.

'Who? Me?'

'Aye, you. You think you're something special or what?'

I've never seen her before. In fact we don't see many women in here. That's one of the main attractions. What's happened? Recovering from the shock I growl at the harridan,

'A pint of heavy and a packet of nuts.' I pay her with a fiver. Seconds later the beer is slammed down in front of me. Half of the contents do a loop the loop before splashing down on the marble counter top, followed by my change and nuts which she lobs into the spilled beer.

As I stand hypnotised watching a river of beer flowing towards me, an experienced hand, gripping a towel, deftly stops its momentum in one practised swoop.

It's Alec the landlord. 'Afternoon Sammy, see you've met the incoming landlady.'

'She's whit?'

'Agnes. She's taking over from me next week.' I'd forgotten Alec was retiring.

'Bloody hell, Alec, for a horrible moment it was like getting served by Ella.'

'Maybe she'll turn out OK…. Agnes, that is.' Even he's heard about, Ella. 'Here let me top that up,' continues Alec, picking up the half empty glass. On his return, he informs me that decrepit old Jock and dozy Mary will still be working there.

'Where - in - the - name - of - the- wee - man, did they dig her up from? The Gestapo?'

I retort, still seething, as I throw out my right hand in a Nazi salute with left hand fore - finger under nose and clicking of heels.

Alec laughs, 'I'd watch yourself, Sammy. She used tae be a bouncer at the Barrowland.' Looking past him, I note that I'm getting the evil eye stare from the camp kommandant.

I can see future problems developing. We'll need to get an escape tunnel started.

The cacophony of babble and animated antics that usually eminates from the bar is somewhat subdued. An eerie, shocked, atmosphere prevails. This bodes ill. However, I'll need to worry about the escape tunnel later because I've just spotted Dugald playing dominoes with one of the cast iron columns.

'Dugald.'

'That you, Sammy?' replies Dugald, addressing the cast iron column.

'Yep. Why don't you put your specs on?'

'Have I no got them on, Sammy,' he mutters, digging into his jacket pocket and producing a pair with lenses like milk bottle bottoms.

Putting them on he continues, 'Ah! That's better. Where's the bloke I was playing?'

'He's just left.' Tell him anything, it makes life easier and preserves your sanity.

'That's a pity just when I was on a winning streak. Dae you fancy a game?'

'Thanks Dugald, some other time. I'm a bit pushed for time right now.' A night at home with toothache would be fun compared to playing dominoes with Dugald.

'Look, Dugald,' I've got to get down to the nitty gritty with him otherwise this inane claptrap will go on all day. '…..Hughie tells me you're thinking about selling the Jag.'

'Aye, Sammy, the old eyesight's shot. I cannae see beyond the bonnet.'

'It's a long bonnet right enough, on them Jags. What about one of these new generation designs with the sloping bonnets that gives you a good view of the road … and even pedestrians?'

'Funny you should say that, Sammy. The wife was on about that too.' Bingo. I'm in.

'Tell you the truth, Dugald, I fancy the Jag for myself. Would you be interested in doing a deal?'

'Well, Sammy, nothing personal right, it's just that I was thinking of a private sale.'

'Why do that?'

'I think I'll get more for it, that way.'

'Listen, Dugald, have you read the morning papers?' Inspiration has at last arrived.

'No, Sammy, wie my eyesight, reading's not exactly my forte nowadays. Why?'

'Well, Dugald, the Footsie's dropping like a lead balloon due to the increase in oil prices. And petrol's gone right through the roof at the same time. It's all due to them oil sheiks stuffing the readies intae their hip pockets.'

'Is that no disgusting, Sammy?'

'It certainly is Dugald - for you. Because you cannae give away big cars, never mind sell them.'

'How's that then, Sammy?'

'I've told you. Because they guzzle petrol, leave their carbon footprint all over the place and damage the ozone layer as well.'

'Aye. I can understand all that, Sammy.'

'And, another thing which wasn't mentioned in the news but is a well known secret, the numpties in Westminster intend to savagely increase the road tax on guzzlers.'

'Is that a fact, Sammy?'

'It is indeed, Dugald. So things being as they are, you've no chance of a private sale. Trust me. I know.'

'Well, you should know, Sammy.'

'I do, Dugald. But you're fortunate that I'm in a position to help you.'

'Very fortunate, by the sound of it Sammy.'

'Now, as luck would have it, I've a wee brammer, a low mileage, VW Beetle.'   Should be, I just re-set the mileage yesterday. 'No bonnet to speak of. You can see for miles, er, well in your case that doesn't really matter. How's that grab you, Dugald?'

'Sounds good, Sammy, but I'll need tae speak to the wife.'

'Tell you what Dugald, I'll throw in lifetime servicing.' He can't have long tae go.

'I still think I should talk it over with the wife.'

'Tell you what I'll do, Dugald, I'll fit it with the very latest high-tech, sat-nav, that'll guide you home, tuck you up in bed and make your cocoa.'

'That sounds smashing Sammy. What colour's the car?'

'The latest fashion statement - gently squeezed lemon.'

'You widnae believe it, Sammy, but that's the wife's favourite colour.'

'I've only got the one in that colour, Dugald. Real popular it is. If you want it, it's yours, but as I've said I've only got the one…. provided Eck hasnae sold it.'

'Phone him and tell him not tae. You've got a deal.' We shake on it.

'Your're a hard man to bargain with, Dugald. You've got a barrow load of extras there for nothing. I must be going soft. Come on round to the garage and I'll show you the Beetle and we'll do the paperwork. We can discuss the difference in price, at the same time.'

'You didnae mention a price difference, Sammy.'

'Don't you worry your head about it, Dugald. It'll be to our mutual advantage. Trust me.'

After all I am Sammy Robb – "The name you can trust".

As I turn into the driveway, Ella is out decapitating the weeds that haven't as yet committed suicide, with a wicked looking disembowelling weapon. On seeing the Jag, she runs to greet it with arms wide, but still holding the weapon. Natural instincts prevailing, on seeing the weapon in her hand, I try to escape out the passenger door.

As she opens the driver's door she catches my trailing leg as I'm half way and pins it, with an ankle twisting jerk, under the hand brake. She then moves swiftly round to the passenger door, pulls me out and, and…… hugs and kisses me!

'Sammy, oh! Sammy, what a lovely surprise. It's lovely. I love it. I LOVE YOU.' Another kiss. By this time I'm reeling. Wake up Sammy. This can't be happening.

'Come on in and I'll make you a nice wee cup of tea,' she coos, leading me by the hand into the kitchen. I look longingly at the kitchen table - the same one from all those pleasurable table edgers of years ago. I wonder if she'd care for a quick ....don't push your luck, Sammy boy, settle for the cup of tea while you're still winning. If Ella offers to make you a nice wee cup of tea it's the equivalent of smoking a peace pipe with Sitting Bull. Finishing my tea *and* a biscuit she leads me by the hand upstairs.

It's been a peculiar day to say the least. Life really does confuse me at times.

# CHAPTER FOUR

## THE SECOND COMING

One week has passed. A week in which I've only fallen foul of the Kung Foo finger twice. Unfortunately, one of the times, I was wounded with a dent to my body that I'll possibly have to live with for the rest of my life. Dirty tactics were used, she speared me straight through the morning newspaper when I wasn't on my guard.  Sorry, digressing again. Well, as I was saying, one week later and normal service has been resumed.

'SAMMY!' The house violently shudders.

'Yes, Ella, dear, how may I be of assistance to you?' No forelock tug. She's on her guard. Everything's on red alert. Remember I mentioned Charlie's arrival was imminent? Well, unfortunately, today's the day.

'Right you. Final warning. First, as I'm sick of telling you, his name is Charles O.K?  Not Charlie and definitely not Chuck. Got that? Next, speak when you're spoken to and when you reply try, just for once, to be pleasant. Do not, I repeat, do not be your usual sarcastic asshole self. I'll be listening to your every word. O.K?'

'Yes, Ella, dearest.'

'What, did I just tell you about your sarcasm? Now, did you remember the camcorder?' She wants to record the second coming.

'Yes, Ella, de…'

'Cleaned the car?'

'Yes, Ella. Spotless.'

'Petrol?'

'Yes, Ella. Siphoned from next door's Merc last night.'

'See you – ya scunner,' The Kung Foo finger darts at me. Two paces back smartly takes me out of the maiming zone '....that's what I mean about you. You just <u>canny</u> answer a straight forward question without some sort of supercilious backchat.'

What's up? All I did was tell the truth. If you leave your car out, you're fair game.

'We're leaving in an hour. O.K?'

'Yes, Ella.' She's turned her back so she gets the middle digit. My feel good factor.


We set off on our journey to Glasgow airport which should thankfully take no longer than half an hour.  It was to prove uneventful by our standards - apart from Ella giving me a severe headache with her continuous sniffling and whining into her handkerchief, about bloody Charlie.  Boy - was I grateful to enter the airport's portals.

On looking for short stay parking meters I find they're all taken.

Suddenly Ella says to me, 'I think that man's waving to you.'

I cruise the Jag up to this apparition, dressed in a navy blue uniform with razor cut brim to his hat and obligatory dark reflective glasses, looking to all intents and purposes like a reject from Hill Street blues.

'Hi!, Sammy. Looking for a place to park?'

'Aye, er – er'

'It's me. Callum - Calum from the pub,' drawled, as he removes his dark glasses.

'So it is. Didnae recognise you at first with the uniform and all that. You a traffic warden then?'

'No me, Sammy, nothing to dae wie the Gestapo. I'm front line security. Keeping the nation safe.  Follow me. You can park in our secure car park. I'll get you a pass.'

Front line security, keeping the nation safe. What's the world coming to? He's just out of Barlinnie prison after doing eighteen months for chibbing parking meters. And where do I find him?  At the short stay meters, obviously casing them for his next heist.

'Right thanks, Callum,' I say, taking the pass from him. '…That's one I owe you.'

'Nae bother. Anything for you Sammy.'


Ella and I then head off in the direction of the main terminal building and on the way Ella tells me that she's impressed with Callum, getting us our own parking slot. With Callum on security, I'll be impressed if the Jag's still got its wheels when we get back.

I really do try to see the best in my fellow man but I can't. Ella says that's only because I know scumbags. A true but harsh assessment.

On checking the arrivals board I find Charlie's flight is on time.

'Isn't it exciting, Sammy? Just think, Charles will come through those doors and back into our lives again.'

'I'm absolutely *ecstatic*, Ella.'

'Whit did I tell you before we left the house, about your antics?'

I should, at this point, have bowed, touched forelock and apologised but unfortunately I lost control of my mouth as is my wont from time to time.

'I still cannae see why the big bullshitter is coming to live with us. As I've said before, wie all his dough you would've thought he'd go to live in the Bahamas.'

'Bullshitter. Bullshitter. There's only one bullshitter I know. Only the world's number one bullshitter of all time. You, ya scunner,' she thunders. Regretfully she's not finished with me yet, '.....If I've telt you once, I've telt you a million times, he's - not - coming - to - live - with - us - permanently. O.K?' I saw it coming the finger. Jumping smartly backwards I unfortunately tread on another ogre's foot who promptly brings her umbrella down on my head.

'Take that you clumsy oaf,' says the ogre lining me up for another wallop. Now you'd think your wife would defend you against this type of common assault. Wrong.

'Give him a wallop for me,' Ella chimes up.

Before the ogre can react I move out of her strike zone taking refuge behind Ella. As Ella turns towards me, I protect my vulnerables with crossed hands, as the footballers do when defending a freekick, since Ella's not averse to taking the odd freekick herself. Being in the contorted posture I'm in, I'm in no position to defend myself against the Kung Foo Finger. As it spears me yet again, in a chest that's beginning to look like a well worn dart board, she asserts, 'And another thing for you to bear in mind, I'm his only living relative, his, his..... next of kin.' She starts to sob. It would bring a tear to a glass eye if you hadn't seen the act before. I have. Umpteen times. She continues between sobs, 'It's you ya nyaff, you bring out the worst in me.'

Final sob and sigh into handkerchief. Step forward Ella Robb to rapturous applause.

The Oscar's yours.

'You swine, that's no way to treat a lady,' rasps the ogre taking another swing at me but fortunately missing with the life threatening blow.

'A lady! Ella, a lady?' I'm about to give the ogre an earful when, fortunately for all, the "arrivals" door flies open and out stream the bleary, weary travellers.

Suddenly he's there. Nothing's changed over the years. Still gormless looking, dressed like a Barnum and Bailey circus clown. Can't miss this. Lights, camera, action.

He's clad in a yellow suit with a red over-check, baseball hat and a giant cigar stuck in the corner of his mouth… only thing that's missing are those three feet long shoes that clowns wear. He's facing Ella with arms wide open, as Armageddon begins.

Ella, projects herself like a shot from a cannon towards the open arms, trips over the ogre's projecting umbrella and ends up rugby tackling Charles low down, with the result that his trousers end up round his ankles revealing a pair of stars and stripes boxer shorts. Down he goes, felled, straight into the trolley, cases flying every whichway. The two of them, with Ella's foot entwined in his wayward trousers, roll about on the floor muttering to each other between hugs and kisses,

"Charles, Charles, after all these years I can't believe it's actually you." Answered by "Ella baby, you darling. I've missed you so much", is some of the drivel emanating from these two embroiled obscenities, as they roll over and over on the floor.

'She needs a bucket of water thrown over her, the hussy.' This from the ogre who two minutes ago called Ella a lady.

'Cover your eyes, children,' says an indignant woman bystander.

'Typical Yank behaviour,' says another.

'Watch your tongue, buddy, I'm a Yank,' says yet another.

'You don't have to tell me. You Yanks are all the bloody ....' The sentence remains unfinished due to the two protagonists trading blows before wrestling each other to the floor to join the terrible twins. Mayhem, total mayhem, and it's all down on film courtesy of the camcorder.

The floor show is broken up and the good natured baying crowd are dispersed by the arrival of armed police. I see Charlie helping Ella to her feet and at the same time grappling to pull up his trousers, as they are shepherded through a security door by the police.

Ella, who is practising her free kicks on two policemen, as they try to haul her through the door, is bawling, 'SAMMY, this is your fault.' Smile please darling, you're on camera, as I use the zoom lens to get the snarling, '.......Dae something about it you, you nyaff.'

I certainly will my love. I'm off to have a cigar.

The airport is on high security alert due to a recent terrorist incident. With any luck the terrible twins might get deported to Guantanamo Bay. As it happens, I've no such luck. An hour or so later, the situation having been satisfactorily explained to the police with the help of Callum, is now deemed over. The sheepish twosome are released into my gleeful custody. I can't wait for the camcorder re-run.

'Howdy, Sa-moo-el, wild homecoming or what, ole buddy,' he bellows as he vigorously shakes my hand and pummels my back. At least he didn't resort to any of that European cheek kissing malarkey. I'm so anti-Europe I've given up French kissing.

'Sure was different, Charles,' I reply to the wild homecoming.

'No need to be so formal, Sa-moo-el. As I've told Ella, call me Chuck.'

'No probs, Chuck.' My, my, Chuck indeed, that should put Ella's gas at a peep.

'Chuck, sounds good to me, Chuck. What about you, Ella?' I query with a satisfying "up yours" sardonic smile.

'Right, let's get out of this....this place. A terrorist indeed. I'll show them who's a terrorist,' growls an irate Ella.

'Never mind, Ella – Karen *will* be proud of you. *She's* never been arrested.... not like her mother,' I take delight in goading as I take shelter behind Chuck.

'I wisnae, er, wasn't arrested, I was... I was, merely helping the police with their enquiries.'

Taking Chuck's arm and gazing longingly into his eyes she continues, over her shoulder, 'Sammy, the luggage, if you don't mind. Bring it round to the Jaguar in the executive car park, there's a good chap.'

'Up yours,' I silently mouth, as tugging my forelock, bowing, and finishing of with the middle digit salute, I set off with the laden trolley in their wake.

I won't bore you with the homeward journey other than to tell you that Chuck has a mouth that would make even the talking clock redundant. He never stopped all the way home. In between all the bull, I gathered some relevant information. He's unmarried, wed to his golf which funnily enough most of my mates are divorced by. Lucky them. And the bullshitting bum claims he's even played golf with Tiger Woods. However, the real thing of interest to me was when he said he would be looking for property adjacent to a golf course. In one of my golf magazines I saw a house for sale next to a golf course - in the Outer Hebrides.

With head throbbing, I drop us off at home and struggle in, unaided by either of them, with the luggage. 'Take the bags upstairs to the West Wing, Sammy, while I get Charles a nice wee cup of tea, after all today's traumas,' Ella instructs me, whilst ushering Chuck into the front lounge. Normally I would react to this. However, the only thought I have is – escape. On completing my enforced task, I track Ella down in the kitchen. The tray is set in her best bone china and laden with cakes, scones, butter and jam.

'I'm for the off. Vera needs help, it's the end of the VAT quarter.'

'It'll be the *end of you*, if you don't stay here and keep Charles company, understand?'

On lifting the laden tray, she growls, 'You're staying in – and that's final.'

As she leads us down the hall and turns in to the lounge, I take my opportunity. Carrying straight on past her, I'm out the front door and in the Jag in under five seconds flat. As I start to reverse out the drive she spirals out the house, like an out of control tornado, straight at me. I immediately lock the door and manoeuvre the window up until only a slit shows. She goes for the door, trying to pull it off its hinges. Foiled. You can't beat experience when you're dealing with Ella.

'I'll attend to you later - creep. Don't think you're getting off with making me look like a stookie, in front of *my* brother,' she threatens. 'Meanwhile, while you're *still* alive, make sure you see William about a van for tomorrow.'

I reverse at speed out the drive causing, Benjie, old Mrs Wilson's dog across the road, to do the splits in the middle of his leg-cocking against my gatepost. He'll be walking peculiarly for a while. Serves him right. He's a pal of Ella's.

Ella's reference to a van is due to the fact that Chuck's main belongings are arriving air freight at Prestwick Airport tomorrow. I'll see Wullie about his van tomorrow.

It's been a stressful day. Some therapeutic encountering required. Lifting my mobile, 'Vera - Sammy. Ah! You're working late tonight on theV.A.T return . That'sss.. ma gal.'

# CHAPTER FIVE

## WULLIE

After a nightmare last evening spent eluding Ella, who's still intent on revenge for my perceived insult to her and Chuck, I'm up bright and early this morning. Deliberately missing breakfast and thereby also the terrible twins, I cruise the Jag towards the city and soon cross the boundary over the River Kelvin into my stomping ground: Maryhill, Glasgow. A short distance further on I stop for breakfast at Ronnie's award winning, "Eggs on Ronnie" greasy spoon bistro. Finding a reasonably grease free table I am greeted with the smoke husked voice of mine host - Ronnie.

'Havnae seen you for a while, Sammy,' he wheezes stealing a look at the clock which shows 7-30 am on the grease splattered wall. 'You on your way home?'

'Very funny, Ronnie. Just you stick to what you do best - poisoning people.'

'You know, Sammy, you can be very hurtful at times. Naebody's died yet.'

'Aye. Yet. Try to make sure I'm not the first.'

Don't worry. All this is kidology. Nothing serious - just friendly banter. I've been coming here for years. You get the best high cholesterol breakfast this side of the Campsie Fells.

'Right Ronnie. Let's have the greasy spoon special.'

'Certainly sir. Dae you want the self service or the silver.'

'Tell you what I'd really love, Ronnie.'

36

'Just you name it, Sammy.'

'I'd love yon incinerated bacon. You know the one? The one that crumbles intae shards at the touch of a fork with yolks surrounded in frazzled white all finished off with your piece de resistance - sausages wallowing in congealed grease.'

'You must be mistaking this establishment for some other that you dine at...*Sir*,' retorts Ronnie haughtily.

'Well you managed it last week.'

'Know your trouble, Sammy? Since you've moved tae Bearsden you've become a food snob,' he retorts as he scuttles into the grease splattered hell known as his kitchen.

Half an hour later after a belter of a breakfast and four indigestion tablets, from experience the absolute minimum, I depart. As the Jag eases itself away from the pavement I wave my goodbye with the time honoured two fingered gesture, to the award winning proprietor standing there in his greased up whites, fag dangling from the corner of his mouth, scratching his unmentionables.


Five minutes later I turn into my forecourt just as Hughie is opening up the premises.

'Morning Sammy.... You on your way home?'

'Very funny, Hughie, *very* funny. Tell me, is Wullie back yet? I don't see his van.'

'Couldnae tell you, Sammy. Havnae seen him since he went tae work in Dumfries.'

To bring you up to date, I haven't seen Wullie either in over a month since he took on, as Hughie says, a contract in Dumfries. He's had to take on work out of the Glasgow area due, as he laments in his true socialist rhetoric, to a recession in the building trade perpetrated by capitalist greed. A rough translation of this - the bank wants its money.

I feel it only fair to give you an insight into what we are dealing with here. This is the man who, on deciding to be become self employed, failed his own job interview. Where was I? Oh! Yes. He phoned me yesterday to tell me his contract, in Dumfries, was finished and after the handover party he'd be on his way home.

As I head for the tenement entrance adjacent to the workshop, where Wullie lives, the bold boy himself zooms out of it jumping the bottom two steps, feet together, landing in front of me with a gymnastic flex of knees.

Springing up, he communicates in a form of algebraic speak with sub-titles which fortunately I'm familiar with, 'Sammy, my man, how's it goin,' giving my shoulder a friendly punch which just about dislocates it. 'You havnae changed a bit since I last saw ye.' He's still well oiled from wherever he's been. Looking at his watch, he chortles, 'You on you way home, Sammy?' Not him as well. I expected better. Mind you in his condition perhaps not.

'No. Are you on your way to work?'

'No. I've nae work to go tae. I'm on my way tae Ali's for milk.'

'Listen, Wullie, I want to ask you a favour...' I don't get finished because Eck, my young gormless salesman, comes belting up the road at full tilt shouting, 'Wullie, Wullie, there's someone in the back of your van, doon the road, bashing on the doors to get out.'

'Tae get oot?' slurs Wullie looking mesmerised.

'Hi, boss,' says Eck noticing me for the first time. 'You on your way home?'

It's a conspiracy. I'm just about to give Eck an earful when I hear a moan from Wullie,

'Shit, shit, it cannae be. I thought I'd taken her home. Listen Sammy, you widnae like to do me a favour, would you?' dangling keys at me.

'Correct, Wullie. I widnae like to.'

'And you call yourself a pal.'

'Right,' I firmly declare, knowing he is about to do his usual and bottle it. 'Wullie, and you too Hughie, let's go and sort this out. You stay here and hold the fort Eck.' And as an afterthought, 'And get the roller shutter up. O.K son?'

'Nae bother, Boss.'


We belt down the road, turn the corner and there's the van in what might loosely be described as parked; abandoned might be more accurate. A wee crowd's gathered. The back doors are getting a fair old pummelling. A female voice is shouting obscenities from inside.

One old crone in a head scarf over rollers, slippers and shopping bag is meanwhile trying to incite a riot, 'What sort of sexual retard wid dae a thing like this tae the poor woman.'

'Send for the polis,' says another. She must be a tourist. Nobody sends for the police round here.

'Sammy, dae something. This is getting out of hand,' cries Wullie in panic at the same time shoving the old crone out of the way. Big time mistake. The shopping bag swings in a violent arch and gets him squarely between his legs.

I wince at the sound and scold her, 'Right you, enough of that, you could ruin his manhood.'

'Couldnae give a shit. A pervert like that yin needs more than a belt in the balls.'

As Wullie continues towards the van doors, in a crab like shuffle due to his recent encounter with the shopping bag, a gnarled old toothless pensioner with a walking stick held threateningly snarls, 'Smell the drink aff him. They're aw alike

wie drink. Aw they think aboot is getting into yer knickers.'
Knuch! What a repulsive thought.

Wullie finally gets to the back doors and inserts the key. The
doors explode outwards, smashing into his face. Down he goes
holding a bloodied nose with both hands.

The next thing is this redheaded wildcat jumps out the
doors, feet first, on top of him and begins to batter lumps out of
him, bellowing and shrieking like a banshee, 'Wullie Leckie,
you big arsewipe. You left me tae freeze in that van overnight.'

Wullie, manfully tries to sit up and is immediately felled by
the old crone's shopping bag.

'Take that you pervert,' wails the old crone.

'Sammy, Hughie, get these loonies aff me,' pleads a
bloodied and bruised Wullie as the redhead is still kicking and
punching him.

'Give him a kick in the nuts,' shouts the tourist. An obvious
sadistic man-hater.

As Hughie and me successfully pry them apart a punch-
drunk Wullie bemoans to the redhead, between kicks, punches
and obscenities that would make a docker blanche, 'Franny,
whit did I dae wrong?'

'Whit. You mean apart from breathing? You take me home,
we get in the back of the van for a goodnight fu ..,' the reason
remains unclear because of the ear shattering erupting hostilities
towards Wullie from the newly formed Maryhill Women's
Liberation Army chanting, 'Baws off, baws off, baws off, cut
his....'

'Then what?' croaks a now petrified Wullie.

'You're so pissed, you get out the back of the van, lock me
in and drive aff.'

'Dead sorry, Franny, so am ur,' replies Wullie mournfully.
'But you should've been dead comfy. That's a brand new
memory foam mattress in there - cost me a fortune.'

'Well, I can tell ye pal, the state my arse is in - it's definitely lost its memory.'

Meanwhile, Hughie and me are fighting a losing battle against holding back the Maryhill Women's Lib horde now surrounding the van and still chanting at the top of their voices. My antenna is twitching like mad - bad vibes. Police.

'Right Hughie. Get her in the back and let's get going before the polis shows up.'

'I'm no going in the back wie him,' hollers Franny at the top of her voice.

'Dead right, hen,' says the tourist as she tries to stick the head on Wullie.

'You stay out of this,' threatens Wullie - nose to nose with the tourist.

'You gonny make me, you dirty perv?' said as she tries to knee him in the crotch.

Wullie by this time doesn't know what planet he's on. Leaning against the van, battered and bruised and fighting a losing battle to stop his eyes looking into each other.

'Right, Hughie. Get them in the back - NOW!'

We hustle both of them into the back. Franny goes in scratching, kicking and screaming for "help" from her new found allies.

'Hughie - passenger seat,' I yell at him as I take the keys out the back door, whilst under a barrage of blows from brollies, shopping bags and walking sticks, 'We're effing off. Now.'

'Get the van's number. She's being abducted by the whole gang,' shouts the tourist.


I drive the short distance, at breakneck speed, straight into the workshop bringing the van to an emergency stop on its nose. Hughie jumps out and before he closes the roller shutter door I can hear the distant wail of police sirens. They'll do me for kidnapping, inciting a riot, driving without a road fund licence. Well you didn't expect Wullie to have it taxed, did you? I'll never learn. How often have I told myself, do - not - get - involved - in - Wullie's - shenanigans…. and failed miserably.

Eck is standing there, goggle-eyed, mouth wide open, 'Whit's happening? We being raided *again* boss?'

'Not yet, Eck…. Away and put the kettle on before we are. And bring us a couple of paracetemol, I'm getting a splitting "head-Eck." If you'll excuse the pun.'

'What's a pun, boss?'

'Sixteen ounces. Boom. Boom.'

A vacant look tells me all. He's been metricated. At times I think it's only Maggie and me standing against the evil advance of the European Union.

I then go round to the back doors of the van to open them. They're locked from the inside. I knock. A muffled voice tells me to "bugger off" and come back in half an hour. The boy's definitely on something. I heard a rumour he likes extra vinegar on his chips.

Half an hour later, sitting in my office, having had to spurn the advances of Vera for no other reason than my nerves are jangling waiting for the police raid to start at any minute, in wanders the bold boy. Battered looking but in high spirits, 'Hi! Sammy. Thanks pal, that's one I owe you,' says mister nonchalance.

Managing to keep my temper under control, realising what's happened was self inflicted I reply, 'You seem to have a thing for redheads, Wullie. After the last time I thought you'd be just a wee bit more wary.' I'm referring to his wife, runaway Rita, a drop dead stunning redhead.

'Franny's, no a real redhead, you know,' he states emphatically.

'Well if anyone *would* know that, it would be *you*, wouldn't it? While on the subject of redheads – do you know where Rita is?'

'I know she's in Tenerife somewhere, wie the chef from Leo's Steak House.'

'I was real sorry when that happened, Wullie,' I reply shaking my head, '….. I cannae get a decent steak since he left.'

'Sorry about that Sammy, but I'm going tae get ma personal life sorted out real soon.'

'Not, for this Franny one….surely?'

'No way, Jose. She's wearing me oot. In fact, I feel like an old man – so what are you doing tonight, Sammy?' he chortles with an impish smile.

I totally ignore him. It ceases to be funny after the millionth time of hearing.

'Aw, alright, be like that. Right, down tae business then Sammy. You're not up at this time in the morning for nothing. So what is it you want?' He doesn't miss a trick.

'I want to borrow your passion wagon.'

'Any time, Sammy. You don't have tae ask, you know that. I don't even want tae know where you're taking Vera.'

Ignoring the wind up I continue, 'If you must know, I need the van tae pick up Chuck's luggage from Prestwick airport. You remember Ella's older brother, Charlie?'

'Never forget the prick. He's finally arrived then?'

'The bullshitting asshole sure as hell has - ole buddy,' I drawl.

'Still cannae see your way tae forgiving him yet.'

'Never. The dirty, conniving, scheming, slime ball. Imagine talking me into parting wie ma pocket money that I'd been saving tae buy a Walkman, tae invest in one of his double your pocket money scams. Told me it was a long term investment and that was the last I saw of it before he shot off tae the States.' A nervous clearing of the throat alerts me to Wullie. Looking at him I instantly recognise the guilty look on his face, 'Not you as well? What were you saving for...a Barbie doll?'

'Aye me as well. Why'd you think I called him a prick? Mind you after all these years our investment must be worth a few bob...shouldn't it?'

'True Wullie, true.'

'However, it's all in the past Sammy. Listen I'd love tae stay and reminisce but I've got tae take Franny home. She's working this evening in a pub.'

'What's the hurry. It's only ten o'clock. Where does she live, Timbuctu?'

'Might as well be - Dumfries.'

'Dumfries!'

'Look Sammy, it's a long story, tell you about it tomorrow, in Rileys.'

As I head for his van and he towards his car he shouts over to me with a wink,

'The mattress is still in the back, Sammy.' You've now met Wullie.

# CHAPTER SIX

## THE ABDUCTION

So where are we regarding the arch villain of the piece, Chuck? Let's have an update.

Having borrowed Wullie's van and by sheer chance discovering that Vera loves the sea-side and aeroplanes, both of us set off for Prestwick International Airport on the Ayrshire coast. After a nice lunch and a cheeky little bottle of Chardonnay in the pleasant small town of Prestwick, (Historic for hosting the very first Open golf championship in 1860, and not St. Andrews as most think. I impart this knowledge from my own personal need that a day without learning is a day lost. Agreed?) the tone of the day was set and with the mattress having regained its memory a Vera therapeutic tone it turned out to be. On the return journey I dropped Vera off at her karate class and arriving home, Chuck, informs me he is about to depart in the next few days to tour Scotland, being armed with the bounteous estate agent brochures and golf magazine ads I had procured for him, in the hope of finding suitable property adjacent to a golf course. I can only hope he finds something to his liking very soon as I can feel myself losing control of my desire not to throttle the bullshitting bum on sight.

Later in the day finds me about to bring another hum-drum working day to a close. Dugald was back in with his VW Beetle. He's determined to get the most out of his lifetime guarantee. Allegedly, his sat-nav took him home to his neighbour's house who happens to be a widow. It apparently tucked them up in bed and made them their cocoa. His wife is unhappy with this arrangement so the sat-nav's been in for removal. Dugald was very unhappy about this. Apparently the widow makes a nice mug of cocoa. Regarding future life time guarantees, if Dugald's anything to go by, I'm going to have to insist on an undertaker's report. They can always smell the clay. Which brings me nicely onto my next topic; one of McGregor's hearses came in for repair. I'm a bit superstitious regarding hearses. I hope it's not the harbinger of doom. Little was I to know.

With Vera already off to her karate class, she's certainly putting the hours in, I catch Eck about to leave for home with a magazine tucked under his arm.

'That, a dirty girlie mag, Eck.'

'No way boss, it's ma Pigeon Weekly,' he blushingly replies as he opens it to show me the front cover.

'Looks like a bird tae me, Eck. A bit pigeon chested but definitely a bird.'

'Very funny, boss. Very funny.' With that he's gone. So's Hughie. Nobody left.

I've tried to contact Wullie, by phone, all day but with no success and I'm beginning to wonder if something's gone wrong, yet again, in Dumfries. So I lock up and take myself up the street to Rileys in the off chance he's there. On turning into the main road I'm confronted by a maw, paw and the weans family, unfortunately going in my direction, strung out across the pavement width in a 4-4-2 formation. After several thwarted attempts to pass a defence that even the great Pele couldn't breach I have to settle for the repulsive rhythmical view of the mother's obese arse bobbing up and down like two buoys in a rough sea. I thankfully reach harbour before seasickness sets in. The first person I encounter at the bar is Toni.

'Did I wina the Pyramid, Toni?'

'You widnae beleva it, Sammy.'

'Let me guessa. There was only one square unsold. You bought it and it won.'

'You musta be psychic, Sammy, you knowa that?'

'If I was, I wouldn't bump into you as often - would I?'

'You no meana that, Sammy.'

'A very detchy Toni,' I chortle, as I move down the bar to someone bearing a resemblance to Wullie. It's hard to see clearly because the donkey jacket's collar is up obscuring the face. On getting closer to him I notice he's sporting a lop sided orange moustache, dark glasses, and a back to front baseball cap. It's him - the master of disguise.

'Hi, Wullie.'

'How did you know it's me?'

'Apart from the crap disguise, could it maybe the "William Leckie Builders" on the back of your donkey jacket?

'Shit.'

'What's with the… er…em… disguise, anyway?'

'I've had a traumatic twenty four hours, Sammy.'

'And what happened to you this time?' prompts me, not really wanting to know after yesterday's near riot.

'Well as you know I was taking Franny back down to Dumfries.'

'M-mmh.'

'Well, after stopping for a meal and a few bevvies, I'm expecting to stay the night wie her. When out of the blue she tells me I cannae stay.'

'And why not?'

'Her *husband's* only in the house minding the kids! So about turn, Wullie, no goodbye leg over. It sickened ma chanker so it did.'

'My, my, that's a real shame, Wullie,' shaking my head in mock sympathy.

'Mind you, I did find oot what happened. She tells me I'd met her at a hen party in the same place as we were having our handover piss up. We some how ended up in the back of the van. I cannae remember a thing aboot it, Sammy. I was totally balootered.'

'And that's when you drove off with her inside and ended up in Maryhill.'

'Aye. So as I'm driving out of Dumfries yesterday afternoon, straight after she dropped her bombshell, I see this newspaper hoarding wie the headline -

POLICE ALERT: LOCAL WOMAN ABDUCTED BY WHITE VAN MAN. I stopped and bought a paper and Sammy, Sammy - It's all about me! Her husband's only gone and reported her missing to the polis,' he ends in panic.

'So, that's why the disguise, is it?'

'Aye, Sammy. What am I going tae dae? I'm now a fugitive from justice. The FBI, Interpol, the whole shooting match will be searching for me.'

'Calm down, Wullie. For a start you didn't mean to abduct her.'

'True, Sammy, true. I was so wazooed, I didnae know what I was doing.'

'We'll, that's not going to help matters telling that tae anyone, is it?'

'No, Sammy, no.'

'Secondly, they haven't got your license number or they would have nicked you by now.'

'True, Sammy, true.'

'And lastly she doesn't know where you live. She never got out the van other than tae wallop you. Right.'

'True, Sammy, true. What a relief,' he gasps, wiping his forehead with the back of his hand. 'I knew you'd sort it out, pal.'

'Now just do yourself a favour and stay away from redheads and….extra vinegar.'

'Extra vinegar?' I hear him query as I get up to replenish our empties.

Arriving at the bar, Jock, is thankfully waiting to serve me. A left over from Alec the previous landlord, he's wizzened, stooped and of an indeterminate age but definitely well past retirement. It is said, amongst the bar worthies that he's, "not the full shilling". This, of course, depends who you're comparing him with. Against Wullie, he's a positive Einstein. Personally, I find Jock a pleasant mannered, sociable, easily put upon and therefore ideal bullying fodder for Agnes, sort of person. I've plenty of time for him.

'Hi, Sammy. What's your pleasure?'

'Two pints of heavy and a packet of nuts for me, please, Jock.'

'See the "Jags" went doon again, last night,' he conversationally says as he pours the drinks.

'Man bites dog, Jock. Now that's news…..'

'No, kiddin. Did he dae that at Firhill, as well?'

Maybe, the worthies have a point.

Taking my drinks back to the table I enquire of Wullie, 'How's the work going?'

'It's not, Sammy. You know yon old warehouses doon the Broomielaw that I've tae convert intae Yuppie apartments? Well, they've been put back.'

'How's that, then?'

'The architect tells me it's something to dae with building control….whatever that is.'

'Well, listen to this, it might be of interest to you. McGregor brought one of his hearses in for repair this morning. The driver of it's got the sack. He left it outside a bookie's shop wie the keys in. It was nicked by some Thistle supporters to take them tae an away match.'

'You're joking. I knew we had a supporter's tandem but a supporter's hearse - now that's mortifying,' he giggles. 'Mind you the way they're playing now…it could come in handy. Why I can remember the good old days when we won the Scottish League Cup back in '71 against the might of Celtic. The Celtic had won the European Cup in '67 wie much the same team that played us that….'

'Aye. Well that's as maybe Wullie,' I had to interrupt otherwise "the good old days" of what the "Jags" did tae Celtic, especially considering he was just out of his nappies in '71 would have gone on for ever. He thrives on the local folklore of the demented and disillusioned souls that brave the Firhill terraces, hanging onto their every word, of that, the greatest triumph in the history of the "Jags". '…so McGregor's needing a hearse driver. That's not a bad wee "fill in job" until your flats get the go ahead, is it not?'

'Good thinking, Batman. Whoever heard of the polis breathalysing a hearse.'

It's truly unbelievable how his mind thinks. Standing up I say, 'Well I'm off home now. Deadline seven - otherwise my dinner's in Benjie.' Benjie, being old Mrs. Watson's dog from across the road, is getting fat on my dinners. 'Make sure you contact McGregor. O.K?'

'Will do.  Here before you go, Sammy. How's the new house?'

'Ella loves it. Personally, I'd rather be back in the Briggs among real people. Enough said.'

'You giving me an invite sometime?'

'When she's out.'

'Why out?'

'You've got to take your shoes off.'

'That's nae bother.'

'Wullie. That's just tae get in the drive. See you later pal.'

With that I'm off home. I'll go via Benjie's kennel just in case.

The following morning, Wullie emerges from his close entrance looking smart in his designer denims, black leather jacket, crisp white shirt and Reebok trainers. Turning left into Maryhill Road, he proceeds a little distance until he comes to a double fronted shop bearing in gold letters on black painted windows the sign-work:McGREGOR FUNERAL DIRECTORS. Entering the shop, an old fashioned door bell on a spring, tinkles. A glass window slides open below a reception sign.

'Aye, whit can I dae for you?' enquires a frizzy permed head, chewing furiously on gum.

'Could I see a Mister McGregor please?' enquires Wullie.

'Dae you huv an appointment?'

'I thought you needed tae be deid for an appointment in here.'

'Well, that's you O.K then, in't it?' mouths the perm, blowing a bursting bubble.

Wullie is just getting geared up for a retort to miss smart arse when a door opens at the side of reception. A very tall gaunt gentleman in black frock coat, grey pinstriped trousers and rimless glasses looks directly at Wullie.

'Has Letitia attended to you, sir?' he says in that slow sombre voice, which seems to be the preserve of all undertakers and tax collectors.

'No she *hasnae*,' replies Wullie glaring at her. 'I'm looking for Mr. McGregor.'

'I am he. Please step this way,' he says, ushering Wullie into his office. 'Now mister....?'

'Leckie. William Leckie.'

'How may I be of assistance to you in your hour of grief?'

'I think there's been a wee misunderstanding, Mr. McGregor.'

'Kindly explain Mr. Leckie,' his eyes peering sternly over the rimless glasses.

'I'm here to see about a driver's job,' replies Wullie.

'How do you know I'm looking for a driver?'

'Mister Robb told me about it. Your hearse is in his place getting fixed. He said he was going tae phone you.'

'He didn't. Are you are a friend of Mister Robb?'

'We're best mates.'

'Would you mind if I phoned Mister Robb to confirm that?'

'Naw, onya go.' McGregor picks up the desk phone.

'Hello Vera, my dear. McGregor here. Could you put me through to Mr. Robb please?' After a slight delay. 'Ah! Samuel. Gregor here. I have in my office a gentleman by the name of William Leckie, claims to be a friend of yours.'

*'Describe him to me. I'll soon know.'*

'Well, he's good looking, dark haired with a clean shaven complexion and slim athletic build. Neatly dressed . Five eleven and three quarters,' replies McGregor casting an accurate undertaker's eye over Wullie.

Wullie preens himself. Could be a description of Brad Pitt he thinks to himself.

*'Good looking? That cannae be the bloke I know. Give's a word with him Gregor.'*

'You don't think it's him,' queries McGregor looking severely over his rimless glasses at Wullie. '…You'd like a word with him. Certainly,' McGregor replies, handing the phone to Wullie who immediately starts shouting down the phone,

'Sammy it's me. Tell the man it's me…' Wullie is met with howls of laughter both from the phone and from McGregor. A dawning look comes over Wullie's face.

What a stookie. They've stitched me up, the pair of them. 'S,s..see you, Sammy..,' to a dead phone.

Turning back towards McGregor he observes a complete change of personality has taken place as McGregor extends his hand with a large beaming smile on his face, 'Right Wullie, pleased tae meet you, I'm Gregor McGregor. Sorry about that, Wullie, but it helps tae break the *dead* monotony of this place, if you'll excuse the pun.'

'Nice one, Gregor. You both had me really going there.'

'Sammy, phoned me last night, tells me you need the job to supplement your income because of your impending divorce.' Crafty Sammy, thinks Wullie.

'That's true, Gregor.'

'If Sammy says you're O.K then that's alright with me. Can you start Monday?'

'Yeh. Nae bother Gregor. Thanks.'

On leaving the premises Letitia is still at her window.

'See ya Monday, Letitia,' Wullie says sticking his tongue out at her.

He leaves to a "V" sign gesture from the gum chewing head.

# CHAPTER SEVEN

## THE HOLE IN THE HEID GANG

As my working day comes to a close I find myself thinking of one of Ella's dad's sayings when he was shutting up shop, "Another day ended, another pound a prisoner". And it certainly was. Once in his clutches every pound was a goner. Never to see the light of day again. Now, I wonder how long we can hold out, as a nation, before I find myself saying, "Another day ended, another *euro* a prisoner". Doesn't bear thinking about.

The pollsters are suggesting a change of government is imminent. Or to use the new Downing Street buzz words, "regime change". Can't come soon enough for me. Anything to get rid of this load of bungling incompetents out of office. Of course there's no guarantee that the incoming incumbents, whoever, will fare any better against Europe since, let's face it, they're all gutless wonders. My advice, for what it's worth would be - fill in the tunnel and put an end to the unending and useless European directives being thrust upon us through it. The first casualty in the de-lousing process should be the ubiquitous Human Rights Act. A one way Act, inflicted on us by an *unelected* bunch of dunderheids, designed for the benefit of crooks, terrorists and the legal profession. If you can distinguish any difference between them.

Why, when we survived for over eight hundred years with the Magna Carta, did we need to change? Stupid question.

Change and ruination of our nation are the foundations of this inept Parliament. Apologies for this most major of digressions but, honestly, doesn't it make you sick every time you hear about our chicken livered judiciary failing to stand up for common sense and decency citing the Human Rights Act for their cowardice at every turn? Pathetic.

Where was I? Yes. Vera's gone off early to feed the homeless under the railway arches before going to her karate class. Eck's away to his pigeon loft. Hughie and Rab have headed for Kenny's Bar. Nothing ever changes. Little was I to know, that not in the too distant future, how glad and relieved I would be to utter those words again.

Ella wants the front lounge redecorated. The décor apparently clashes with her new dress. You'd think it would be easier to get a dress to match the décor, but no it has to be redecorated. So after locking up, I head up the street for Rileys and on turning right into the main road I notice what I take, at first glance, to be a pony on the pavement outside Rileys. Nothing by now surprises me what you find outside Rileys. On closer inspection it turns out to be Pek, a Great Dane, held on lead by its master Zato. He's our local Czech émigré. Zato that is, not the dog.

'How goes it, Zato?' I enquire, as I stretch up head height to scratch Pek's ear.

'Not so good Zammy. The Agnes wan, she put me an Pek oot.'

'What for?' Stupid question. With Agnes the list is endless.

'Pek, he taking up two of her drinking places standing at the bar.'

'Does Pek not like sitting?'

'Naw, he a bar person, like me.'

While this banter has been going on Pek has cocked his leg against Rileys wall.

'Sorry about that Zammy. She put him oot before he had time tae go tae the gents.'

'I'll tell Agnes you're sending your love, Pek,' I say, as I stride the torrent. Pek woofs with delight, licking my head with his giant tongue and on thumping me between the shoulder blades with his great paw sends me sprawling straight through the swing doors.

Picking myself up, totally disorientated, I find myself looking into the demonic eyes of the harridan herself – Agnes, who immediately snarls at me, 'You been drinking, pal?'

'No, Agnes. Just tripped over my shoelace,' I reply hoping she won't notice I'm wearing slip-ons.

'I'll be watching you. Anyway, whit dae you want?' she growls, with her small beady Quasimodo's mother's eyes staring me out.

Having spotted Wullie sitting down, I order, 'Two pints of heavy and a packet of nuts.'

She disappears to the font. On her return she slams them down on the counter. They do their now famous loop the loop.

'You a member of the Magic Circle, Agnes?' I enquire of her, at the risk of eviction.

'Whit dae you mean by that?'

'You've just, by magic, turned two pints into two half pints.'

'Tell you whit I'll dae. I'll turn you intae a door. It'll save me putting you through that yin,' she growls pointing to the main doors with an arm rippling with tattooed muscles.

Lifting the drinks, not daring to further criticise the measure, I casually mention, 'See you've barred Zato.'

'Aye, he's my first bounced Czech.'

'Very funny, Agnes.'

'I don't dae jokes, smart arse.'

'I was only checking,' I reply.


Happy at having the last word I take the drinks over to Wullie's table and sitting down I mention, 'Met Zato outside. She's barred him.'

'Zat no a shame,' he replies with that inane grin he uses when he thinks he's funny.

Before he can start his idiotic nonsense again I get in first with, 'Listen Wullie, I need your help – it's Ella.'

'What's she done tae you this time?'

'She wants the front room re-decorated. Clashes wie her new dress.'

'How many times is that since you moved?'

'Lost count, Wullie. Cannae remember how many new dresses she's had.'

'Anyway, no can do, Sammy. Just sacked ma painter this morning. Interviewed him yesterday. I honestly thought I was in the presence of a reconstituted Leonardo Da Vinci....wie all the things he could dae.'

'Reincarnated,' I correct.

'That's whit I said....anyway it disnae matter. I discover today he disnae know which end of a brush tae hold.'

'So you gave him the brush off.'

'Put the lid right on his tin, Sammy. So there you go, fresh out of painters. Try Joe. He'll be at Ned's party tonight.'

'I'm not going.'

'You're kidding.'

'No. Ella says I've to go to her operatic society tonight. She's the treasurer.'

'Operatic society? Whit are you daen wie them toffy-nosed Tory poofters who've never done a proper day's work in their lives.'

'Listen Wullie, that class warfare thing went out with the Dinosaurs. We've all been hi-jacked. The real enemy now is a bunch of arrogant Islington wankers making decisions round their posh dinner tables. Tories or New Labour, it doesn't matter which, they're one and the same - only interested in themselves and the easy money. So no need tae go on about Tory poofters, which by the way you've enough of in your own party.'

'How'd that happen?'

'Whit?'

'Tory poofters in the Labour party.'

'I didn't say that, you galoot. What I meant was you've got enough poofters in your own party without starting on the Tories.'

'Well O.K then, Sammy, but these Islington wankers what are they then, Liberals?'

'Do's a favour Wullie. I'm talking educated hoods here. Real villains. Not plastic mac, sandal wearing brainless wazoos. And another thing, where have all the Commies gone? They haven't just disappeared, you know. They've infiltrated your lot…. As usual.'

'Well, that's all as maybe, it disnae matter. What does matter is that for the price of that opera ticket of yours you could feed a family of four for a month in Angola.' He sounds just like Karen, my daughter, only difference is she knows where Angola is.

'Whatever you say, Wullie,' I reply, tiring of his inane left wing rhetoric. Hastily changing the subject I ask, 'What are you going as tonight?'

'A knight looking for a knightette.'

'Are you taking that bird from McGregors? You know the one you, er, mmd...in the back of the hearse.'

'How'd you know that? Wis it that, Tam? See him, when he's had tae much bevvy...'

'Wasn't Tam. You think the dead don't talk? Remember I repair the hearses.'

'Ha. Ha. Very funny, Sammy. But, if you mean is it Letitia going wie me tonight the answers - no. So, I'm on my tod. Well, that's it, Sammy,' he declares, downing his drink, 'I'm off tae get ready for to-night's soiree. Pity you're not coming, I've a feeling it's going to be a belter.'

'Don't count me out yet.'

'Who are you trying tae kid? If Ella tells you you're no going, you're *no* going and that's final.'

The truth be known, I'm glad I'm going to the Opera even though I hate it with a passion.

It's saved me the embarrassing real reason for not going to the party tonight. That being; Ella now feels these parties, which we attended for years, are now beneath her dignity. Sad. Pathetic in fact.

I'm busy thinking it's a dog's life, as I turn into our avenue. With that I suddenly have to do an emergency stop as Ella wanders into the road with a shovel held at arms length coming from the direction of old Mrs.Watson directly across the road. Turning into the driveway I stop and get out to meet Ella coming towards me still with the shovel held at arms length in front of her but now holding her nose.

'What's *that*?' I ask, as if I can't see the large dog's do-dah, the size of a Cumberland sausage, lying steaming on it.

Ella replies, bursting out in sobbing tears, 'Sammy, Sammy, I'm fair affronted. What will the rest of the neighbours say?'

'Why? What's happened now?'

'When I returned home about ten minutes ago this thing was lying on the front lawn. So I went and got the shovel and scraped it up, took it across the road and dumped it on Mrs.Watson's front lawn.'

'Quite right too, Ella,' I utter to comfort her. This just results in a further outbreak of the vapours.

'Mrs.Watson, having seen me do it, says to me, "What did you do that for?" I said it was Benjie up to his old tricks again. Then she says, "Benjie got run down and killed yesterday". Poor... poor old Benjie. What - a - lovely - dog,' sobbed through tears.

'Ella, the last I heard from you, you were going to kick Benjie's tail up its jacksie....'

'Right, that's it you. I'm not going with you tonight. Between you and that Mrs.Watson, who has a mooth the size of the Clyde tunnel, everyone will know. You go to Ned's on your own. It's all right, I want to be alone.' This last recited theatrically, a la Garbo.

'Ella I couldn't go without you..... It just wouldn't be the same.... But if you insist....'

I'm out of the door and into my study in a flash before she can change her mind.

I lock the door of my sanctuary and phone Wullie.

'Wullie, it's me. Ella's flung a wobbly and she's not going to the opera. She's told me I can go to Ned's, but I've no fancy dress.'

'Great. How'd you manage that? Never mind tell me later and don't worry about the fancy dress. If you remember when Rita and me used tae go to fancy dress parties we went as Bonnie and Clyde. I've still got all the gear. Will you be wanting both suits?'

'Seems a shame not to.'

'Vera?'

'Vera likely.'

'No surprise there then. Coming down to the office to change?'

'Good idea. See you in half an hour.'

When I get to the office the lights are on and Vera's scooter is in her allocated slot. Just as I'm parking the Jag, Wullie comes out of his close entrance with a suitcase in one hand and a violin case in the other with a Tommy-gun tucked under his arm. Coming into the light of the office he is, as he said, dressed as a knight. Looking closely the effect is achieved with a ladies white full length sleeveless nightdress with a crusader's red cross on the front and "Once a knight's enough" printed on the back. This over a black polo neck sweater over a pair of lady's black tights. A black page boy wig and a pair of black Chelsea boots round off the very imposing ensemble.

'You'll have nae trouble pulling a damsel in distress wie that get-up,' I compliment him giving him the thumbs up.

'Ta, Sammy. I've got yours and Vera's suits in the suitcase. The violin case has the carry-out in it.'

Unpacking the case I slip into a black suit with chalk stripe, black shirt, white tie, black trilby with white band and tommy-gun under my arm.

While waiting for Vera to change I inspect the tommy-gun and pass the comment, 'First time I've paid any attention to the gun, Wullie. It's very real looking.'

'Should be – it is. It's ma faither's from the last war. Family heirloom.'

'Jesus Christ Wullie, you'll get us the jail. They were all supposed tae be handed in.'

'Nothing tae worry aboot, Sammy, it's legal - there's nae firing mechanism in it.'

That's all we need; tae be stopped by the police toting a real tommy-gun. However, before I get a chance to mention it further, Vera finally arrives from the ladies dressed identically to myself. That's it. We're all ready for the off. We're taking the Jag. Wullie's driving since he knows Ned's new address.

Wullie, while shrugging himself into his car-coat says, 'Right Vera, assuming you're only having your usual vat of sherry, I'll drive us there, you drive us back, O.K?'

'Oh! Goody, William. The Jag - I love it,' she enthusiastically trills, continuing,

'I must say you *do* look abby fabby in your tights, William.'

'Thanks babe, you look not so bad yourself. Let's burn rubber,' he replies in his usual lousy pseudo American accent.

Going outside we encounter a change in the weather, the evening has turned into a fog-shrouded mist-laden night. Nasty driving conditions. Wullie sets off, crouched over the steering wheel with his nose inches from the screen in an effort to see where he's going. After about thirty minutes Wullie eventually sighs with relief, 'I think we've been over the Kingston bridge twice but we're finally here folks. If yous want to get out I'll park and join you as soon as poss. It's number seven.'

Vera oozes out the back seat followed by me into what has turned out to be an old fashioned "pea souper". Holding Vera by the arm and with the tommy-gun tucked under my arm we set off hopefully in the right direction. We're feeling our way along the garden walls with me in the lead when a figure suddenly emerges scarily out of the murk. Unfortunately, I was adjusting the position of the tommy-gun, which had started to slip from under my arm, so that it was a pointing at him as he broke through the fog. Seeing it he throws his arms up in the air, pleading, 'Please don't shoot, I've got an expensive wife to keep,' as he slides one of his upheld arms down to retrieve his wallet from inside his jacket and throw it at us crying out, 'Here take this only don't shoot.'

As I bend down to pick up the wallet he runs of into the gloom shouting something lost in the murk. The incident has allowed Wullie to catch up with us who, panting from his exertion, gulps out in deep breaths, 'A guy just passed me shouting, "Help! I've been robbed – call the Police."'

'It must be nutters night out, Wullie. One just jumped out of the fog and flung his wallet at me, then ran off shouting something I didn't catch. There's bound to be a name in it. I'll return it in the morning,' I explain, as I slipped the wallet into my jacket pocket.

Looking for Ned's proved all too easy; all we had to do was follow the blasting, reverberating Quo's, "Rocking all over the world" ethereally stealing through the fog. Arriving at the open door we are greeted by Ned, a Rick Parfitt look-alike, and his air guitar gyrations. Nodding our hellos to mine host, as he does the splits to the rending of his denim's crotch accompanied by an ear splitting scream suggesting rupture, we enter the kitchen to off-load our carry-out from the violin case. The "good fairy," burping and farting, is in full flight. Looking at Wullie with a one eyed-focus he slurs, 'Love your tights. Big man.' Then with puckered lips pouts, 'Gie's a kiss big boy.'

'I'll give you a kick up your effing tutu - you wee fairy,' retorts Wullie.

'Another night of culture ahead,' observes Vera. And so it was to prove.

At this point I take the opportunity of giving Vera her token dance reducing the minute waltz to thirty seconds before I set out people hopping. One of my last sober recollections of the evening was a Red Indian doing a war dance with Hiawatha to the beat of an upside down waste bin acting as a tom-tom, played by a Mexican bandit. I think there was an Egyptian sand-dancer as well, because I vaguely recall thinking at the time of Toni and his pyramid scam where Tooty Cameroon met his bird at the sand dancing.

Meanwhile, Wullie, shoulders swaggering, heads towards a female in the fancy dress of a punk with purple spiked hair, tattoos, safety pins and studs in every conceivable orifice all wrapped in a black bin liner. He opens his chat-up in his pseudo American accent with, 'They call me Brad, babe. You know like Brad Pitt.'

'Brad Pitt! You look mair like my auntie Mary's arm-pit - Wullie.'

This response brings a one eyed study of her from Wullie and a burped, 'Who's you?'

'Sasha.'

'So it is then. Long time no see. You look smasha Sasha, but you know it's supposed tae be a fancy dress party, don't you?'

'You've got a way wie women, Wullie. The further away the better.'

'How's about you an me for a bit of action then, Sasha?' slurs a swaying Wullie.

'Like making up your Horlicks....'

'Aye. Then tucking *us* up in bed...hic.'

'Wullie, get a grip. You're staunin there, swaying all over the place, pissed as a fart boasting, "Once a knight's enough" on your nightie. Whit good's that tae me?'

'That's no fair ....Och! Whit the fu...'

The "Good Fairy" has just snagged Wullie's tights with his magic wand.

'See you, ya menace.....these tights cost a fortune.'

'See you, ya menace these tights cost a fortune,' mimics the "Good Fairy" mincing round with hand on hip, waving the wand in a limp wrist gesture, continuing. 'Away you go you big poofter.'

'That's it pal, your tea's oot,' Wullie growls as he lunges at the "Good Fairy" wrestling it to the floor and swinging a punch. No contest. All over in two seconds flat. The "Good Fairy" is lying face down with the magic wand sticking up his rear end.

As Wullie is examining the damage to his tights Vera passes by saying, 'Oh! William, what a shame. I was hoping to get into those later…..,'

'Nae time like the present, Vera.'

'I have to hand it to you, Wullie, your're a trier,' interrupts Sasha.

'……..I meant when you had finished with them, William,' finishes Vera.

'Not your night Wullie,' comments Sasha waving her goodbyes as Wullie watches Vera wriggle her swaying pert-bottom into the next room where Sammy is finalising a sales pitch.

'It's a wee bramer, Joe. Allowing you discount, for decorating the front room, you couldn't do better at the money. It comes with central clocking, er, locking. How's that sound to you, Joe?'

'Hick, burp…sh..sh…shounds good tttae me, Shammy.' Replied as Sammy guides Joe's hand in signing the contract and a sealing handshake. Joe then collapses - snoring.

'How could you do that to a pal, Sammy?'

'Just doing him a favour, Vera. If it wasn't for me he might have fallen into the hands of some unscrupulous dealer. There's a few about, you know….hic.'

'*That's* my boy. All heart,' coos Vera putting her arms around Sammy while pointing him in the direction of the door and home.

The party ends. Well sort of. There's still bodies about but in a non compos mentis state, including Ned, who is still in his splits pose but has been laid aside prone against a wall surrounded by the debris of discarded beer cans, bottles and up-turned furniture.

Getting outside, Wullie collapses. We lug him into the back seat. The fog has lifted and the first rays of dawn are peeping between the stately Pollokshields mansions as Vera takes the wheel of the Jag and we set off. We haven't been going minutes when we encounter a car stopped askew across Pollokshaws Road with a police car, light bar flashing brilliantly in the gloom, across the front of it. Unfolding before our eyes is the unforgettable sight of a Red Indian chief, Hiawatha, an Egyptian sand dancer and the "Good Fairy" all with waving palms to their mouths whooping and dancing a Red Indian war dance to the beat of a tom-tom, tucked under the arm of a Mexican bandit, all cavorting around the stationary cars being chased by the police.

I chuckle to Vera, 'Let's have some fun,' as I point the tommy-gun out the window at the police and start making loud immature shooting noises, "Rat-a-tat-tat. Rat-a-ta..."

The police, seeing the tommy-gun sticking out the Jag's window, dive head first over a garden wall much to the delight of the dancers who take the opportunity to make themselves scarce. As the Indian chief passes he gives us the peace sign drawling, 'Heap big cavalry sure took their time getting here, pardner.'

'Let's vamoose from Tonto, pronto. Hit the gas, Bonnie.'

Unbeknown to me the day of reckoning looms large.

Ring, ring, r.......ing. A bomb has been detonated behind my eyes. Ring, Ring.....

Thankfully it stops. Somewhere in the distance I hear a faint voice.

'Hello, Sammy Robb Motors. The name you can …..' The next I am aware of is a thump on the head, as a phone receiver bounces off it and dangles on its cord before my eyes. From the mouthpiece I hear this sledgehammer of a voice reverberating in my beleaguered brain, 'Hello! Hello! Is Sammy there? Answer when I speak to you…do you hear me? Whoever's there, tell the dirty stop-out nyaff I'm on ma way in tae put his lights out.' An elegant hand, in the ethereal mist, removes the receiver from my view.

The next I feel is my face being gently slapped and a voice in full panic mode screaming,

'Sammy! Sammy! Wake up. *Please* wake up. That was Ella. I think she recognised my voice. She's on her way …here.'

There's nothing like a shock to sober you up and as shocks go they don't come much bigger than that. As I rise from the carpeted floor, I thump my head on the underside of the desk. The reality of the situation sinks in.

Suddenly, like Vera, I too am in full panic mode as I run towards the general office. 'Wullie! Wullie! Wake up. Please wake up,' I'm shouting at the top of my voice to the prone figure on the floor. His wig, having slipped down his face, is thankfully helping to reduce the noise of his snoring which by this time must have reached a trillion decibels. 'It's Ella she's on the warpath.'

A hand removes the wig to reveal eyes looking like a road map of Spaghetti Junction.

'Hi! Sammy. What's the problem?' sleepily mouthed through a yawn.

'It's Ella, she's on her way in. Do - you - hear - me?'

'Zzzz.'

He's nodded back off so I kick him awake, 'She's - on - her - way - in.'

'That's nice,'….yawn.

'Wullie, the one thing in the world it's not is – nice. It's a disaster. Now please, please wake up, we're in the shit.' I can't resist another kick at him. It does the trick.

'You couldn't get me.....' Vera is at his side with the paracetemol and Irn-Bru. Every Glaswegian's answer to a hangover.

Downing the elixir of life he enquires, 'Right. What's the problem again?'

'Wullie, for- the - umpteenth - time, Ella is on her way, here!'

'Sammy! We've been to a party - she knew about. We slept the night here. So what?'

'*Vera's* the so what, you dickhead. She's just answered the phone tae Ella.'

'Shit!'

'That's what I've been trying to tell......'

'Let's think. You've got an answer phone, haven't you?'

'Yes. But we didn't have it on. It's broken.'

'What's the usual message?'

'Hello, Sammy Robb Motors. The name you can trust. We regret there is no one in at present to speak to. Please leave your...' relays Vera.

'And what did you say to Ella?

'Hello, Sammy Robb Motors. The name you can...then I dropped the phone on Sammy's head, in panic, when I realised it was Ella.'

'That's it then,' replies Wullie, snapping his fingers. 'No time to explain. Hurry! Change clothes with me.

Stripping down to my boxers I pull on the laddered tights to a giggle from Vera, followed by the polo neck sweater then the nightdress which I manage to get on back to front showing "Once a knight's enough" to its front. Wullie at the same time slips into my suit and accessories.

'What about Vera?' I enquire, expecting him to get her to strip down to her undies.

'She keeps her suit on and puts on my wig and shades.'

This Vera does, to such an affect that even her mother wouldn't have recognised her.

'Now this is what we tell Ella.' Wullie hastily outlines his plan. 'Got that?' he finishes.

'What happens now?' I enquire of Wullie.

'We sit and wait. Nobody panic,' he says staring pointedly at me, 'And all will be well. Trust me,' he finishes as he leans his chair back against the wall nonchalantly. Patting his jacket looking for cigarettes he stops, withdrawing a wallet, 'What's this?'

'That's the wallet that bloke flung at me last night,' I reply.

Wullie then throws the wallet across to me. Catching it I open it to find out who the owner is. Delving through it I find what I'm looking for, the owner's business card, along with several other cards. I study them, then spread them out on the coffee table saying, 'Cop this Wullie, "Sexy Sue – Discreet home visits", followed by, "Raunchy Roma – Stress relief", then, "Lulu – Parisienne Nights", and "Big Butch – Gentle masculinity".

'Wow!' exclaim Vera and Wullie together.

'Who's the perv?' queries Wullie.

'You'd never ever guess in a million years....It's only Sheriff "It's - a - pity - I - can't - give - you - life" Deighton.' The bane of our life.

'Never. No kidding?'

'The very same one, Wullie,' I reply, as I return the cards and Vanessa Viagras to the wallet.

With that a door slams. I'd recognise that slam anywhere – Ella.

'Nobody panic, nobody panic,' I squeak, as I'm busy panicking. With that the office door bursts open burying its handle deep into the plasterboard wall. The top hinge sighs and removes itself from the door. The door stopper, in sympathy, whines across the room burying itself in the opposite wall. Ella has arrived.

'Right where is she...the tramp?' said as she wallops a rolled up newspaper on the desk.

'Ella my love, what *are* you talking about?'

'Don't you Ella me, buggerballs. Where is she?'

'There's only Nancy here,' pointing to Vera, 'Wullie's girlfriend.'

'Who answered the phone then,' she slyly enquires.

'The answer phone, of course Ella.'

'It sounded human to me.'

'Well it would, would it not. It was recorded by one after all.'

'Don't get smart wie me, smart arse..... Why did it stop?'

'It's broken. It only goes, "Hello, this is Sammy Robb Motors, the name you can...."'

'I heard snoring as well.'

'No Ella. What you heard was it rewinding. I'll need to get it fixed.'

There's a long silence as she studies me suspiciously. Then, 'I suppose so. But it still sounded like the tart.' Next, turning to Vera who gets the stare, 'Sorry about this Nancy but wie these two scunners you can't help but think the worst of people.'

Vera who has kept a petrified silence replies, in a shaky disguised local vernacular voice,

'I can understaun that Mrs. Robb. They don't half take liberties wie you so they dae.'

'Now Ella love.....' I interrupt, trying to take the heat off Vera.

'Shut it *asshole*. Where did you get to last night?.... Out tom-catting wie the tart?'

'Ella, you know very well where I was. I was at Ned's with Wullie and Ver....,' realising my near error, I burst out coughing, hopefully recovering, '..and veery nice it was too.'

Deadly silence. Broken by, 'I'm sure it was but why didn't you come home?'

'So's not to bother the neighbours or you so early in the morning.'

'Not like you to be so considerate, Sammy. Then cunningly without warning, 'Tell me, where did you get your fancy dress then?'

Panic, I've no answer ready. But before I can start my incoherent babble Vera takes over, still using the local vernacular, 'I did it, so I did Mrs. Robb. Used an old nightie of mine and an old pair of tights. Wullie gaed him the polo neck, so he did.'

'Well that appears tae be that then. But there's something not right. Everything's too pat. If I put ma finger on it and I find out you're lying tae me Sammy…'

'Would I lie to you, Ella?'

'*You*! You're so warped you widnae know you're doing it.'

With that Ella turns and in a sharp voice which has reverted to her Bearsden posh, 'William!'

'Yes Ella,' he replies startled, having fallen asleep again.

'What were you and your girlfriend supposed to be dressed as last night?'

'The notorious gangsters, Bonnie and Clyde, Ella.'

'That figures,' Ella says turning the paper she'd arrived with over to its front page. The *Globe's* glaring banner headline proclaims: POLICE SHOT AT BY BONNIE AND CLYDE. Underneath a sub-title, "Bonnie and Clyde Rob Well Known

Sheriff at Gun Point - Police Warn Public Do Not Approach. The Gang Are Armed And Dangerous".

We all gasp. Ella continues, 'I wonder what Sergeant McLeod would give to find out the whereabouts of the "Hole in the Heid Gang". You know the Sergeant McLeod I'm talking about - don't you Sammy? He certainly knows you.'

'Ella, my love, you wouldnae shop us to that balloon......'

'Shut it Sammy. I've had enough of you for one day. Just make sure you're in tonight or else...and another thing,' pointing to the motto on the tunic showing, "Once a knight's enough", '........you can get that changed tae, "When pigs fly".'

With that she abruptly departs. Abruptly being what she does best. We wait until we hear the slam of the car door. With tyres howling, she's gone. We all burst out cheering, jumping up and down, clapping and hugging each other.

'We did it gang. We did it. What a brilliant piece of acting Vera. And as for you Wullie – what a master planner,' I ecstatically declare, with the enormous relief of ridding myself of the pent up emotions of the last half hour.

'Sorry to spoil the party boys but haven't we forgotten something? The police,' queries Vera.

'Sammy. Sammy. Vera's right we're still public enemy number one. Shooting at the polis, robbing a sheriff. We'll get life. They'll throw away the key. I need tae lie down.'

He's about to have one of his traumatic headaches.

'Look Wullie, there's absolutely nothing to worry about.'

*'Nothing tae worry about?* I don't have to tell *you* anything about the polis, Sammy, after what we've been through wie them. They'll be everywhere looking for us. A worldwide dragnet. The FBI, Interpol, Taggart, the whole shooting match.'

His mind's pickled with all these TV cop shows he watches.

'Now listen, both of you, and - stop - panicking. What I have in my hand,' holding up a business card, '...is our - get - out- of - jail - card. Trust me. It's the good Sheriff Deighton's business card with his *home* phone number. Following me?....' Both of them are sitting there goggled-eyed and nodding their heads. Clueless. '...Good. So let's give the good sheriff a ring and find out his views on "Big Butch and his gentle masculinity" to start with.

Using my mobile, I thumb in the numbers. 'Hello, is that Sheriff Deighton, I'm speaking to?' Pause. 'It is. Good. This is "Big Butch" here Sheriff. Just to let you know I'm the "Clyde" in the "Bonnie and Clyde" gang the polis are looking for......."

I suspect my partying days are about to draw to a close.

# CHAPTER EIGHT

## SAINT ANDREWS

Since the now infamous "Bonnie and Clyde" party, the trail has gone cold on Glasgow's most wanted. I suspect this might have something to do with Sheriff Deighton's generous intervention. This kindly act was possibly due to the fact that around the time of the party the good Sheriff was, unbeknown to me, about to be short-listed for elevation to High Court. It goes without saying that any form of scandal would have ended his ambition of high judicial office. It would appear they're not allowed to do "naughties" before they become judges, only after. So you can imagine his shock on being contacted by "Big Butch". The rest is history as they say.

Ella, in retaliation to the party going-ons has grounded me for the last two weeks. You know the usual. Home in time for meals. No drink. No sex - well not at home. All this I've managed to cope with admirably due to the blissful absence of Chuck from my life being as he's wandering his way round Scotland armed with my recommendations for suitable property adjacent to golf courses. However, being resigned to the fact that any form of bliss in my life is relatively short-lived, it comes as no surprise to me when I was informed last night that Chuck is due back from his travels today. Let's find out if there's any further news.

Entering the kitchen I leave the door open in its usual escape position .

Ella looks up and in that demure cultured voice of hers growls at me,

'What are you looking so happy about?'

'Because today, Ella – today, is about to become one of the happiest days of my life.'

'You're leaving me,' she intones, in a no - emotion - matter - of - fact voice.

'I wouldn't *leave* you, Ella.'

'I know Sammy, I know. I just don't carry that sort of luck. Well since you're not leaving me what's your problem then?'

'Not so much a problem, more like good news.'

'Like?'

'Like, when Chuck arrives we'll find out when he's going tae bugger off *permanently* and give me the peace I've enjoyed these last two weeks.'

Ella, gives me one of her slit-eyed malevolent stares and replies in a low scary voice, '*Maybe*, he's just on holiday. *Maybe,* he's joining the local golf course. *Maybe,* he's going to buy that empty house up the road or *maybe* he's even going to live with us - *for ever.* The house is big enough.'

I'm flabbergasted, speechless. She has his ear. She never jokes. I need to sit down.

I feel a deep depression descending over me. I need a dark room.

I'm awakened out of my bad dream by a razz–a–ma–tazz– jazz playing car horn. It can only be - Chuck. Rising unsteadily to my feet, still in shock, I look out the kitchen window and sure enough there's – the pink monstrosity. The car. Not him. His pink vintage, circa 1960, Cadillac complete with white wall tyres and space-craft tailfins rising above the bodyline is in the driveway. Fortunately, Ella can't blame me for this design abortion lowering the tone of the neighbourhood. He bought it off the internet from a specialist dealer in London. Digressed again, didn't I? Sorry. I'm still traumatised and babbling. I need to get to my calm-me-down pills.

The back door bangs open reverberating on its hinges. What is it with the pair of them? They're not happy unless the hinges need replacing on a weekly basis.

'How's you good folks, this fine morning?'

'Chuck, darling. I'm so glad you're home safely. Did you have a pleasant journey?' greets Ella as she rushes to embrace him.

'Sure as hell did, sis.'

'Hi! Chuck. Did you find a place to stay?' I ask, cutting right to it.

'Sammy means, did you find a nice place to stay when you were away, *didn't you,* Sammy?' Looking at me with malice. I'm about to reply, "No I didn't mean that" when I notice my escape route is blocked. Chuck is covering the back door and Ella craftily the hall exit. I surrender.

'To answer your question Sa-moo-el, I sure as hell did find a nice place. It was one of those quaint old guest houses you have over here. Something called the Old Course Hotel right on the ole St. Andrew's golf course. Now if you'll excuse ya'all I'm in need of a shower. Once I've freshened up I'll be right down to give ya'all the low down.'

'You go right up, Chuck, and when you come down I'll have a nice wee lunch ready for you,' says Ella at her creeping smaltzy best. Pass the sick bag.

The bullshitting bum has only gone and reduced one of Scotland's finest hotels to guest house status. The hotel runs parallel to the famous seventeenth fairway or "road hole" as it is known locally. It stands on the site of the old railway sheds demolished in the sixties. The hotel was formerly owned by British Transport Hotels - you, me, us the people. It was disgracefully sold off along with Gleneagles and Turnberry hotels for peanuts to who but - the multi-nationals as you no doubt guessed. I wouldn't suggest for a moment that there was any skulduggery involved but bear in mind, it was a political decision - enough said. This was, in my humble opinion, just a precursor to the loss of many publicly owned jewels; first and foremost among them being our Public Utilities. I mean to say our gas, water, electricity owned by the multi-nats and even worse - foreigners. All skinning us alive. Don't get me wrong I'm not in favour of full scale nationalisation but I do draw a line at our public utilities. What were they thinking of? Are any of our diabolical European partners' utilities in foreign hands? I think not. Haven't we been, and aren't we now, run by some of the biggest chancers ever to have crawled out a mother's womb. I'll maybe leave my hung office photo of Maggie permanently facing the wall in disgrace since I regret she is responsible for much of these ills. Forgive me, I know I've digressed big time but I feel a victim of an unsolved crime.

On the departure of Chuck upstairs, Ella takes up her battle station posture, finger extended, 'What is it with you? You're always picking on him. Now I'm telling you, just this once, you lay off him. Do you hear me? He's done you nae harm.'

'Done me no harm? How would you like to be called, *Sa-moo-el*, every time he claps eyes on you? It makes me sound like a coo mooing……..,'

'……Oh! Dear. Poor ole, *Sa-moo-el*,' she retorts mockingly.

'……not to mention that non stop bullshiting of his.'

'Look you. He hasnae been here for two weeks to do any bullshiting.'

'You don't have to tell me that. It's been…..' I stop. She's heading for the utensils. Now the problem of having these sort of friendly chinwags in a kitchen is the handiness of the life threatening equipment available. She's going for the old favourite, the meat tenderiser. I'm off - through the open door. Not even time to give her the finger.

I return an hour later having fortified my sagging confidence not to mention my fraying nerves with several large whiskies at my local in Milngavie. I sneak a look in the front lounge window. They are both there. Ella sitting sedately on the sofa, with sherry glass and a smug look on her face. This bodes ill for me. As I enter the lounge, Chuck is standing with Martini glass in hand and a foot long cigar in his mouth, still unlit - the coward. He greets me with, 'There you are Sa-moo-el. Come on in and join the party.'

Something's afoot and it's not just his cigar. Ella is now looking complacent as well as smug. I don't like this. She's right. He's *not* leaving. He's going to live with us for *ever*.

I head straight for the whisky and with shaking hand pour myself a good stiff measure. Armed with the glass of golden nectar I sit at the opposite end of the sofa from Ella leaving the usual safety gap between us.

Chuck, already standing, starts off with, 'Well folks, I'll bet you've all been a wondering what lil ole me's been up to these past weeks?' I certainly have, Chuck.

'Well, first off Sa-moo-el, I'd like to thank you ole buddy for your good efforts on my behalf with regard to your choice of real estate. Unfortunately I found the Outer Hebrides and Orkney islands just a lil off the beaten track.' I steal a look towards Ella and find I'm getting the demonic stare.

Chuck continues, 'Now as well intentioned as this act of kindness was, an even allowing for the fact, as Sa-moo-el says, that these islands are gifted with an all the year round tropical climate, I feel that they'd be just a lil too remote from being able to visit you good folk regularly.'

I've suddenly noticed Ella has slid up the sofa and is now within maiming distance. What's with her? I was only trying to help Chuck. Sensing the immediate danger I'm in, I quickly stand up and replenish my glass with another stiff measure then sit down at the other end of the room.

'As you both know I'm a golf nut.' He takes an air swing to prove it. Continuing, 'So I takes lil ole me off to St. Andrews, as I don't have to tell you the home of golf and fell in love with it. Its lil ole historic university, quaint streets, lovely beaches, harbour an of course the Old Course itself.' Hello, this sounds a bit better. Continuing, Chuck adds, 'Now to have all this on your doorstep would be a dream come true….. and I intend to make it mine, folks.' Sweetness to the ear. Should I kiss him, do a cartwheel or both?

As it happens, I stand up clapping exuberantly and shouting, 'He's the man. He's the man.' Not knowing exactly what that means but it sounds American.

'It's just his way of showing happiness at your good fortune,' espouses Ella through clenched teeth. She gets up from the sofa and stealthily moves in my direction. I seek sanctuary behind Chuck who puts his arm around my shoulder hugging me to him.

'Thanks for everything ole buddy. Really appreciate it.' My eardrum bears the full brunt of this but who am I to complain being in the arms of safety. Still with his arm around me he continues, '….To conclude folks, I've found myself a hunky-dory piece of real estate in Saint Andrews. So what I propose is that you and me, ole buddy, play golf on the Old Course next week and conclude all the legalities with the realator at the same time.'

'Sounds good to me Chuck.'

'Sorry, I've been such a drag on the kindness of you good kind folks. You'll no doubt be glad to see me go.'

'Never. Not me, Chuck. Just sorry you can't stay longer. We'll really, really, miss you,' I gush, sneaking a look at Ella who has a handkerchief to her eye dabbing it and giving a faint little sigh.

'Oh! Charles, I'll miss you terribly,' she sobs, as she slips the handkerchief up her sleeve and advances towards me with open arms. She's forgotten that I've fallen for that old knee in the crotch move of hers before.

I duck from under Chuck's arm and dash for the door. Tapping my watch, as I go, I remark over my shoulder, 'Late for the VAT man. The superplod don't like to be kept waiting. See ya'all. Have a nice day.'

With that I'm out the door, in the Jag and gone in under ten seconds. Ella's voice is ringing in my ears as I motor smartly out the drive.

'Sammy Robb. You lying, two faced hypocritical shit, get back here and apologise tae Chuck. Dae - you - hear - me?'

Tut, tut, Ella. What will the neighbours say?

A week later finds me and Chuck in St. Andrews. We've attended to the legalities and it looks like Chuck could be in residence within the month. That's the good news.

The bad is: I find myself on the first tee on the Old Course. The first tee and eighteenth green being adjacent to each other are surrounded on this beautiful morning by golf wise holiday makers and sightseers, all passing knowledgeable comments and clapping the fine shots being played. This was soon to change. Chuck has just teed off, to my surprise left handed, and hit an absolute screamer down the middle of the fairway. Maybe he does know Tiger after all. Now it's my turn. My nerves are shot to pieces and my legs have turned to jelly. Everywhere a sea of faces. Standing over the ball I'm desperately trying to remember the rudiments of my new "bionic thumb" method when I receive a prompt from the starter in his lilting Fifeshire accent.

'You gonna hit the ba son or staun there aw day hypnotising it?' said to the delight of the crowd. Well, you can imagine what that did to my already shattered confidence. I swing, eyes closed, and feel a contact with the ball. I look down the fairway; nothing in sight. 'At your feet, yells someone in the crowd.' To my embarrassment I look down and there it is lying there, winking at me, having just dribbled off the tee peg.

'Is he a golfer, mammy?' This from a ten year old urchin directly behind me.

'The tee box has more chance of being a golfer,' replies his mother.

That's all I needed. Several hacks and gouges later out of the sacred and hallowed turf finally sees me make solid contact with the ball. To the triumphant roar of the crowd, off it flies down the fairway, a real daisy cutter, soaring to the awesome height of two inches off the ground. As I swagger off the tee I hear the urchin saying to his mother, 'Is he deformed, mammy?'

'Naw, he's just using that new "bionic thumb" method, son.'

I don't have to tell you that's the "bionic thumb" method heading for the bin. However, all is not lost. In this month's "Golf for Duffers" I've just finished reading about the "Cyclops" method. You apparently use only one eye. Early trials are proving inconclusive. I think I might be closing the wrong eye. I've digressed again, haven't I?

Right. Where was I? Yes. After the nightmare of the first hole I settle down into something like my normal game; total crap. We eventually arrive at the second green where Chuck, on putting out, walks over to me and puts his arm round my shoulder and turns me to face the auld grey city of St. Andrews. There, rising through the shimmering heat being given off from the first and eighteenth fairways, on this most glorious of days, is the silhouette of the most famous golf clubhouse in the world: The Royal and Ancient. What a majestic sight!

Chuck, with free arm outstretched towards this truly magnificent vision and with trembling emotion rising in his voice declares, 'You know Sa-moo-el a man could die real happy looking at that view, yes Sir-eee.'

With that, something whizzes past my ear accompanied by a distant cry of "FORE!" causing me to duck my head. The cry came from the direction of the sixteenth fairway behind us. There's a sudden dull splat of ball - to - bone as a ball, travelling at great speed, strikes Chuck behind the ear and bounces into a bush. His knees give way as he slowly pirouettes and crumples to the ground on his back, poleaxed.

I bend down to him and in a voice of utter panic cry out, 'Chuck, Chuck, *talk* to me. *Please talk to me. Please.*'

With that a plus-foured gent comes bounding up to me and lisps, 'I say old chap, you didn't see a jolly old ball come in this direction. Eh. What! Shouted "fore" an all that.'

In a confused haze I find myself pointing at Chuck and saying to "plus-fours",

'After it bounced off his head it rolled into those bushes.'

Returning my attention to the unmoving Chuck, what I see I don't like. He's deathly white and I can't find a pulse. Still in panic mode I find myself yelling, 'Come on Chuck. You cannae do this to me. What'll Ella say. Please, Chuck *please*.'

Nothing. As I'm getting my mobile out of my golf bag, "Plus-Fours" comes bounding up to me again and says, 'Found my ball, old chap. In the jolly old bush as you said. Not too au-fait with the rules. Do I get a preferred lie from the bush?'

I don't believe this, it's surreal. I vent my anger, 'Listen you, dickhead, the only thing getting a preferred lie is him – an by the looks of it – it's going to be in a cemetery.' Pointing towards the prostrate Chuck.

'Oh! I say. Do you think I've hurt him?'

'Hurt him! hurt him! You've only gone and *fuckin*g killed him.'

And so ended one of the worst days of my life. Right up there, on hindsight, with my marriage to Ella.

The ensuing period after the tragic accident I am trying desperately to forget. At the coroner's inquest, held in St. Andrews, the finding of accidental death was in keeping with the evidence presented. Seeing "Plus- Fours" at the inquest my mind replayed for the umpteenth time his cry of "fore" which had caused me to duck my head fractionally. The problem I'm having trouble dealing with is that if I had not ducked my head would Chuck be still alive? Conversely, would I be dead? My dilemma.

Ella, contrary to my expectations, on that fatal day has attributed no blame to me. Quite the reverse in fact. She has found time to comfort and help me with my dilemma. Soothing it away by insisting that "what's *for* you won't go *past* you." It was Chuck's time, she says. She calls it "Fate – Serendipity". She can be lovely when she wants to be.

I've been told that Chuck's lawyer has found a codicil in the will asking for a burial at sea. I have arranged for Chuck to be moved to the Glasgow mortuary of McGregors, the family's undertaker. Swing easy, Chuck. R.I.P

# CHAPTER NINE

## THE FUNERAL

Wullie has now been in his part time driver's job at McGregors for nearly three weeks. In this period he has befriended Tam, the head embalmer, head pallbearer, head usher and general factotum. Tam's a real nice guy but by Wullie's reckoning is as thick as two short planks. For Wullie to think that of you, you must be a real thicko. As Wullie enters the mortuary, Tam is just putting the phone down.

'That was the boss, Wullie, he's got a special for us back end of the week. Some bloke's died and wants buried at sea. You and me's tae prepare the coffin right away. Let's go.'

'Go where, Tam?'

'Tae the merchant tae buy the lead.'

'The lead?'

'Aye. It's to weight doon the coffin so it sinks tae the bottom.'

'Tam,' says Wullie putting an arm around Tam's shoulder, 'A wee word wie you, son.

Does it no strike you as a bit daft to weight doon a coffin wie lead when concrete blocks would do just as well?'

'You cannae do that Wullie. The bloke's paid for lead.'

'Why not, Tam? The blokes deid. He's no going tae tell anyone, is he?'

'But it's unlucky tae steal from the deid, Wullie.'

'Look Tam, it's not your *actual* stealing. It's more a swop.'

'So we buy concrete blocks instead of lead?'

'No Tam, no. We still buy the lead.'

'Right got it. Then we give the lead back after the funeral.'

Wullie, sighing heavily, replies, 'Tam. - What's the point of buying the lead in the first place just tae give it back?'

'Aye right, Wullie.' He hasn't a clue. I'll need tae spell it oot for him, thinks Wullie.

'Tam, watch my lips. We - buy - the - lead. Bring - it - back - here. Let - McGregor - see - it. Then - we - do - the - switch. Are you following or is it still too complicated for you?

'Naw, naw I'm following nae bother, Wullie.'

'Then we take the lead tae Nutters scrappy and flog it. We go fifty-fifty. O.K'

'You sure it'll work, Wullie?'

'Trust me Tam. Trust me.'


Later in the week finds Tam, now in his guise as head usher, dressed in top hat, black frock coat, pin stripe trousers and gleaming shoes, sitting in the hearse with Wullie awaiting the exit of the mourners from church.

Tam breaks the silence with, 'Wullie you know yon brick wall around the rubbish bins back in the yard?'

'Aye.'

'Well, it's no there anymore. McGregor's asking where it went.'

'I took it down. It was in a dangerous state.'

'What did you dae with it?'

'Don't ask Tam.'

'Wullie, you didnae use it for...' Tam's voice tails off as he turns round and points at the coffin. Wullie, with an abashed look shrugs his shoulders with hands held palms up.

'You're not going ta believe this, Wullie. McGregor's asked me tae ask you if you'll rebuild the wall. Says he'll pay you tae dae it.' How lucky can you get thinks Wullie.

He was very soon to find out.

'Look out Wullie, here they come,' whispers Tam as the mourners start to file out.

'Bloody hell, Tam! That's Sammy and Ella. Christ, that must be Chuck back there,' exclaims Wullie with thumb gesture to rear of the hearse. 'Sammy, told me he was going tae Chuck's funeral but I didnae realise it was this wan.'

'How'd you know no it wis this wan?'

'You're the heid usher and you didnae tell me the name of the deceased.'

'Why'd you no get an invite tae it, in any case?'

'I didnae really know him when we were wee. He was really Sammy's pal and now that Ella's nobbin it wie high society she's no likely tae invite me, is she?'

'That's for sure,' This draws Tam a stinker of a look from Wullie. '...Well, why didn't you recognise the house when we picked them up?'

'Because he's moved house and I huvnae clapped eyes on the new one.'

'Well why didn't you recognise them when I ushered them intae the car when we picked them up?'

'Look you, what's going on wie aw these questions. Am I auditioning for brain of Britain or whit?..... If you must know I was listening tae football focus.'

'You didnae hear if Thistle were successful with their bid for Beckham. That's Billy no the....'

'Tam, shut it. This is serious. Why didn't *you* recognise them?'

'I don't know them, Wullie.'

'Well you must be the only one in Glasgow that disnae know them. If Sammy finds out what you've did tae *him*,' says Wullie with a thumb gesture to the back of hearse, 'He'll never speak tae me again.'

'It wis *your* brilliant idea tae use the bricks from oor rubbish bins,' replies Tam indignantly. '...If you hadnae talked me intae *stealin* the lead we widnae be in this mess.'

'Aye O.K Tam. Off you go and dae your ushering,' groans Wullie as he stretches into the glove compartment and comes out with with his ever-present disguise kit of dark glasses and orange moustache.

The chosen port of departure is Leith Docks, Edinburgh, home of Brittania, Her Majesty's former yacht, now a major tourist attraction. The coffin as per Chuck's late instruction has to be laid to rest in St. Andrews Bay within view of the Old Course.

Wullie and Tam have been told by McGregor to deliver the coffin to the boat, help load it on and return to Maryhill. The mourners will be brought back by the remainder of the cortege. Wullie, on arrival at Leith, due to the weight of the coffin, has to get out to give the cortege drivers and boat crew a hand to load it aboard. Standing to the side of the loading, with heads bowed, are Sammy and Ella. Ella is naturally distraught. Sammy, naturally suspicious, as he whispers to Ella, 'Ella, does that funeral bloke, the one with the top hat and orange lop sided moustache, dark glasses and limp, look familiar to you?

'Sammy! Show some respect. My poor brother Charles, his last few feet on earth before a watery grave and you ranting on about nothing. Show some respect.'

'He still looks familiar to me,' mutters a still suspicious Sammy under his breath.

Wullie and Tam, their job over, set off back to Glasgow. On the way they decide to stop for a beer, as is their wont. Wullie, pulling off the motorway, parks the hearse outside the rural pub. The landlord, who is standing outside with others having a cigarette, asks them to park round the back out of sight telling them, 'Sorry lads, having tae ask you to dae that. But due tae they numpties doon in London and their smoking ban, business is dead. If you'll excuse the pun. So hearses, parked outside, are no going tae help me any. Are they now?

'Fair comment, pal,' agrees Wullie as they move the hearse round the back before adjourning to the pub.

Tam, the decent guy that he is, is feeling a bit guilty about all the happenings bemoans,

'I've got a bad, bad, feeling aboot this Wullie.'

'Don't be daft, Tam. As Humphrey Gocart once said, "Dead men don't talk" so get them in.'

'Whit aboot the drinking and driving, Wullie?'

'Ask yourself, Tam, when did you last hear of a hearse being stopped by the polis.'

'Nice wan Wullie. Same again then?

Returning to Glasgow and after garaging the hearse, Tam and Wullie proceed to demolish what's left of the day in Rileys. When Wullie finally gets home he switches on the TV and goes into the kitchen to make a mug of tea to go with his fish and chips from Giovanni's which were served by his old flame Tina, recently returned to Glasgow, who he still loves but hasn't plucked up the courage to ask out yet due to his situation with Rita. The tea made, he returns to the lounge where the late night news reader is announcing, "The new Chief Constable of Glasgow today stated his intention to bring in a zero tolerance policy on all crimes, in an effort to stop the spiralling crime wave".

'And about time too,' agrees Wullie, through a mouthful of well vinegared chips.

After outlining the Chief's policies to blunt the local villains activities the announcer continues - "Regarding the coffin found on the foreshore of St.Andrews bay earlier today, we are informed the police are treating this as a suspicious incident". The TV picture shows a coffin lying on a beach with police and crime scene investigators dressed in "space suits" surrounding it. "More on this matter in later bulletins", continues the reader. "Now to sport. Partick Thistle had their bid for Billy Beckham...."

Wullie snaps off the TV and with head in hands groans in despair, 'Bloody hell! The coffin. It *cannae* have surfaced already. It *cannae*. They was good heavy bricks, still had the mortar on them! Christ almighty, wie that new Chief Constable and his zero tolerance – I'll get life.'

He reaches for his mobile and punches in the numbers,

'Tam, you bam, answer me. Answer me. Where are you?' By this time shaking the life out the phone. No reply.

A few minutes later Wullie, complete with false moustache and dark glasses, was to be seen slipping furtively out of his close heading for McGregor's garage. Letting himself in he slips into the back of the hearse. Within minutes he is asleep in a drink induced stupor. The next thing Wullie is aware of is a hand on his shoulder, shaking him awake.

Sitting abruptly upright and banging his head off the hearse roof in the process he squawks, 'It's no me. I'm innocent. I was framed.' His stock answers to the police.

'Wullie, it's me, Tam. You've been dreaming.'

'Bloody hell, Tam. You just aboot gave me a heart attack, sneaking up on me like that. And no, I've not been dreaming.

You and me's in big, big, trouble,' said as he rubs the stiffness out of his joints.

'How's that then Wullie?'

'The coffin, Tam. The coffin on the beach at St. Andrews. We're wanted men.'

'Wanted for whit?' quizzes Tam.

'Wanted for whit, he says. It was on the news last night. They found *our* coffin on the beach at St. Andrews.'

'Naw Wullie. They found *a* coffin but it wisnae oors.'

'Wisnae…wisnae.. o..o..urs?' stutters Wullie in utter amazement.

'Naw. According tae this morning's news the coffin was found yesterday *morning* - *before* ours even took tae the water in the *afternoon*.'

'So we're no fugitives from justice then?'

'No, Wullie. Never were. Just listen tae this. The coffin that was washed up was fifty years old. You widnae believe it but them undertakers, all those years ago, stole the lead and used bricks!'

'And that's it just coming tae the surface now,' gasps Wullie with delight.

'Aye. Can you credit anyone doing a thing like that? Gets the profession a bad name. Eh! Wullie?'

'Just goes to show you Tam. You cannae trust anybody nowadays.'

'Wullie?'

'Whit.'

'Your moustache's at a funny angle.'


Work finished, I head for Rileys where I am served by old Jock.

'Evening Jock. Where's the ogre?' Having noticed Agnes's absence.

'The old bag's doon at the sweetie shop mugging the waens. Just jokin, Sammy. She's actually doon in the cellar getting the rack ready for the next victim.' Thumb pointing to the raised hatch in the floor behind the bar. 'Now what can I get you – the usual?'

'Aye. And a pint for Wullie, as well,' I reply, having noticed Wullie in his usual seat.

'I'll bring your nuts over to you, Sammy, when she closes the hatch.' The nuts being hung from the display gantry directly behind the open hatch which he can't get at.

'That'll do fine, Jock.'

Lifting the drinks I head for Wullie. It's a racing certainty he was the pall bearer at Chuck's funeral so I deliberately sit opposite him to see his reactions.

He opens our conversation with, 'Havnae seen you since you went tae Chuck's funeral, Sammy. How'd it go?'

'Spectacular, Wullie, spectacular. Did I tell you that Chuck was buried at sea.'

'My, that's a coincidence. McGregors had a sea burial this week as well.'

'That must have been, Chuck's!' I reply, stringing him along.

'Well, I didnae know that,' replies Wullie, who I just know is lying through his back teeth, '....McGregor had me attending tae another one. We're so busy just now, people are dropping like flies. It's all this global warming you know.'

'I'm sure I saw you at Chuck's funeral,' I reply, staring straight at him.

'Definitely no me, Sammy.'

'I must've been mistaken. So answer me this then, who's the weirdo wie the orange lop sided moustache, dark glasses and a limp?'

'Couldnae think who that could be, Sammy. Maybe McGregor used a casual.'

'A casual wie a lop sided moustache and looking dead weird. McGregor must be getting desperate,' I reply, noting that Wullie is beginning to look a bit fidgety and guilty.

'Geez,' Wullie says, snapping his fingers, 'I've just suddenly remembered, Sammy. Vince did his back in and we did have tae get in a casual at the very last minute.'

'Is that a fact, Wullie. Its just that I don't usually forget weirdos,' I state, continuing to stare penetratingly at him, '.....Especially ones that forget which leg tae limp on.'

'Don't blame you, Sammy. He sounds weird to me. I'll have a word wie McGregor next time I see him.  He's bound tae know who it is.'

'Incidentally, Wullie, I hear McGregor used lead to weight down the coffin,' Wullie looks totally mesmerized. '....Now that's a risky business with so many light fingered weirdos about. If it would've been me, I would've flogged the lead and used bricks. What would you've done Wullie?'

Wullie has a fit of coughing before spluttering, 'All I can say about that Sammy is, that it's all "Hearse - say".

'Nice one Wullie. Nice one.'

Well that's laid that to rest.

That seemed years ago. I knew it was Wullie at Chuck's funeral, he'd used the same orange coloured moustache as a disguise when he went into hiding from the Dumfries police, the FBI and Interpol as his over supercharged brain would have you believe. What made me laugh was that he kept forgetting what leg to limp on. He was welcome to the lead. Chuck could well afford it and it'll help towards the loss of Wullie's stolen pocket money all those years ago. He'll maybe now get his

Barbie doll. These thoughts are coursing through my mind as I listen to Chuck's lawyer droning on about how many millions Chuck has left Ella in his will. Most guys in my position would be delighted. Not me. She was impossible before. Can you imagine what my life's going to be like now? Amen. Another chapter in life finished.

# CHAPTER TEN

## ROUGH JUSTICE

In the months that that have elapsed since Chuck's ill fated demise, life appears to be returning to hum-drum normality. Now that all the legalities, on both sides of the Atlantic, have been successfully completed Ella is, as Wullie would say, as rich as Creosote. Me? I've inherited a puke pink Cadillac and Chuck's set of left handed golf clubs; more on these later.

On the personal front, the kindly compassion shown to me by Ella during *my dilemma*, is on the wane – extinct to be exact. This appears to have coincided with her own period of mourning coming to an end. While not conclusive, I base my assumptions on various clues that have come to my attention. Primarily, that she has recently become a highlighted blonde, dripping bling, and sporting a Mediterranean tan straight from the sun-kissed beaches of the local tanning parlour. A scarlet Ferrari coupe now sits centre stage in the drive replacing the company Fiesta. What are my thoughts on it all? Well, the fact is that *if* Chuck was still alive, and how I now wish he was, the situation would not exist. '*If,* as we know, didn't happen - as it never does. So, sad to say, Ella, on inheriting this immense wealth, has allowed herself to be swallowed by all its tenuous promises. She's ignored her humble and admirable working class roots. To explain I need, of course, to digress.

The gap site between the tenements, from where we operate our business, at one time had two magnificent red sandstone buildings on it. Unfortunately, due to the uncharted meanderings of the Maryhill mine workings, subsidence took place in the early nineteen hundreds with the resultant demolition of these fine buildings. The gap site was ironically turned it into a coal yard with stables because in those far off days the wagons were mostly horse drawn. It remained a coal yard until just after the last war. The one with Germany that is – there being so many of late, due to the present incompetent "Weapons of Mass Destruction" warmongers at Westminster, that you tend to get lost as to which war was the last *last* one. Sorry, I appear to have digressed on a digression. Continuing. In the early fifties Ella's father acquired the site and turned the stables into a workshop for his garage business and when the ground floor flat of the adjacent tenement building became vacant he acquired that and turned it into a car showroom. Through subsequent shrewd business negotiations he acquired the remainder of the tenement with all those imprisoned pounds at the end of his working day. A clever entrepreneurial move forming the basis of the business we now run. But his real good fortune was as yet to happen. He employed a suave, good looking, apprentice motor mechanic – me. I met Ella, his daughter, and we married. Her parents retired and passed the business to us. Ella's brother Chuck had by this time emigrated to America with my pocket money. This was during a period in American history when they were allowing *anybody* in. After many years of hardship, long hours and hard work Ella and me built the business up to the level it is today. Successful enough to give us a good standard of living such that we were able to move from our one bedroom tenement apartment, next to the garage, to a three bedroom bungalow in suburbia – Bishopbriggs. We'd arrived – or so I thought. All this Ella has now forgotten and forsaken. Me?..... Never…. That's my heritage.

My relaxation from the stress of every day life as inflicted on me by Ella – is golf. I'm not particularly good. In fact I've heard it said of me that I get rabbits a bad name. Even the club professional has given up on me. Every time I make an appearance at the club a closed sign appears on his door as if by magic. His gripe is based on previous lessons I had from him. Apparently "reverse tuition" took place. This means he has been inflicted by my full armoury of faults: head-ups, fresh air swings (missing of ball), topping, slicing, hooking and shanking. The latter, being the jinx of all jinxes was, according to the professional, the last straw. He's a wimp. Sam Torrance (my hero) wouldn't worry about minor faults like that. This is the reason I've had to seek alternative methods in my quest for "*The Secret*". As you already know the "bionic thumb" method bit the dust at St.Andrews along with Chuck and the current "Cyclops" method will, if I don't stop, render me cross-eyed for ever. The article did not explain the inventor had a glass eye.

Why do I put myself through so much torment? Well, as any golfer will tell you, once you're smitten, you're hooked for ever. An addict - with no known antidote. The quest for golfing immortality - the secret held by those golfing gods: Hogan, Nicklaus, Palmer, Woods and Sam Torrance (my hero) to name but a few of the carriers of this, the most contagious of diseases, continues throughout one's lifespan. And some say even beyond. Those who claim to have successfully given the noble game up are but a hollow shell of their former selves. There are regular reported sightings of them wandering the streets after dark, in a zombie like state, taking air swings at imaginary balls and shouting that dreadful Americanism, "get in the hole". Is there no help available I hear those of you with compassion in your heart, ask. Simple answer - none. The nearest thing to help, I am aware of, is that offered by several unfinished tomes on "How to give up golf". Being unfinished due largely to the authors being led off to the "funny farm" before completion. So there you have it – a curse worse than that of Tutankhamen and I call that relaxation. Mind you everything is relative. I mean compared with Ella….it's par excellence and that's about the only par I'm ever likely to score.

However, an article in one of my golf magazines quotes from "The Freedom of Information Act" an HM Government white paper on the "Mental stability of golfers and their suitability for becoming cabinet ministers". Allegedly the current incumbent at number 11 Downing Street, having fallen asleep during a cabinet meeting listening to his neighbour from number 10, "The First Minister of Fairy Tales and Porkies", suddenly awoke from his deep slumber shouting "fore to the right". The remainder of his colleagues, awakened by his cry, ducked under the table. From this insight it is fair to assume that the Chancellor is obviously a golf addict but of his fellow colleagues it's wrong to imply that they are true addicts since their adopted position of ducking is the norm to them during their working day. The last I read of the matter was that the Chancellor was setting up a task force to look into golf addiction. This can only be but good news to all us addicts.

Now, where was I? Yes. As you know, I've inherited Chuck's left-handed clubs. But I'm right handed – or am I? I mean I could be left handed and not know it. This could be the missing link to my golfing salvation, *"The Secret".* Well, as luck would have it, Dougie, the *Justice* on the *Sunday Informer*, rang me this morning suggesting a game at his club tomorrow morning. Having not had star billing in his column recently I felt it safe to accept the invite. It will also give me the opportunity to try out being left- handed.

I mean it can't be all that much different from being right-handed, can it?

The following morning finds me up bright and early. A few back garden swipes, I've given up using the word swing to describe my golf action for fear of contravening the trades description act, finds me completely at ease being left-handed. A hasty look at my watch tells me I just have time for a quick high cholesterol "Desperate Dan" breakfast at Ronnie's Greasy Spoon before teeing it off, up the road at Dougie's club. After a belter of a gut busting breakfast I bid mine host, bedecked in his usual grease splattered attire, the usual two finger farewell which he reciprocates with the same gesture whilst scratching his rear. I then point the Jag towards Dougie's club. After the short journey up the road, I turn in between two ancient sandstone gateposts with the club name, Maryhill Golf and Country Club, carved into them and picked out in, now flaking, gold paint. As I then proceed up the tree lined avenue of Glasgow's most exclusive golf club to the stone built mansion, home of a former nineteenth century tobacco baron, now the clubhouse, the nagging doubts begin regarding being a lefty. Do I use the same grip? Which knee do I bend on the backswing? Too late now - I've arrived at the clubhouse car park and there's Dougie, standing beside his car, waiting. We greet each other with the customary shake of hands and exclamations of what a fine morning it is for golf before entering the clubhouse to change into our gear.

On the way to the first tee I happen to look up at the large, stone mullioned, square bay window overlooking the tee. A myriad of faces are pressed against the window to see who Dougie is playing with. Dougie, being the *Justice* in the *Sunday Informer,* the people's crusader for good against the evil forces of rip-off merchants, usually has a game with his intended victims before crucifying them in his column. I should know having had star billing on several occasions.

Arriving on the first tee Dougie turns and says to me in a low but threatening voice,

'Remember, Sammy, we're playing "pure" golf... none of your "rogue stuff." O.K?'

I tell him "cross my heart and hope to shank for ever" should I resort to such tactics; more on this later. We toss a coin for honour. This to see who goes first. Dougie wins and tees off, hitting a topped running shot that scampers into the rough some one hundred and eighty yards distant. Now my turn.

Removing my *left-handed* driver from the bag, Dougie, showing his newshound sharpness observes, 'Sammy, what's with the lefty clubs? Didn't know you were ambidextrous.'

'It's my first time being a lefty.'

'You mean your, *first - first time?* You haven't played the other way round before?'

'Correct. Well not quite. I had a few practice swipes this morning in the garden.'

This answer brings on a coughing fit as his face turns the same colour as the ash of the cigarette he's choking on. Taking up my stance which suddenly feels unnatural, like wearing your underpants on back to front, I hear this wheezed whisper, 'Don't you think you should stand the other way round, Sammy?'

Silly me, I've only gone and taken up my usual right-handed stance. Embarrassed, I correct my stance to suit that of being left-handed. This left handed lark is all getting far too complicated but not as complicated as the actual horror when my situation becomes stark reality. In the past when I've played here right-handed, the bay window of the clubhouse was behind me, now the bay is in front of me with a sea of leering faces pressed against it. If there ever was a "beam me up, Scotty" moment in my life then this is it. My knees, as usual, have turned to rubber as they always do on first tees. Why do golf courses have first tees? Why don't they start at the second hole instead?

With that, I'm shocked out of my daydream by Dougie's whispered words, 'Don't want to hurry you Sammy, but the next game is heading for the tee.'

Nothing for it then – let's rip it. A full corkscrew backswing with the momentum of greased goose-shit, followed by a jump assisted forward lunge results in an eyes closed contact with the ball. Opening my eyes I witness the ball projecting itself, with *Scud* missile velocity, towards the bay window. The faces in the window disappear nano seconds before the ball strikes one of the stone window mullions and ricochets off it up the fairway some two hundred yards distant. I'm impressed - two hundred yards!

'Sammy, for fuck's sake, you just about took out the Captain, the committee and the clubhouse window,' wails Dougie in a panic-stricken voice.

I ignore this remark as I stride off the tee, putting it down to petty jealousy, being as I'm twenty yards ahead of him off the tee. With my new "lefty" method off to a flying start, I stride confidently to my ball and swipe it similarly to my first swipe. Unfortunately, there is no window mullion this time to deflect the ball back onto the fairway as it ploughs its merry way into the deep boondocks. Dougie, having already hit his second shot first, a clever trick if you think about it, is in similar trouble on the other side of the fairway. Entering the woods I find my ball in a bush – totally unplayable. Nothing for it but to play the old hand mashie. The main weapon in the "rogue" golfer's armoury. This shot comprises the lifting of the ball into the throwing hand and projecting it back onto the fairway or green as the predicament warrants. 'Good shot,' I hear Dougie cry as my hand mashie bounces onto the green. I better go across and help him find his ball, as "pure" golf etiquette demands. On searching I find his ball, which unfortunately for me, is lying with a clear view to the green. I stumble and in a classical "rub of the green", a sort of "God's will" manoeuvre, inadvertently kick it into a bush shouting as I do, 'Found it Dougie.....but I'm afraid it's unplayable.'

From my actions you mustn't conclude that the art of "rogue" golf is a cheats' charter. Far from it. It was designed as an equaliser to give the less talented, in fact the no-hopers like me, a fairer chance to win against those good enough to have risen to the dizzy heights of obtaining a handicap. Further, any promises forced on you by a "pure" golfer, apropos Dougie's first tee coercion of me, are not recognised by "rogue" golfers.

Sorry, about the digression, but I felt it necessary to lead those uninitiated through the minefield that exists between "rogue" and "pure" golf.

Reaching the sixteenth hole I unfortunately hit a wayward shot, which on ricocheting off yet another tree, narrowly misses Dougie who has to throw himself into a bush to get out of its deadly hurtling path. Extracting himself from the bush, bearing a multitude of lacerations to his face and hands and with a *Julius Caesar* halo of twigs around his head, he furiously splutters at me, 'Right-that-does-it, Sammy. I better tell you why I invited you here before you end up *killing* me.'

'Don't joke about a thing like that, Dougie,' I reply sadly as my mind drifts back to Chuck on that fateful day in St. Andrews.

'I'm not joking. You're a bloody menace.'

Accepting this, to my mind unfair criticism, I reply in a peeved tone, 'You know you can be very hurting at times, Dougie.'

'You - ain't - heard - nothing - yet,' replies Dougie near to an apoplectic fit.

My antenna's twitching. Something's up, so I innocently ask, 'How's that then, Dougie?'

'Well, Sammy, as I don't have to tell *you*, I'm *The Justice*......' So that's it. The two faced-crud - pretending it's a friendly game, '.....and the mail bags have been bursting at the seams with complaints about you for years.'

'As I've told you before, Dougie, if you bothered to read them closely you'd find most of them's fan mail,' I yell up at him from a deep greenside bunker.

'Fan mail! If that's fan mail I'd hate to read the complaints,' comes his sarcastic reply.

Right that's it - a state of war now exists. Being in the bunker and out of sight I effect a quick hand mashie, followed simultaneously by a handful of sand flung in the air, which sees the ball roll onto the green. This action is known as a "Sahara" to all "roguers." On climbing out of the bunker and stumbling up the steep slope to the green I notice that both the balls are lying next to the pin. How did Dougie manage that? The last I saw of him, before my visit to the bunker, he was in the "fucarwe" rough - right up to his neck. I hope he hasn't resorted to "rogue" golf. I hate cheats.

Leaving the green Dougie puts his arm round my shoulder saying sympathetically,

'How many years have I known you, Sammy? - Years,' answering his own question. '.....I know you're a rogue Sammy, in everything you do. You can't help it. It's inherent in your nature. How many complaints have I suppressed? Too many to count,' answering himself again, '....but.... this time you've overstepped the mark.'

'How's that then, Dougie?

'You sold my editor's wife a run-around - only it doesn't.'

'When was this?'

'Ten days ago.'

'How unlucky can she get. Out of warranty by nine days.'

'That's typical of you. Everything a joke.' What's he on about? I meant it.


We tee off and next meet on the green - eventually. Leaving the green I start with,

'I still can't place her, Dougie. Maybe Eck sold it to her. What make was it?'

'A Corsa.'

'The Corsa! It was a *wee* cracker. As I remember, it was minted, low mileage (of course) wie bundles of extras like revolving wheels, see through windows, ....'

Dougie exasperatedly rasps, 'Right, Sammy stop right there. I've heard enough of your crap. You've gone too far this time. My boss wants blood - yours'.

'Can't understand why. I mean it even came with Embassy Coupons.'

'SAMMY! Embassy Coupons went out with the ark.'

'I know, Dougie. But they're collectors items now worth....'

'Sammy! Stop. Please stop. I can't help you anymore. You know what to expect.'

'The usual. Would you buy a car from *this man* - type headline?'

'Yes.'

'Well, you did.'

'Please, please, don't remind me, Sammy. Have you seen the state of it?'

'Yeah. I'd be ashamed to bring it here if I was you. Now I've got the very thing for you - a lovely clean, low mileage (of course), Volvo estate which I could let you have at a *bargain* price of......'

'Sammy, do's a favour....shut it.'

The game is by some miraculous means level with two holes to go even after using the "rogue" golfers, time-honoured, recommendations of nerve jangling tactics like key or loose change pocket rattling, tuneless whistling, sneezing and coughing just as your opponent is about to strike the ball. So my diversionary tactics, which have been successful against Dougie in the past, are proving to be of no avail this time. He's either playing to, or below, his handicap, considered by most "rogue" exponents to be a form of cheating. A closer scrutiny of his every move is now required. But how?  Considering the only time we ever meet is on the tee and the green. The green sward of fairway being treated, by both, as a no-go area.

As we are about to tee off at the seventeenth and with all other efforts failing I am left with no option but to use the most admired of all diversionary tactics – the "fartfolong."

This tactic is, whilst never having as yet used it myself, I am assured is guaranteed to break down the most inured of "pure" golfers. Reducing them to whimpering wimps. Waiting for Dougie to reach the zenith of his backswing I let go a whistling cheek vibrating emission of body gases, increasing in volume throughout his swing, climaxing in a loud thunderclap as he hits the ball. Not a flinch from him as he hits a screamer all of two hundred yards straight into the rough to join my already taken shot which has, as is its norm, found its way into the woods.

As he leaves the tee he mutters to me, 'Weather could be changing, Sammy. Thought I heard a rumble of thunder.'

I am totally deflated in more senses than one. Why did the "fartfolong" fail? It could be, being inexperienced, the way I executed it. However, having had the "Desperate Dan" breakfast at Ronnie's I really felt qualified to join those accepted experts in the noble art of "fartfolonging" - the partakers of vindaloo curries, spiced kebabs and copious amounts of lager. A cautionary word of warning - this is the only time, in golf, when it is not advisable to follow through.

The fairway, for the last seventeen holes, has been treated as sacrosanct - our preferred route to the green being through the rough or woods. This hole proves to be no different. On arriving at the green Dougie enquires, 'How many shots did you take?'

'A chip and putt six,' I reply.

'So did I,' he mumbles, 'but I thought I heard you taking at least six shots in the trees.'

'What you actually heard - Dougie, was three shots and.... three echoes.'

He doesn't look happy with my answer but it is bad form for the "pure" golfer to query his opponent's honesty. What was there to query?

So all square it is with one hole to go.

Standing on the eighteenth tee I confide in him, 'Tell you what, Dougie. Since it's you, and provided you promise not to tell anyone, you get your boss to send his wife back with the car and I'll refund her money. Can't be fairer than that.'

'Sorry, Sammy, I told you there's nothing I can do. He wants to nail you.'

Teeing off at eighteen a miracle of miracles happens - we both find the fairway. Watching each other like hawks on every shot, we proceed onto the green in three shots each. The advantage lies with Dougie being only three feet from the hole as opposed to my ten. I putt first, narrowly missing the hole, and tap in for a five. Dougie, sensing the opportunity of victory, with a flat straightforward three foot putt, gleefully gloats,

'This to win the money, Sammy.' Not if I can help it.

As he is about to strike his putt my body is racked, once again, with a bout of consumptive coughing. Totally oblivious to my spasm he strokes the putt sweetly into the hole for the winning four. He gives a jubilant jig of ecstasy throwing his hands skywards.

'I've won. I've won,' he joyfully cries almost in tears.

It's now or never time. I step forward with hand outstretched to congratulate him, 'Well played, Dougie. Allow me,' I enthuse, bending down to retrieve his ball from the hole. I pick it out, examine it and ask, 'What ball are you playing?'

'A Trueshot 4. Why?

'Because, Dougie,…this is a Trueshot 2. I'm sorry to say you must have played the wrong ball at the last hole.' This in "pure" golf means the loss of hole, or in this case the game, being as it's the last hole of an all-square match.

'I, I, I……' The poor sod, who has unwittingly fallen for the old "now you see them - now you don't" two ball switch, is too dumbfounded to speak.

'What a way to loose a game,' I console him.

'I, I, I…..,' stammers the bold boy now somewhat deranged, 'I, I, I,…….'

Being of a compassionate nature I comfortingly say to him, 'Don't worry, Dougie, I won't tell anyone. It's not as if you *deliberately* tried to cheat.'

I think the Dougie has, in billiard parlance, been well and truly potted.


On the way to the locker room we pass a duck pond. The splash, followed by ever increasing ripples is the last ever seen of Chuck's golf clubs. Being left-handed's not for me. You need to be a contortionist to play that way round, well at least the way I play it. However, in this month's "Golf for No-Hopers" there's an article on "The Deep Lung Theory." This, in the ever continuing quest for "*The Secret,*" could finally be the answer.

In the locker room there is a funereal silence as Dougie, counting off the holes on his fingers, tries to figure out where it has gone wrong. In an effort to cheer him up I console him with, 'Just in case your Captain was still looking out the window would you like me to find him and explain, that it wasn't as it looked, that you didn't *really* cheat.'

Turning a shade of purplish puce he stammers, 'No! No thanks, Sammy. I've just remembered I've got another pressing appointment.' With that he rushes me out of the locker-room and into the car park.

Standing alongside Dougie's car I casually remark to him, 'I see what you mean. It *is* beginning to look a bit tatty. Now about that Volvo estate...'

His door slams, he's off, no farewell just a growled, 'I know it's tatty. I bought it that way from *you*.'

Bad loser. Just no gratitude anymore. I mean how was I to know it was his editor's wife?

I can now expect a no-holds-barred, full frontal, attack from the *Informer*. So I best be off and start preparation of my defence or maybe - an idea is forming - my attack.

# CHAPTER ELEVEN

## HERITAGE BETRAYAL

The ensuing days find me beavering away, head-down-ass-up, in the determination of one trying to meet a deadline. In this case Sunday's edition of the *Informer*.

Late Saturday night everything is in place ready for the attack. Early Sunday morning finds me pulling the Jag to a stop outside Andy's newsagents.

'See you've got star billing again, Sammy,' says Andy slipping the early morning edition of the *Sunday Informer* in front of me. Sure enough there's the article on the front page in banner headlines, WOULD YOU BUY A CAR FROM THIS MAN? above an unflattering grainy photograph of me.

'Is it no time you gave them a better mug shot of you since you're now back in demand. Maybe no, mind you, since yer actually *beginning* tae look like a dodgy second hand car salesman.' Rolling the paper up I take a good natured swipe at him before departing. This headline has triggered the start of "Operation Informer".

I then gun the Jag down Maryhill Road and on turning off into my street I see, already waiting on the forecourt wall, Hughie, Eck and Rab. On my "thumbs up" signal they hop into the basket of a cherry-picker and hoist themselves to near the top of one of the lamp posts, outside the forecourt, and attach one end of a banner to it. Descending, they repeat the performance tying the other end of the banner to another lamp post across the street. What they have achieved is a three foot deep banner strung overhead between the two lamp posts. In the dim light of dawn, filtering between the high tenement buildings, can be read on the banner:

THE HOME OF SAMMY ROBB MOTORS – AS ADVERTISED IN THE SUNDAY INFORMER. Borrowed police road cones, indicating a reserved area in front of the forecourt, are put in place. Phase one complete.

Hughie, Eck, Rab and myself then retreat to Ronnie's for his "Desperate Dan Special" breakfast to prepare us for the avalanche ahead. Eck asks how I know there's going to be an avalanche. If there's one thing I know, being a car salesman for over twenty years, it's human nature I inform him. Prior to leaving Ronnie's the team are issued with their sales instructions: Cash only deposits. All vehicles sold as seen. No warranties. Keep your sales strategy as simple as possible has always been my modus operandi. Fired up and raring to go we set off for the showroom.

Entering our street I notice Vera's pink scooter in her parking slot. She's today's cashier. I de-briefed her last night. As I turn my attention to the forecourt, I feel a swelling of pride overcoming me. There they are, polished and gleaming, my thirty proud sentinels in the fight against the oppression of the press. We have no sooner put the kettle on than the first of the sightseers arrives on foot. The knack is now to turn them into punters. I'll show you what I mean. Before the unsuspecting punter has a chance to sidle past the premises I emerge from the office and meet him at the forecourt entrance. He looks at me, a good sign, for from vast experience this can go two ways, he'll either drop his gaze while contemplating his navel, and walk on, or stand his ground and have a go at me. Thankfully it's the latter.

'You that Sammy Robber guy in the *Informer*?'

'Aye, that's me. Maryhill's answer tae Dick Turpin.'

'Ah don't know how you have the affront tae make a joke of it, efter what you did tae that poor woman.'

'You don't know what I did tae that poor woman, as you call her.' Keep them talking.

'Aye, I dae. I read it in this morning's *Informer*.'

Shaking my head in disbelief I continue, 'Did it mention a bull had stuck the heid on the motor?'

'N..no, it didnae. How'd that happen, then?'

'She lives out in the sticks, Balfron. Among the woolie-backs. Right?'

'Aye. If you say so.'

'Well, she's doing a twelve point turn in a lane out there when she stamps on the accelerator instead of the brake. Right?'

'Aye. Onya go Sammy.' Note that, first name terms now. He's a cert.

'Well, before you know it she's jumped the pavement, through the farmer's hedge and hit a bull. The motor's red, well that's like a red rag tae a bull, so Toro lays intae it in grand style. It's a wreck and I'm expected tae refund her money just because she's the wife of the *Informer's* editor.'

'Whit a cheek, Sammy. Just goes tae show you canny believe all you read.'

'Especially not in the *Informer*.'

As *bull* goes I can be right up there with them.

'I saw you surreptitiously giving the Cavalier a wee look out the corner of your eye.'

'I used tae own wan aboot ten years ago.'

'And you got rid of it?'

'Aye. Upgraded tae a Vectra.'

'That was a big mistake. Dae you realise you got rid of a design legend in its own time. A real classic.'

'Nae kiddin. And tae think I got rid of it. Whit a mug.'

'Well, now's your chance tae make amends. That one, in the condition it's in (weary, but with low mileage, of course) will treble its asking price, believe me.'

'Will it really?'

'Trust me.' After all I am Sammy Robb the name you can trust.

As I'm sticking a sold label on the Cavalier windscreen I notice Eck heading, with a punter, towards an ancient, er, vintage classic Cortina. Another lamb to the slaughter.

What followed was total mayhem. By eleven o'clock the police had to put a constable on point-duty at our street junction with Maryhill Road due to massive traffic congestion. Nothing like it has been seen since the halcyon days when Thistle used to play the might of Rangers and Celtic. This was before their slide into obscurity – Thistle that is. The ice cream and hamburger concession vans are doing a roaring trade from their reserved area in front of the forecourt. Their nominal site rental being paid to my favourite charity -"The McMillan Nurses." Toni, Glasgow's favourite pseudo Italian, is also out there - no doubt flogging his pyramids.

All of this witnessed by the *Daily Globe*, the *Informer's* bitter rival, who apparently received an anonymous tip off. As our stock dwindles fights break out over those vehicles remaining. Absolutely crazy. Even two cars parked overnight in the street have sold stickers on them. Nothing to do with me. If I was to hazard a guess at who - Toni would be high on my suspect list.   Eck has prepared a SOLD OUT notice -

photographed by the *Globe*. It's all over by mid-day. We're battle weary but ecstatic.

Kettle on, tea and biscuits served, Eck queries, 'How's it possible to get a slating like you did in the *Informer* boss and end up wie everything sold?'

'Well, Eck,' I reply, stretching my red braces outwards in a bombastic pose, '…as I told you, human nature being as it is everyone loves tae see everyone else's disasters. I knew they'd come to look.'

'Me. I would've gone intae hiding,' declares Eck.

'There you go then, Eck. You've learned something. It's called nous.'

'*The Sunday Informer* made a real balls up of it, doing that tae you,' states Eck emphatically.

'No Eck – they didn't. Without them it wouldn't have happened. As I've repeatedly said, it always pays to advertise, especially when it's a freeby from,' my finger pointing at my team who chorus, '*The Informer',* breaking out into peels of laughter.

It's been my kind of day - so far. Now to face Ella. Not a pleasant thought.


Turning in the gateposts of home, I cut the engine and glide to a halt. I then let myself in the kitchen door quietly and head for the safety of my den, when suddenly the penetrating voice of Ella shatters the quiet, 'Sammy, in here NOW.'

'Yes Ella dear. How may I be of assistance?' I enquire as I open the lounge door.

I immediately notice the *Sunday Informer* lying on the coffee table, front page up, with its gruesome banner headline and my photograph to the fore.

'Explain,' bellows Ella with an exaggerated sweep of her arm towards the paper.

'All I can say Ella, is they must have used an old photograph. Doesn't do me justice.'

'Don't try my patience – you nyaff...' When did she acquire patience I'm wondering as she continues, '....What will the neighbours think of this....this obscenity?'

'Not a lot. Seeing as they're mostly crooks themselves.'

'What dae you mean by that?'

'Well how do you think they got money tae live here in Bearsden?'

'Something *you* widnae know anything about – hard work and honesty.'

'Honesty! They're all lawyers, accountants and bankers for Christ's sake. They widnae recognise honesty if it bit them on the...'

'Enough of that kind of talk. It disnae matter in any case.' Ella logic. Pointing again at the headline she continues, 'What does matter is that this is typical of you, always has been. You just don't give a rat's arse about anything.'

'Ella! Ella. Calm - down. Calm - down. There's no problem.'

'What do you mean, *no* problem. It's a *calamity*. That's what it is. A calamity, dae you hear me. I'm going to be the laughing stock of the whole of Bearsden due tae you - you waste of space. You're all talk and nae do.'

'Nae do? Wait till your mates read tomorrow's *Daily Globe*....'

'My *mates,* as you call them, dickhead, don't read that sort of rag. They're *Herald* readers.'

'......all will be explained. Trust me.'

'Trust you? I wouldnae trust you to sit on a toilet seat the right way round.' This said as she threateningly advances towards me with *the finger* in strike mode. I'm off at the double through the open lounge door. I hope the *Globe* delivers the goods tomorrow.

Otherwise, ….. I don't want to think about otherwise.

I'm up with the lark, straight down to our local newsagent. There on the *Globe* news - board, set against his wall, is my dream headline - LOCAL MAN VINDICATED. They've done me proud. I've made the front page. There I am, complete with cheesey smile, handing over one of those giant cheques to my favourite charity, "The McMillan Nurses". The contents of the article, as you will have guessed, concentrates on the rubbishing of the *Informer's* claim against me of which I don't want to bore you.

However there is one line in the article I must quote to you, "The much maligned Mr. Robb, on being vindicated as an *honest* man of the people, has elected to take no further action against the spurious content contained in last *Sunday's Informer"*. That'll keep the *Informer's* gas on miser rate for the foreseeable future.

I then buy every *Globe* in the shop and waylay the paper boy and slip him a tenner to delivery my *Globes* to all his *Herald* customers as well. All bases covered I return home leaving a copy of the *Globe* on the kitchen table. I then take myself off out to the garage to sort out a couple of minor flaws that are showing up on my new "Deep Lung Theory" - namely breathing. I have just fastened the oxygen cylinder to my back when my mobile rings, picking up, 'Sammy Robb speaking.'

*'It's Ella, Sammy. If it's not too much trouble do you think you could pop into the lounge to see me please?'*

'Eh, er, yes. Right away, Ella.'

That's a first. Summoned for execution by phone. Entering the house, I tentatively stick my head round the edge of the lounge door fully expecting the usual abuse to start. No. She's sitting there, on the sofa, with a sherry in hand and a large glass of whisky on the coffee table. On seeing me she pats the seat beside her saying ever so politely, 'Do sit, Sammy.' I am about to sit when she continues, 'but don't you think you should take that thing off your back first.'

I've only come in with the oxygen cylinder strapped to my back. Wrestling myself out of the harness I carefully take up position at the opposite end of the sofa.

'Silly me,' I say feeling er….. silly.

'Not always, Sammy,' she says handing me the whisky, 'You did a fine job stitching up the *Informer*.'

'Er..thanks. I told you everything would turn out the bees-knees.'

'Indeed you did, Sammy. For that I thank you.' This conversation is getting unreal.

'It says the *Globe* received an anonymous tip off. Any views on that?'

'Not really. Why?'

'Oh! Just curious. You being a drinking buddy of the *Globe's*, on the spot, reporter and all…,' said with a knowing smirk and wink. She knows.

Continuing in the serene calm tone she's used throughout, my nerve ends fraying and twanging because of it, she murmurs, 'What I want to speak to you about is, your health. All these constant trials and tribulations you're going through can't be good for you – *at your age*. I'm absolutely convinced your problems lie in the quality, or lack of it, in the cars you sell…….'

'Now listen, Ella, not all my cars…' Her hand takes up the "talk to the hand" position.

'….Sammy, kindly let me finish. Now when I bought the Ferrari it was an experience I'll never forget……,'

'So what – most of my punters say the same thing,' I retort indignantly.

She lets me finish my objection, then continues, '....a beautiful showroom, in a salubrious location, gleaming prestigious cars, immaculately dressed salesman.....'

I can't control myself. That bit about salesmen was the last straw, 'Salesmen! Salesmen! - they're not effing salesmen. They're just booking clerks (With apologies to all *real* booking clerks except that awkward bastard in Maryhill post office ) They want to try a week in Maryhill. Flogging someone a motor they don't want. Now *that's* selling.'

Incredibly, still no reaction other than with a regal flip of the wrist, she calmly replies,

'Quite so, Sammy. Quite so. What I propose is, that I open a new showroom, possibly in town, selling up-market cars – to make your life, that little bit easier. After all that's what money's for, isn't it? What do you think, Sammy?' She's asking *my* opinion! This is getting *scary*. Am I hallucinating? Maybe I've sucked in too much oxygen from the lung.

I'm brought out of my hypnotic trance by a *delicate* double prod on my arm from the usually violent Kung Foo finger, 'Yoo-hoo! Sammy. Anyone in?  All I asked for was your opinion.'

There it is again – I'm actually being asked *my* opinion. I must be having one of these "out of body" experiences that you read about. I'll be talking to aliens next. Mind you, after talking to Wullie that might be something to look forward to.

'Er, er, yes.' I manage to mumble, in reply, still being confused by it all.

'Er, er, yes – what Sammy?'

'Yes – that sounds good to me.'

'Good. That's it settled then. A new showroom it is and you close your Maryhill thing…. whatever you call it,' she says rising to her feet and kissing me on the forehead signalling the end of her quality time with me. That's brought me back to reality.

'My - Maryhill - thing - or - whatever - I- call - it,' I repeat, '……is all part of my heritage. But I wouldn't expect you to understand that anymore, Ella.' Said more to myself than Ella, as she has already disappeared out the room.

How could I have agreed to betray my heritage?

# CHAPTER TWELVE

## THE NEW LOCATION

Staring mournfully into my morning coffee I can't help but feel, as I watch the last of the dissolving granules swirl around and disappear into the vortex, that I too am about to disappear into a black hole. Several weeks have now elapsed since my hasty agreement to open a town centre showroom with Ella, who views it as yet another step in her social climbing ascendancy. I couldn't care less about the new showroom; it's her money but of my mind blowing, shameful, agreement to close Maryhill, well that was a step too far. The ultimate betrayal of my heritage of which I am always boasting.

My musings are brought to a juddering halt with the kitchen door blasting open under the usual squealing protest from the hinges.

In strides Ella and with a sweeping arm gesture opens happily with, 'Good morning Samuel dear.....I didn't hear you come in this *morning*.'

Not quite the response I was expecting after the lateness of this morning's arrival.

'Er, mm, I worked late last night, Ella. End of VAT quarter and all that. Didn't want to disturb your beauty sleep.'

'How very considerate of you Samuel,' still in that happy placatory tone, '... Now, if it's not too much trouble, do you think we could have a discussion about the town showroom, please.'

*Please?* This *is* getting scary...*scary*...When did I last use ... *scary*? My brain which has been idling in neutral suddenly clicks into gear. I remember. The last time I used it was when I had *that* discussion, with Ella, about her new showroom and ......and I ended up surrendering Maryhill and my heritage. Crafty Ella, she's trying the same smooth verbal seduction on me again. She wants something. All senses are now switched to red alert. Two can play at her little game.

'Co-eh! Samuel. You appear to have drifted.'

'Of course we can have a discussion, Ella dear.'

'Excellent. You may be wondering why there's been a delay regarding the showroom. Yes? Well, I employed an agent to find me a suitable location for my, er, our venture.'

'Which is where?'

'Bothwell Court.'

'Wouldn't have been my choice. Parking meters, up a cul-de-sac.' The rebellion has now started.

'Fortunately, your opinion is of little consequence,' she replies with an edge creeping into her voice, 'There's the report and the keys. Go take a look at Barrington-Bell Automobiles'

'Barrington-Bell? What sort of nancy name is that?'

'Well you don't expect *quality* to be branded under the title of Sammy Robb Motors, do you?'

With that nasty retort, she turns on her high heels and heads for the door. On reaching it she abruptly stops and with all ladylike finesse gone, the Kung Foo finger pointing threateningly, snarls, 'And another thing, Sammy boy, when I appoint the architect I'll make sure I get a recognised builder to do the job not one of your usual *fuck-up* mates and ... that includes Wullie and the galoot that did Maryhill.'

'No problem there, Ella. Big Owen's skipped tae Tenerife, owen everyone. Get it? Owing every…..'

'Clown.' With that she turns her back and storms off. She gets the finger of satisfaction. She's twigged that I've rumbled her little game. A state of war exists.

Not letting our little contretemps upset me, I set off for work in high spirits. Reaching my premises and parking up I notice Wullie about to get into his van.

'Wullie!' I shout over to him.

'Morning Sammy. Saw your lights burning late last night. And…'

'End of VAT quarter,' I retort sharply not wanting a continuation of where I think this conversation is going.

Ignoring me he continues, '…And a pink scooter,' with a knowing wink.

'Yeah, yeah. Well spotted Sherlock. I just happened to be repairing the scooter if you must know….it was overheating.'

'Nae wonder. So would I be, if I had Vera sitting astride me.'

Ignoring that remark, since I need a favour from him, I enquire, 'Are you busy?'

'Yup. Yup. My yuppie flat conversion's started. But for you, Sammy - nae bother.'

'Good. Well, Ella wants tae convert shops into a car showroom. Could be a nice wee earner for *both* of us. Interested?'

'Of course.'

'Can you take a look at it now?'

'As I said, for you Sammy, nae bother. Where aboots?'

'In town. Jump in.'

On the way into town I find myself struggling for inoffensive words to explain the situation to Wullie. Finally giving up I blurt out, 'Ella doesn't know you now trade as WL Builders so we might get away with it.'

'Get away wie what?'

'How can I put this without offence. Ella doesn't want me to use any of my "*fuck-up*" mates on this job.'

'Well, she's no so daft is she? What, wie some of the chancers that you deal wie.'

Ignoring this idiotic nonsense, I press on, 'And another thing, she wants a recognised builder.'

'Sammy, how long have you known me?'

'Too long.'

'Right. And what's my name?'

'Wullie Leckie.'

'There you go then. Long established and recognised. Nae problemo.'

Fortunately for him we arrive just then at our destination and park outside the premises. Slipping on a recently acquired "Out of order" hood over the meter we view the vacant premises from the pavement. The premises turns out to be two adjacent shops in a four storey red sandstone building. I start with the agent's recommendations, 'The report suggests the two shops be knocked into one and a new shop front sympathetic with the area be fitted. O.K wie that?'

'Nae bother, Sammy.'

'Right let's go inside.'

As I step inside the recessed entrance way I kick aside old battered cardboard boxes.

A voice from inside the boxes complains, 'Whit dae you think your daen pal. You widnae like it if I came into your hoose and kicked you awake, wid you?'

With that, this stinking bundle of rags emerges from the box. What a pong.

'This your usual doss?' I ask him, stepping briskly back into the fresh air.

'Only when I cannae get intae the Central.....station that is.....no the hotel. Since you woke us up any chance of a couple of quid for a café latte?'

'A couple of quid? It used to be a shilling.'

'That's what's called inflation. This government's ruining the country. Affecting ma shares something awful.' He's not wrong there.

'There's a quid. Away an treat yerself tae a bar of soap.'

'God bless you, sirs. The name's Bertie.'

'Pleased tae meet you Bertie. My name's, Sammy, your new landlord. You've just had notice tae quit.'

With that Bertie disappears in the direction of the Central station, off to see if there's any vacancies ....over the hot air vents.

'But by the grace of God there goes me,' sympathises Wullie.

'Cock this job up and that *will* be you....an me.'

Opening up the shop we have a good look around. Spacious and including next door I estimate room for at least twenty quality vehicles excluding my pet hate - the "Chelsea tractor". Except for farmers and a few drainage contractors out in the sticks, what *is* the point of them, especially in towns? They were designed as rough terrain vehicles and conceding that some of our roads are a pot holed disgrace, possibly passing as rough terrain, who in their right mind would buy one? They're massive, ugly, gas guzzling, carbon footprint enemies of the ozone layer and should be banned from the roads. But will they? No chance. More fuel guzzling - more revenue for HMG.

More an irritation than a digression. Now where was I? Yes. The showroom.

Sitting down on two discarded packing crates I continue to read out the report, 'The report requires the load-bearing wall between the two shops to be removed. Do you have the nous to do it, Wullie?'

'Nae bother at all Sammy. Did a big one like this a few years back in the Dumbarton Road.'

'Was that Vinnie's Vehicles?'

This question elicits a reluctant, 'Aye.'

'Was that where, in building terminology, you might call a structural collapse took place?'

Another reluctant, 'Aye.'

'The one where a poor woman was having a bath one minute and the next she was flat on her back?'

'Aye. But to be fair, due tae her profession, she was used tae that position.'

'Jesus C Christ Wullie. This is not exactly a glowing recommendation is it?'

'Sammy, I said I had experience of Vinnie's, not that I actually did the job. I was just the brickie, the builder was Big Owen…'

'Cairney.'

'Aye, of course. I forgot he did your Maryhill showroom when I was doon in London working.'

'Please, Wullie, don't remind me about Owen and Maryhill. Know what he tells me when he finishes Maryhill? He says, "Sammy, you're now the proud owner of the eighth wonder of the world". Never a truer word. It's a *wonder* it's still standing. It comes as no surprise he took himself off to Tenerife if all his jobs were like mine and Vinnies.'

A feeling of total helplessness now sweeps over me on having my memory jogged by Wullie that he had worked for Big Owen. Big Owen being the building trade equivalent of

Frank Spencer. Who's Frank Spencer? Remember the TV series "Some Mothers Do Have 'Em". Yes? Well, now you know what I mean. Total mayhem.

I'm getting very, very, bad vibes about this which is not helped by Wullie's effort at consoling me, 'Don't worry, Sammy. Look on the bright side - you've got me now tae take the strain. Nae worries.'

'Well now, that's a *real* comfort to me, isn't it? What wie walls falling down, buildings collapsing, and you a fully paid up member of Big Owen's demolition team doing tae Glasgow what Hitler couldnae do, and you tell *me* not to worry. This is Ella we're dealing with Wullie, not the "Good Fairy".'

'There you go again Sammy, exaggerating as usual. The walls havnae fallen down, *yet*. Have they? Trust me, the job's a doddle.'

On hearing the word *yet* a blinding headache started to kick lumps out of my eyeballs.


Why, did I ever involve him?  All I need now is Ella to appoint an unapproachable architect and all is lost.

# CHAPTER THIRTEEN

## PLANNING PERMISSION

During the ensuing weeks, Ella, informs me she has appointed an architect, Leonard Payne and Associates, and that the showroom has been submitted for planning permission. She asks me how my plans are going for the closure of Maryhill and is informed, in no uncertain terms, they aren't. What's the point in closing Maryhill when the showroom is nowhere near fruition. Reluctantly she agrees to this common sense logic thereby giving me more time to solve the quandary of Maryhill which, in all honesty, I'm still no nearer solving. Fortuitously, as it transpires and unknown to Ella, the architect is a drinking colleague of mine from various watering holes I frequent throughout the city. He's *approachable*.

Time to put *approachable* into action. Knowing that where I'm heading no prisoners are taken, I hop into a taxi. Paying it off at a restaurant well known for its building trade clientele I head for the lounge bar. Sure enough, Lenny's there in his usual corner with his associates. Noticing me he raises his glass, normally a large *Glenmorangie*, in acknowledgement. The grey shoulder length hair atop a bearded and bespectacled face is showing its customary whisky flush. A polka dot bow tie lost in a swathe of beige corduroy, leather patches and hush-puppies

125

completes his ensemble. I return the acknowledgment and nod to a vacant alcove table.

Having only ever previously dealt with Big Owen, when I was re-building Maryhill, and his "cash only – everything's an extra" contract conditions I want to know how a real contract worked. I'm sure Lenny can enlighten me.

As I arrive at the alcove and place two large *Glenmorangies* on the table we shake hands vigorously as is his style. He opens in his curt cultivated Kelvinside accent, 'Samuel, my boy. How's you? Well, I trust.'

'Razor edge, Lenny, razor edge. Hear you're busy.'

'As you well know Samuel, you can never be *too* busy. So if you or any of your colleagues are looking for an architect, I'm your man.'

'You already are my man.'

A puzzled look comes across his owl like face, 'How so Samuel?'

'Car showroom, Bothwell Court.'

The puzzled look remains on his face, 'But that client's a Mrs. Robb. No offence intended Samuel but she's, how can I put it?....'

'Classy. Different from me,' finishing the unsaid for him. 'She's my wife.'

'Well I never. Fancy that. You always lead me to believe she was a bit of an ogre.'

'You want to try living with her, Lenny.'

'Quite so, Samuel. Quite so,' he agrees with a distant pained look on his face obviously remembering his three previous attempts at marriage.

At that moment I hail a passing waiter, order replacement drinks and ask for a menu.

'Trust you can join me for lunch, Lenny?'

'Delighted, Samuel,' he replies having regained his composure after his faux-pas. Adding, 'Well, Samuel, I suppose with this expenditure you require my assistance in some way or t'other.'

That's what I like about Lenny. Straight to the point. No dancing round the chanty.

So over a somewhat protracted and liquefied lunch he advises me of contract procedures. I won't bore you with all the details but the main criteria I'm interested in appears to be: the monthly valuation of work carried out by the builder is presented to the architect, in this case Lenny, for payment by the client, Ella, to the builder with any unforeseen extras being taken from a "contingency item" already built into the contract. Bingo! I've found what I'm looking for – *any unforeseen extras.* Sounds to me like a license to print money. With Lenny now on board all I need is the cooperation of a friendly builder. So we agree that after "competitive tendering", as demanded by Ella, that the *friendly* builder will be WL Builders - Wullie. Job done.

That settled, the *Drambuies* are called for, the bottle left at the table. Oblivion beckons.

On a very slow re-entry into the world, the following morning, I awake to the reality of the nightmare that has been haunting me. In the nightmare Ella discovers that Wullie is WLBuilders and evicts him bodily off the job along with my "heritage" compensation. This would not be in my best interest.

Now if Ella were to be absent during the contract period. A plan is forming…..

Over breakfast I casually enquire of Ella, 'Can we have a wee serious chat, Ella?'

'Why, what's wrong this time?'

'Nothing. Nothing *yet* that is.'

'What do you mean by *yet*?'

'Well, it's you Ella. I'm worried about you.'

A suspicious look comes over her face as she queries, 'You're - worried - about - me?'

'Yes, Ella, I am,' I reply with all the sympathy I can muster. Continuing, 'Ever since Chuck's unfortunate demise you've been under enormous stress, haven't you?'

A hanky appears by magic, dabbing her eyes. A little sob is emitted from behind the handkerchief, 'My poor dear Charles. May his soul rest in peace.'

'Why don't we take a little holiday soon, say during the showroom alterations.'

'What are you up to?'

'Nothing. Honest Ella.'

'You. Honest. Don't make me laugh.'

'Thanks very much, Ella. And there's me about to offer you a world cruise. Just think you could be rubbing shoulders with Chris Tarrant's Millionaires, celebrities from Coronation Street and Eastenders and…..the like,' I reply in a hurt tone, playing for sympathy by mentioning her favourite TV shows. I draw the line at Noel Edmonds.

A long pause takes place during which the stare intensifies. I feel it penetrate.

Finally, 'You know, Sammy. Maybe just for *once* you could really mean it. I have, as you say, been under considerable stress and a holiday might well be the answer.'

She's taken the bait. I reply in all innocence, 'Now you *are* being sensible, Ella.'

'But a world cruise...... Couldn't we go somewhere else? Somewhere nice and quiet.'

Before I can stop my big mouth from screwing everything up, I idiotically give forth with one of my usual sarcastic thoughtless retorts, 'Certainly Ella. I'll just nip out and get us two cheap day returns to Mars.'

Silence. Big, big, silence.

Broken by a snarled, 'Now that's more like the Sammy I know. A facetious, sarcastic loud mouthed, nyaff. You can stick your holiday where the monkey sticks its nu..'

Lost as she disappears round the slammed and hinge damaged door.

I'm too deflated to give her the finger. Well that's blown that.


On reflection it's fascinating how problems can resolve themselves when you least expect it. Especially when the problem resolves the problem.

The World cruise episode behind us, but not forgotten by Ella as is nothing I allegedly do wrong, finds us sitting having breakfast together during one of the rare lulls in our ever increasing hostilities.

'Busy day ahead?' I ask out of curiosity knowing that with her chairperson duties of various charities and associations not to mention the jam making industry, which by this time must rival Robertson's in output, usually keeps her going full blast.

'I've got to take the Ferrari into their technical sales division for a service this morning.' I love the waffle these main dealers use – technical sales division indeed - their workshop being what they really mean. Suddenly the old antenna begins to twitch like mad with good vibes. Of course! That's it! Problem solved.

'Sammy! Are you listening to me?'

'Yes Ella,' I reply coming out of my ecstatic daydream. 'Listen, these *quality* cars we intend to sell, where do we service and valet them? They just don't do themselves you know.' A blank look tells all, 'Erm.....just the usual place Sammy.'

'But that's Maryhill and we won't have it anymore.'

The blank look just became a vacuous void. Enjoying every moment of her discomfort, I hit her with my piece de resistance, 'May I suggest we retain Maryhill and rename it Barrington-Bell *Technical Services*.'

'Sammy, what a brilliant idea,' she jubilantly replies seeing an immediate solution to her embarrassment. 'But what about the selling of those crap cars of yours?' I hoped she'd forgotten about that but having the answer ready I can afford to ignore her cheap jibe, 'I'll franchise it out.'

'You do that and you've got a deal.'

'Done,' I excitedly declare. Continuing, 'How's planning going?'

'My architect informs me he expects a positive decision any day now.'

With that I get up from the table and taking my leave I can't resist giving Ella a big kiss.

'Mmm. Nice one, Sammy. Make sure you come home early tonight, won't you?'

I hear seductively from behind me on my way out. Could I be on a promise?

The drive to work has never been more enjoyable. My Maryhill fiefdom has been saved. Planning permission is now imperative for the showroom.

When I arrive at my newly saved fiefdom I go straight to Eck, to inform him he's about to become the new franchisee of Sammy Robb Motors - in name only of course. Then to Hughie to inform him of the name change to Barrington-Bell Technical Services.

That settled, I set off for my office. As I enter I hear the chill freeze words, 'Yes, Mrs Robb. He's here,' Vera has her hand over the mouthpiece silently mouthing, "Ella."

Nodding, I take the receiver thinking, she usually uses her mobile.

'Yes, Ella, what's wrong with your mobile?'

*'Forgot to charge it. Hope I didn't disturb anything.'*

'What do you mean by that?'

*'Who's the sexy voice?'*

'The cleaner.'

*'Is it indeed. Maybe I'll have to take a look at this one as well. Eh! Sammy?'*

The applied inference here being that, Ella, having taken an unreasonable dislike to Sonia, Vera's predecessor, because of her large boobs, long legs and mini skirts, came in one day and flung her bodily out into the street. I still fear the same fate for Vera.

Not liking the way the conversation is going I hastily change the subject, 'Now Ella, you're not phoning me for the good of my health so what's the problem?'

*'Bad news I'm afraid, Sammy. My architect's just phoned to inform me that we have been refused planning permission.*

'What!' I groan in despair. 'Did he say why?'

*'No. I think he's to stunned.'* Not half as stunned as me. This is disastrous.

'Right, leave it with me.'

*'Sammy?'*

'Whit?'

*'Don't forget tonight.'* What a time to become an object of desire.

I then phone Lenny. He informs me that the building, unbeknown to him, recently acquired listed building status and has been refused planning by a Victor Fenwick. He will of course appeal the decision. How long will that take? Couldn't say for sure – could be years. Yes, he was aware his fees were going down the tubes not to mention his bung. What was it listed for? He reckons it's because the fortieth illegitimate second cousin of Queen Victoria had slept there. No, not in a cardboard box in the doorway.

Later in the day having exhausted all my brain cells regarding this latest catastrophe I bow to defeat and phone Wullie on his mobile. 'Wullie, Sammy here….Got a problem with that job I showed you. Where are you?.....You're already in Rileys ….Right. I'll see you in five min…' With that Vera oozes her body round the door and perches herself, legs crossed, on the edge of the desk '…..make that ten minutes, Wullie. Something's just popped up.'

Hurrying up the road to Rileys, I encounter Archie our local news vendor on the corner of the street shouting out the latest news,

'GET YOUR DAILY GLOBE LATEST HERE - TRAFFIC LIGHTS WIPED OOT - POLICE HOLD DUG AS SUSPECT - DUG SAYS THEY'RE BARKING MAD.'

'Archie, what brings you up here. You're usually down at the lights.'

'It was those lights that got wiped oot by a motor, Sammy.'

'Surely the police, even that loopy dingbat McLeod, cannae suspect a dog?'

'Not a dug Sammy. It was old DUGald. Blind as a bat. Shouldnae be driving. Criminal whoever sold him that car,' I cough gently at this. '…I've got tae resort to this kind of subterfujie due tae TV and now the Internet. I'm an endangered species, Sammy.'

'Not you Archie. You could sell "yesterday's news",' I reply, slipping him a quid for the proffered paper. Before entering Rileys, I decide to quickly peruse the article just in case *I am* mentioned. No chance of that - it is *"yesterday's news"*. I hear the old rogue's mocking laughter of me as I enter Rileys.

Reaching the bar I am greeted by that ever ugly ignoramus, Agnes, 'Aye. Whit dae you want?' she asks in a voice that jars every nerve in my being.

Not being in the mood to bandy words with her I reply, 'Two pints of heavy and a packet of nuts, if it's not too much trouble. Once served I head for the table to deliver the drinks but on arrival discover I've forgotten the nuts. I return to the bar; she's waiting there with hands on hips. Being as there's no way of putting it to her without her taking the double entendre offensively, I ask her as innocently as I can, 'Any chance of my nuts, Agnes?' No expected violent outburst. Instead removing her hands from her hips she looks me over at length, turns and heads for the nuts hanging on the gantry. On her return she slips the nuts into my hand, squeezing it as she does, and with a wink making her look like Quasimodo's mother, whispers, 'I know what you really want, Sammy. I can always tell. You're special - a sex bomb.' I'm shocked by the use of my name but not half as shocked as when I read the semi-literate contents of the note wrapped round the nuts. It gives me her phone number and the best times to contact her when her husband is out. A husband! I look towards her. She winks. Shit. Double shit. Hastily grabbing the nuts, stuffing the note deep into my pocket, I return to the table.

Still being in a state of shock and not daring to mention the happening to Wullie, knowing he'll broadcast it to the nation, I mumble, 'Did you know she's married.'

'You - are - kiddin. You'd need tae be seriously roond the twist tae marry that thing. Can you imagine crawling in beside her at night.' I shudder at the thought. He continues, 'This problem you've got has tae be serious you look as though you've seen a ghost.'

Pulling myself together I manage a squeaky, 'The showroom, it didn't get planning permission. That means the deal is in danger of going belly-up.'

'That's bad, but don't dae your usual and panic. Stay cool man. Let's start from the beginning. Who's the architect?'

'Lennie Payne.'

'The alcy-tec? Is he not one of your town drinking mates?'

'Aye.'

'Has he been looked after?'

'Well bunged.'

'Who's the planning officer?'

'A guy called Victor Fenwick.'

'Mm. Fenwick. ….Fenwick.'

'You know him?'

'Something's ringing a bell. Need tae make a phone call first. I'll just nip outside.'

As Wullie departs to make his call Geeza sidles up to me and out the corner of his mouth conspiratorially whispers to me, 'Pst, Sammy. The grapevine tells me the cops think auld Dugald's M.O.T was dodgy. Just thought you'd like to pass it on to whoever. Know what I mean?' Finished with a knowing wink.

With that he disappears to the bar. What a day this is turning out to be.

Wullie eventually arrives back and taking his seat confides in me, 'When you mentioned, Victor Fenwick, it rang a bell. So I phoned Big Owen.'

'In Tenerife?'

'Aye. Now listen to this. When Owen did Vinnie's job.......'

'The one that collapsed.'

'Correct. Well, it turns out that when building control asked Owen tae confirm the status of the wall to be taken down between the shops he tells them it's wallpapered on both sides but damp at the bottom. Following O.K Sammy?'

'Yep.'

'They tell him that status means, is it a load bearing wall. As you know Owen wouldn't recognise a load bearing wall if it......' He points at me.

'If it bit him in the balls,' I finish for him.

'Correct. So they tell him to get somebody technical to advise him. So Owen asks the bloke if he knows anyone. The bloke says he does. Himself. For a fee. Tae you an me a.......' He points at me again.

'A bung,' I reply.

'Correct again. Now here's the nub of the matter. The bloke is none other than...... Victor Fenwick.'

'Come to papa,' I gleefully exude, rubbing my hands together.

Wullie continues, 'So, Owen agrees tae let Fenwick advise him. Now, Owen might be many things but dolly dimple's not one of them. So he tells Fenwick he wants a receipt and confirmation in writing. Fenwick baulks at this but an increase in his inducement sees Owen getting his way. Deal done. Fenwick in his pocket. You possibly don't know this, Sammy, but these council guys aren't allowed to work both sides of the counter.'

'You dancer, Wullie. We've got the slimey bastard by the short and curlies.'

'Hold it Sammy,' hand held outright in stop position, '......that's all hearsay so far, no proof. Now here's the real deal. Fenwick's letter to Owen confirmed the wall as *non-load* bearing. Owen went ahead and, as you know, down comes the wall and most of the building above. Mercifully no one was killed. Well, because of the letter, that's Fenwick's career up shit creek and Owens's not looking too bright. Still following O.K?'

'Sure am, Wullie.'

'Well, Owen was on the verge of doing a runner in any case due as he says to extenuating circumstances. You can take that as the tax man. So he does a deal wie Fenwick involving muchos, muchos, euros. Takes the rap, keeps his mouth shut, and scoots off tae Tenerife. Fenwick is now in the clear, or so he thinks, because Owen still has *the* letter and *the* receipt for the money. He calls them his insurance policies which he is now prepared to cash surrender to you. How's that?'

'Caught and bowled. Tell Owen it's a deal.'

'Knew you'd agree. He says he'll fax you a copy of them today.'

Thanking Wullie, I start back to my office. On the way out Agnes winks at me. I shudder. Owen, as good as his word has come up trumps. There the copies lie on my desk along with a cover note, "Sammy, trust yur keepin well. Hope this helps you screw the wee bastard. Wethers bewtiful here. Come and enjoy." That's Big Owen, tells it, spells it, as he sees it.

The following day finds me entering the City Chambers, a swaggering Victorian masterpiece, through the grand entrance portal in George Square. Entering you are faced with the cool marble opulence of the great staircase. Climbing the stair to the first floor I wend my way through the beautifully designed and decorated labyrinth of corridors to the planning department. By-passing the general office I happen upon a door with the name V.Fenwick - Senior Planning Officer sign written in gold leaf. Knocking and entering in one movement I enter a large reception room, to be confronted with a grey haired matronly type sitting behind a desk.

In a refined voice she asks me, 'Can I be of assistance to you, sir?'

'Yes, I'd like to speak with Mr. Fenwick, please.'

'And you are?'

Not wishing to give my real name I reply, 'Samuel Leckie.'

Making a pretence at studying her appointments diary she retorts, 'You don't appear to have an appointment Mr.Leckie.'

'I don't,' I confirm.

'Well, I regret without one you cannot see Mr. Fenwick.'

'I am not here on business. It is an, er, delicate personal matter. Could you just mention to Mr. Fenwick I have a message from a Mr.Owen Cairney of Tenerife for him, please.'

She looks long and hard at me then rises and disappears through the door behind her.

Moments later the door opens and in a surprised voice at such an occurrence trembles, 'You may go in now Mr. Leckie.'

Entering an oak panelled room I notice sitting behind an enormous desk this weasel faced upside down head, you know - bald with a beard, that barely comes above the desk top.

In a squeaky nasal voice to match the face he whines, 'Now Mr.Leckie what's this all about? I'm a very busy man.'

'Busy… but not for long I suspect,' as I lay before him the copies of Owen's insurance policies. Fenwick on reading them turns ashen and goes rigid. Had it not been for his Adam's apple going up and down, like a motorised sludge gulper drain cleaner, I would have assumed rigor mortis had set in.

Coming round he feebly moans, 'What do you want?'

'That's more like it Victor baby. Now about a recent planning application for..........'

A week later when I arrive home I am greeted with an elated Ella, which is as rare as a sighting of Lord Lucan. She kisses me and leads me to my favourite arm chair where I am given a large whisky. Ella then pours herself a sherry and sits opposite me with a large smile on her face. Another surreal "out of body" moment in my life.

Raising her glass towards me we chink glasses and she toasts exuberantly, 'To the showroom.'

'How come?' I reply in all innocence.

'Well, my architect has just informed me that we have retrospective planning permission for the showroom.'

'Never,' I reply, feigning surprise. '.....how did that happen?'

'How indeed, Sammy,' she replies looking suspiciously at me. 'My architect also informs me, through his contact in planning, that a certain Samuel *Leckie* paid a visit to Fenwick. You wouldn't know anything about that either would you?'

'Not a thing Ella.'

'So what do you think happened?'

'I suppose you could say this Sammy *Leckie* joker got Fenwick tae, *"Owen – up"* tae his mistake.

'Sammy, you rascal. "Sammy - *Leckie*" indeed. Who do you think you're kidding?'

Putting her empty sherry glass on the table she rises embraces and kisses me passionately. I feel a little tremble as my DNA dots slip into place.

Life can be very confusing at times.

# CHAPTER FOURTEEN

## TWO MANY MIXERS

With planning permission having now been granted, Wullie has made a start on the showroom and I'm heading into town to find out how the job's progressing. Town traffic being light I find myself turning into the Bothwell Court cul-de-sac within ten minutes.

As I arrive, Wullie is standing on the pavement supervising his joiners who are putting the finishing touches to the temporary hoarding around the frontage of the showroom. The hoarding is an eight foot high plywood elongated 'U' shaped fence forming a solid barrier between the job and pavement. The long face of the barrier runs parallel to the pavement and the projecting return ends are butted against the building. The area within the hoarding being used for general storage and offering an external area for the cement mixer. The projection of the hoarding is such that it leaves little room between the face of the hoarding and the edge of the pavement.

Parking the Jag I sidle up to an almost unrecognisable Wullie who beneath his hard hat is wearing a lop-sided moustache and is admiring his WLB logo on the hoarding.

'Hi! Sammy. What do you think?'

'Nice simple logo, Wullie. I like it. None of that, "we're here to serve you" or "we're the way forward" crap that all these loonie left Councils love to waste our money on.'

'Well, all that aside Sammy, what I really meant was, do you think Ella would recognise me?'

'Don't think so Wullie…..if it wisnae for your name on the back of your donkey jacket, again.'

Before he can reply there's a "Toot - Toot" behind us. Sitting on a mobile pavement sweeper is an agitated Council Cleansing Department employee who complains to us,

'Yous two mind moving. It's hard enough trying tae get past as it is.'

'What's up with him, Wullie?' I query as the sweeping machine just makes it between the hoarding and the parking meters.

'Don't worry about Malky. It's just his dukes playing him up again.'

'Dukes?'

'Duke of Argyll's – piles. Fancy a cuppa…..?'

Everything going well at Bothwell Court, I arrive back in Maryhill to be informed by Hughie that one of the cars has been vandalised and is in need of a touch-up paint job. I use Alfie, a self-employed spray painter, who does an excellent job provided he's not on the cratur. It being lunch time and knowing Rileys to be his rendezvous I might, if I'm early, catch him sober. As I turn into Maryhill Road, I notice almost outside Rileys, old Eddie standing on the pavement edge leaning on his walking stick. He's obviously waiting to cross the very busy road. Also outside is Bertie, the tramp, my almost tenant from Bothwell Court with a supermarket trolley containing all his worldly possessions. Noticing a gap in the traffic I grab Eddie's arm and start escorting him across the road. As I'm doing this I'm aware of him glowering at me as we cross. Suddenly, without warning, he slashes at me with his stick and snarls, 'What are you doing you daft ejit?'

'I thought you might show a wee bit more appreciation than that. Eddie.'

'What for you stupid bugger.' This he's savagely growling as I'm trying to dodge further vicious decapitating blows from his walking stick. Breaking free of him I dash recklessly back across the road to the accompaniment of horns blaring, curses and two finger gesticulations. Reaching pavement safety, I ask Bertie, 'What's up wie him?'

'Well, Sammy. I watched him take twenty minutes to get across the road. He just gets across, leans on his stick, then you take him back. I widnae be here when he gets back.'

'Thanks for the warning, Bertie,' I thankfully mumble slipping him a couple of quid. 'Away and get yourself a café latte.'

As I move towards Rileys swing doors I hear Bertie's complaining whine, 'Whit aboot ma croissant?'

'Tough, pal,' I reply over my shoulder as I enter Rileys. Mary, doing her early shift barperson, pulls me a pint. Listen to me – "barperson". I'm allowing myself to be P.C brainwashed by the loonies. Looking around there is no sign of Alfie but I spy his side-kick Geeza who I reluctantly join on account of him being a total pain in the bollocks.

'How's it going Geeza?'

'Smashing Sammy. You couldnae geeza a fag…. naw you don't dae you?

'No. Where's Alfie?'

'Bit tricky that, Sammy. He's indisposed at the minute. Like for thirty days.'

'No joking. What happened this time?'

'Well it's like this Sammy,' he says looking at me and rattling his empty glass on the counter.

'Another pint of heavy, Mary,' I shout to her, getting caught by "king ponce" again.

'Ta, Sammy that's very good of you. Dole's no until Friday. Now as I was saying, me an Alfie's in town this morning walking past the Sheriff Court when he says tae me, 'How's about us going in for a laugh.' Well with nothing else to dae it seemed a good idea at the time. I wisnae to know that Alfie was about to have an "Alfzeimers" attack. We go intae court and guess who's presiding? None other than your old pal .......
Sheriff Deighton.'

'Please Geeza, you shouldnae say things like that when I'm no expecting it,' I splutter, having just taken a mouthful of beer.

'Well the case is a non-English speaking German seaman charged wie allegedly assaulting a prossie doon in the docks. His interpreter has failed tae show and Deighton is asking the court if anyone speaks German. Before I can stop him, Alfie, wie hand up says tae Deighton, 'Aye. Me your honour. I spraken the Dutch.'

'Your name, please?' asks Deighton.

'Herr Alfredrich Scott.'

'Your fluent in the German language, Mr.Scott?'

'Ja, Herr Sheriff.'

'Excellent Herr, er, Mr.Scott. Can you ask the defendant his name please?'

'Vat es your name,' goes Alfie. The German draws him a blank so he goes on,

'Ach! So you vill not tell me svinehound. Vell we have vays of making you talk….'

With that Deighton is on his feet shouting for the court officers tae arrest Alfie.

Alfie says to him, 'What for your honour, I'm effluent in German.'

'Never a truer word, Sir. Thirty days for contempt of court.'

'You couldnae make that up, Geeza.'

'I'm no finished yet Sammy. As they're taking him away he's shouting tae me that he's going tae spend his time learning French and Italian tae add to his language portfolio.

So there you are, your man's having a thirty day holiday at Her Majesty's expense.'

'Well thanks Geeza that was very enlightening.'

With that I down the rest of my pint, ignoring the rattling of Geeza's empty tumbler on the counter, and leave retracing my steps to the office. Old Eddie is still on the other side of the road. So is Bertie but in the café supping his latte. He gives me a royal wave.

Reaching the office Vera greets me with a light sensuous kiss murmering, 'How did it go, Sammy?

'It didn't. Alfie's been excused working. Anything else?'

'Yes. Two things, Sammy. Firstly the Volvo's back with an oil leak.'

'Red Adair couldn't sort that one.'

'Red Adair?' queries Vera.

'Way before you time, Vera. He used to put out fires and sort oil leaks in the Iraq war. The first one. The *legal* one.' This I vent with feeling as I look at Maggie's photo on the wall. I could swear she knowingly winked back, 'And the second message?'

'Willie's taken to his bed with a traumatised headache. Something about the new showroom.'

'Right. Hold the fort again Vera. I'll just nip up to see him.'

Wullie rents the whole of the top floor of the tenement, next to the workshop, from me in return for the maintenance of all the properties. There's three flats up there. Two of them his living accommodation, which were once the home of Ella and me before our move to Bishopbriggs, and one his registered office. Vera does his officework and through a link to our office answers his phone when he's out. He's got it made.

I knock. A theatrically weak voice answers, 'Come in Sammy.'

Being on his CCTV I wave to him as he buzzes my entry.

As I open the door he, in the same theatrical voice, groans, 'Don't put the light on, Sammy. I'm having one of my traumatised headaches.'

'What's the problem?'

'Going tae jail's the problem.'

'What's happened this time?'

'Put the light on slowly and I'll tell you. It's your showroom.'

'Ella!' I shout, with rising panic in the voice. 'She's recognised you?' As we know if she ever does the game's up for us.

'No. That's sound man. Don't worry about that. But listen tae this. I get a phone call from my foreman, Brasso, last night, wanting a cement mixer for this morning. Not one of the big ones but one of those dinky half bag ones that sit on a stand, wee crackers. Know the ones I mean?'

'No.'

'Good. So first thing this morning I buy a mixer and deliver it. I warn Brasso that his job is on the line if it gets nicked, so make sure it's chained up. I then leave tae attend tae other business and call back about an hour later. I don't see the mixer so I shout intae the building, Brasso! You there?'

'Here I am boss, he replies tae me.'

'How's it going?'

'Well I've good news and bad. What dae you want first?'

'Make it the good, I reply.'

'I've sacked myself to save you the bother.'

'That's good. And the bad?'

'The mixer's been nicked.'

'It's what?.... Fucking hell, Brasso, what did I tell you? You've got tae chain everything doon roond here, I bellow at him, having completely lost my rag.'

'It was when I went tae get the chain, tae chain it doon, that it got nicked. By the way someone's nicked the chain as well.'

'When did it happen? I ask him.'

'Today, he replies.'

'I know it was today you, moron. I delivered it this morning.'

'Oh! Aye. So you did.'

'What I meant was how long ago was it nicked?'

'About ten minutes ago.'

'So, Sammy, I jumps in the van thinking the sod might not have got far. Following?'

'Yeah. No wonder you've got a headache. I'm developing one myself.'

'You havnae heard *nothing* yet. So I gets in the van and drives off. I'm stopped at the lights at a tee junction in a one way street. Just then, round the corner comes a wee bloke pushing a brand new cement mixer – mine. I jump out the van and run after him. Stop you thieving little bastard, I'm shouting after him. He looks round and wie that he clutches his heart and collapses against a wall slipping down onto the pavement. Shit, I'm thinking to myself I've killed the wee barra. Just then all hell lets loose. Horns are blaring and there's guys out their cars shouting at me. The lights have changed and I'm causing a traffic jam. To a barrage of "V" signs and the finger I manage tae bump the van up on the pavement. As I get out the van I sees the wee barra get up and run away leaving the mixer. So I goes up the road gets the mixer and struggles wie it into the van. Then going round tae the driver's seat there's a polis waiting. By this time that's all I need. I'm totally traumatised.'

'So am I, Wullie.'

'I'm still not finished. So the polis says to me. Was it you they were hooting at, sir?'

'No me, officer. I was up the street reclaiming my property, I reply.'

'Well let's hope it was a tax disc, sir.'

'Don't tell me the wee bastard stole that as well.'

'Tut, tut. Language, sir, he says taking out his notebook tae do me.'

'You'd be glad that was it. What a day.'

'Sammy. It's not finished.'

'You're kidding?'

'No, I'm not. That was just starters. I then drive back round tae the showroom. I poke my head into the building shouting to Brasso, You there?'

'Yeah, boss. Just coming.'

'On his arrival I explain to him, I've got the mixer back, Brasso. Caught the wee bastard red-handed. There's a long silence, with Brasso looking peculiar like, at me. Well, aren't you going to say something like thank you for saving my job, boss.'

'I don't want to appear unappreciative boss. It's just that we've got ours back. It wisnae stole.'

'What dae you mean it wasn't stole?'

'Well, when you off-loaded the mixer this morning you blocked the passage between the hoarding and the pavement. So while I was away getting the chain the mixer was blocking the sweeping machine from getting past. So, Malky, the operator, moves it round the side of the hoarding out of my sight.'

'So you mean it was here all the time? I says tae Brasso, wantin tae strangle him.'

'Aye. That's what I've just telt you. Malky, telt me where it was on his return journey, just after you left.'

'So there you are Sammy. That's the whole sad story. So *whose* mixer have I got?'

'Whose mixer have you *hi-jacked* would be more like it.'

'Exactly, Sammy. It's a disaster. A total disaster.'

'Mind you, looking on the bright side you now own two mixers. So what's the problem?'

'Sammy, the mixer's *not* mine. The owner will have reported it to the polis and wie my track record, remember I've been done already this morning, for no road tax and obstruction and now, as you say, hi-jacking. - I'm for the high jump.'

'Wullie, the plods have to catch you first and right now they've got more to worry about.....they're all out booking double-parked skateboards.'

'Very funny, Sammy. Look wie your contacts dae you think you can get the mixer to disappear? No questions asked?'

'Not a problem, but it'll cost you.'

'Just get it done, Sammy, as long as the polis aren't involved.'

As I come out of Wullie's, a pick-up truck enters the garage forecourt. I recognise the driver, another of Wullie's great unwashed clan of Shuuuu - sters. You know, the inward breath sound all builders give you before they tell you the bad news.

'Frankie, my boy. Long time no see. What can I do you for?'

'This,' he replies giving the front tyre a kick. 'It's punctured and so's the spare. It's an emergency, Sammy. I've got to get to my merchant before they close.'

'For you Frankie, nae bother. You're looking a bit flustered. What's up?'

'Hell of a day, Sammy. Hell of a day. Weird in fact....'

'Hold on Frankie, I'll get Rab to do your punctures right away then you can tell me all about it over a cuppa.'

Having organised Rab, Frankie and me are sitting in my office when Vera oozes in with the tea and biscuits. Having greeted us in her usual polite manner she then takes her leave in her customary pert bottom sway, all noticed by the bulging eyeballs of Frankie.

'Wuf,' he sighs, '…I wouldn't mind…..'

'Frankie!.......You were about to tell me about your problems.'

'Aye, so I were,' he replies still looking longingly at the door no doubt wishing Vera to reappear. She has that effect on lechers. I do not include myself in that category.

'Well it's really my own fault Sammy what happened. I was so busy I sent Wee Mac to pick up our new mixer. One of those dinky wee half bag jobs. You know the ones, Sammy?'

'No.'

'Good. Right then, because the wee fella cannae park outside our job he has tae wheel the mixer to our site. He's just got round the corner of these traffic lights when he's attacked by a demented maniac, shouting and swearing at him. Mac legs it, fearing for his life, leaving the mixer.' My antenna starts twitching. 'The next thing this maniac puts the mixer in his van and scarpers. In broad daylight Sammy, would you credit it?'

'Absolutely unbelievable, Frankie. There's certainly some loonies on the loose nowadays,' I reply, with positive conviction, already knowing the culprit. '…...It'll be one of them care in the community.'

'No Sammy. Wee Mac says it was a pro job. A hi-jacking.'

At this I splutter into my cup, 'Down the wrong way, Frankie,' I choke. '…..What are you going to do about it?'

'You mean the polis?'

'Aye.'

'Wouldnae waste my time. They're all out booking double-parked skate boards.'

'So I hear. Bit of an epidemic apparently.'

'So, that's why I need my truck. I need a mixer for the morning.'

'Listen Frankie you're not going to believe this. A punter traded his car in last week, and wait for it, you're not going to believe your luck, to make up the difference he offered me a mixer. It's brand spanking new. I gave him two big one's for it.'

'Did Wullie not want it?'

'Asked him but he's got two already. Would you be interested?'

'Sounds good. Let's have a look at it.'

'Hold on a tick I'll go and see where I left it.'

'Any chance of another cuppa?'


Ignoring the lecherous sod I leg it up the stairs to Wullie. He's up, dressing gown on and a bag of frozen peas held to his forehead.

'Wullie, I've been talking to one of my contacts. For a ton he can he can disappear the mixer, guaranteed.'

'Done Sammy,' said as he takes his wallet out and hands me five twenties, '…Cheap at the price.' Now he tells me.

I then leg it back down the stairs to Wullie's yard located behind my workshop and wheel the mixer round to the rear of Frankie's truck. Frankie on seeing me from the office joins me at his vehicle.

'There you go Frankie. What do you think?'

'As you said Sammy, a wee stoater, brand new as well. Just like the one I had stolen.'

This brings on a fit of nervous coughing from me, 'Sorry, Frankie that biscuit's still stuck in my throat. So do you want it then?'

'Smashing Sammy, there's your money,' he agrees pulling off two hundred from a roll that would have choked a pig, '..... Cheap at the price. I would've paid twice that.'

'You would've?'    Him as well. They've no sense of decorum. Neither of them

'Thanks Sammy, that's one I owe you,' he says jumping into his truck and driving off.

As the tail end of his truck disappears Wullie arrives, 'Was that Frankie Paterson's truck?'

'Aye. Why?'

'Just curiosity, Sammy. He's doing a job round the corner from the showroom.'

'Do you know a Wee Mac?'

'No. Should I?'

'I've got this feeling you soon will.' I leave him scratching his head.

I'm sitting counting my easy gotten readies when Vera puts her arms around my shoulders and whispers, 'Looks like a profitable day, Sammy.'

'A *mixed* batch of a day, Vera.'

'That guy's back in about the Volvo. What are you going to do about it?'

'Nothing. It's an oota car.'

'An oota car?'

'Oota showroom, oota warranty,' I reply, as Seamus gets blindfolded and Maggie turned to the wall.

Then disaster. It suddenly dawns on me – Frankie didn't pay for his punctures.

# CHAPTER FIFTEEN

## THE POSH SALESMAN

The town showroom is now finished and open. Ella, never did find out that Wullie was WLBuilders. Between them Lenny and Wullie have done a superb job creating one of the finest, including all the mega bucks main dealers, showrooms in and around Glasgow. Ella's so proud of it she's doing conducted tours on a regular basis.

In all modesty I have to say I played my part too. During the contract period I was busy stocking the showroom with quality one owner, low mileage (goes without saying) vehicles.

Departing Maryhill to take up my new town showroom duties, I bid Vera a very tearful farewell as I borrow her handkerchief to dry my eyes. I've told her to keep in touch, by phone, daily. Also to keep a watch on Eck and don't let him turn the premises into a pigeon loft. Any serious trouble let Hughie handle it, not to go karate chopping the local neds on her own, as I know she is capable of doing. She doesn't understand why she can't join me in town. I have to remind her Ella doesn't do understanding.

Will I come up and see her most days, she asks? No. Due to a major oversight on my part, I have no cover for time off for myself and will remain a virtual prisoner in the showroom until I sort the situation out. Ella won't allow me a secretary unless she picks her. So no rush there then. What about Eck? Can you

151

imagine him let loose in town with his sales spiel, "How's it goin, china. Out tae buy a new set of wheels then?" Tolerable for Maryhill but not for the town showroom where class counts.

Since opening, some two weeks ago, business has been very brisk but very, very, boring. The boring is doing my head in. These top of the range super cars sell themselves. The challenge of selling someone a car they don't want has gone and with it all the fun of Maryhill. The irony of my situation is, that having referred to Ella's Ferrari salesmen as booking clerks, I now find myself one. So with Eck being of no help and Ella content to let me rot in here, action is called for. But what?

To break the tedium, I make faces at window gawpers. In fact, being really bored stiff, I'm off to do that right now. Fortunately, a gawper arrives at the window as I take my position behind the Porshe Carrera, the object of the gawpers desire. Even with his hands shielding his eyes from the sun's glare on the window there's something familiar about him. On close inspection I realise the familiar figure doing the gawping is none other than Wullie. Springing out from behind the Porshe I beckon him inside. Recoiling in shock, he shakes his head. I beckon again. Again he shakes his head.

What's the matter with him? I get to the door, open it and holler, 'What's up with you? Come on in.'

'Not on your Nelly, Sammy. If I go in there, I'll come out wie a motor I don't need, don't want or cannae afford.'

'Don't be daft. Would I do that tae you?'

'Aye. Without even batting an eyelid.'

'Funny you should mention that. That Porshe you were looking at…..'

'That's it - I'm off.'

'Oh! no you're not, I'm only joking,' I reply grabbing his arm as I haul him back towards the showroom, '....I need someone to talk to. Even you.'

'This looks good for business, you out grabbing people in aff the street.'

'Shut up and get inside.'

Finally getting him inside he looks around in amazement; he's never seen it finished.

For obvious reasons prevailing at the time, it was vital that he did not attend the opening albeit he suggested the use of one of his master disguises. Having witnessed his disguises in the past he might just as well have shown up with a placard round his neck proclaiming, "I'm Wullie Leckie". So while I really felt he deserved to be at the opening, but due to the stakes being so high, I had to put the veto on that idea.

As I was saying, he's never seen it finished. The combination of Ella's modern stainless steel, together with the right blend of antiques sets the background to the gleaming marques sitting on the highly polished imported marble floor.

Taking a seat I open the conversation with, 'What do you think of it now it's finished?'

'I'm gobsmacked, big time, Sammy. It looks smashing. I'm real proud tae be associated wie it. Even though I didnae get an *invite*.'

Ignoring that last remark, but knowing I haven't heard the last of it, I console him with, 'And so you should. You done brilliant.'

'Thanks, Sammy, nice tae be appreciated. Even though I didnae get an *invite*.'

'Wullie, I've told you already why you didn't and you told me you understood.'

'Correct. But it would still have been nice tae get an invite so's I could've said no.'

And to think….. *I forced him* into the showroom. I would've been better off talking to one of the parking meters outside. At least I would've got some change out of it. Being desperate to change the subject I try with, 'What brings you down here anyway?'

'I've just priced a job up the road so I've took the opportunity tae pop in tae tell you we're all missing you at Rileys. It's not the same without you. Even Agnes sends her *love*,' he finishes with a smirk. A shudder runs down my spine at the mention of the ogre.  Pulling myself together I reply, 'Aw! That's real nice of you all, Wullie. I'm missing you lot as well. It's only been two weeks but it seems like two years. I'm bored out of my mind, being stuck in here all day. What - am - I - doing - in - here? I keep asking myself. It wasn't meant to be like this. I was supposed to be in Maryhill running Barrington-Bell Technical Services. Not down here rotting away.'

'My, that's a sad wee story, Sammy. Does Ella know how you feel?'

'Ella, doesn't do feelings. You know that.'

'So what do you do now?'

'Well that's the problem. How do *we* get me out of this predicament without Ella twigging? Any ideas?'

'*We?*'  No thanks Sammy. I'd rather take on Vlad the Impailer, than Ella.'

'Thanks a bundle, pal. Have you forgotten that I rescued you from that redheaded wildcat from Dumfries?'

'So you did Sammy. I forgot about that. Sorry, it's just the thought of dealing wie Ella that gives me a dose of the sh...shakes. Tell you what, Sammy. Meet me in Rileys once you've finished here. I'll see what ze leetle grey cells can come up wie.'

'Look forward tae that Inspector Clouseau.'

Due to a combination of a late punter buying a Merc and heavy traffic it's well gone five thirty by the time I arrive at Maryhill and park in my old spot . Eck's gone to his pigeon loft.  No doubt Hughie's gone to Kenny's bar and Vera I know's gone to her karate class. We only keep in touch by phone now. What a life. A flood of nostalgia overcomes me. How I miss them all.

However, it feels just like old times as I set off for Rileys. As I near Rileys a taxi draws up alongside me, 'You McNab?'

'No he is,' I reply, pointing at McNab who is hugging a lamp post for support, '...But he lives on planet Zog.'

'Nae problem, pal. I do that run regular.'

Nothing's changed. I love and miss it all.

Entering Rileys, Agnes awaits me with a smile, 'Hello there stranger. Glad to see you again. I've missed you these last two weeks. Wullie's in, so will that be two of heavy and your *nuts* then? The tiresome innuendo obvious, I shudder. I'm now a shuddering wreck. She then continues in a whisper, 'You still havnae phoned me yet.' Looking around in panic in case anyone heard her I notice Twazzle, the bar drunk standing next to me, giving me the one rheumy eye treatment. After a couple of false spluttered attempts, which I manage to dodge, he finally blurts, 'S..S..Sammy, how c..come you get S..S..Sammy and a smile an aw I g..get is, "right p..pal whit dae y..you want?"'

'We cannae all be as lucky as you, Twaz,' I reply, meaning every word. Grabbing my served drinks I beat a hasty retreat towards Wullie and safety. Before sitting I look back towards the bar. I get the Quasimodo wink. This is getting seriously out of order. Taking my seat, Wullie opens with his usual diabolical impersonation, 'I've been using my leetle grey cells.'

'And what did they tell you, Inspector Clouseau,' I squeak, still in shock.

'I keep telling you, it's no Clouseu, it's Poirot.'

'Well, what did the leetle grey cells tell you? Pure rot.'

'A posh salesman.'

'A *posh* salesman?' I repeat.

'Aye. Eck and the posh salesman take over in town……..,'

'Have you taken leave of your senses, Wullie? Eck - in - town? You couldnae inflict him on the townies. They'd think he was from planet Zog.' Well, he *is* a pal of McNab.

'Let me finish. Not only do you get to take over the running of Barrington-Bell Technical Services as you planned but you also get to sell your own motors again. What dae you think of that?'

'I think it's a brammer of an idea Wullie, except for Eck.'

'Look, if we get the *right* posh salesman he can teach Eck that etty-quetty posh stuff.'

'Fine. But where do we get a *right* posh salesman. You cannae advertise for one. The politically correct loonies would have a hairy fit. I don't know about you Wullie but these politically correct creeps get right up my nose. It's ever since we joined that European lot and their nanny state politics happily endorsed by your New Labour gang. Now if Maggie was still in power she'd….'

'Is that it, you finished now? Or dae you want my view on *her*?'

Having heard his treasonable opinion of Maggie I elect for, 'Finished.'

'Good. Because I've just spotted the answer tae your problem going intae the gents.'

'Well, who is it?' I tetchily reply, still annoyed at his attitude towards Maggie, just as Geeza double shuffles past the table.

'How's it goin,Geeza,' hails Wullie on seeing him.

'It's yerself, Wullie,' he wheezes, 'you couldnae gie's a fag?'

'Here you are you poncing git,' replies Wullie offering up his cigarettes. Geeza on accepting the pack takes the mandatory two tucking them behind his ears.

'For efter,' he explains, 'now that they numpies in London willnae let you smoke.'

Before I can vent forth on this Geeza continues, looking at his watch, and with a finger to his lips, 'Sh! Quiet.This is it lads.'

On the stroke of six the pub phone rings loud and clear. Silence breaks out all over the pub. You could hear a pin drop. Agnes wrenches the receiver off its cradle and growls,

'Aye. Whit dae you want? I'm no an answering service you know……It's an emergency is it?.......All right, but just this wance. Who dae you want tae talk tae?.... Willie? There's plenty of Willies in here.' This brings a rude snigger from the bar worthies. 'A mister who? Right, I'll try again but this is it pal.' Turning to face the bar worthies once again she snarls, 'IS THERE A WILLIE PULLER IN HERE?'

'Aye, me,' answers a female impersonated male voice from the worthies at the bar. 'Tell him I'll dae it for a tenner.'

A look of dawning comes across her face changing to red-faced embarrassment then purple rage as she shouts into the phone, 'See you, you dirty pervert if I find out who you are I'll cut your……' We never did find out what part of the callers anatomy she was going to chop off because it was lost in a tidal wave of convulsed mocking laughter from the worthies which immediately stopped on her turning to face them.

Silence - everyone in innocent conversation.

I loved it. 'My congratulations to whoever the caller was, Geeza,' I compliment.

'You're about tae meet him,' he wheezes pointing in the direction of the gent's toilet. The door opens and out glides a tall, slim, elegant, silver haired, extremely well dressed, distinguished looking gentleman in his early fifties.

Moving towards Geeza he chortles, 'That got the old bag going, Eh! what, Geeza.'

'Nice wan, Nigel. Wullie would like a word with you.'

'Well, well, William my dear chap, pleasure to see you again...' this spoken in the most aristocratic of accents, '....Whatever did we do before mobile phones? Eh! what.'

'Cracking piss take, Nigel. Have you met my mate, Sammy Robb?'

'Delighted to meet your acquaintance Samuel,' said as he extends his hand, '....Not *the* Sammy Robb of *Sunday Informer* fame and persecution?'

'At your service, Nigel,' I reply, taking a bow. 'Loved your wind-up.'

'Long overdue. Can't abide ignorance.'

'Me neither, Nigel. Can I get you a drink?'

'Love one old chap. A whisky with a splash of water, please. I'll leave the measure up to you. Har, har.'

I then set off for the bar hoping to be served by someone other than the ogre. I'm in luck, but it's a very worried looking, Jock, who on looking around, obviously to see where Agnes is, greets me in a very low, confidential whisper, 'Wis that you that made that phone call, tae the auld bitch, Sammy?'

'Not me, Jock.'

'Sounded like wan of yous yins tricks. She'll no doubt take it oot on me, you know.'

'Why, what'll she do to you?'

'She'll have me up and doon they cellar steps all day long,' pointing to a hatch in the bar floor behind the counter. 'Aw for nothing. Just tae take her spite out on me. Hurts ma legs something awfy so it does, Sammy.'

'Sorry tae hear that, Jock, but I'm not surprised. She's something else that yin. By the way, while you're here, give's two pints of heavy ….'

'And a packet of nuts,' finishes Jock.

The bitch. What an evil thing to do to an old man. We'll need to sort her out.

Lifting my drinks, and still seething with Agnes at her treatment of old Jock, I head back for the table and re-tell what happened, finishing, 'Wullie, we've got to do something about *her*. Imagine doing that tae an old geezer like, Jock. Sorry about this, Nigel, but I'm reaching the end of my tether with her.'

'Us all, dear boy, us all. That's why I did what I did to the old bag just now. Didn't of course know she takes it out on poor old, Jock.'

'Sadly she does….Right Nigel, down tae business. What do you do for a living?'

'I'm a double glazing-counsellor.'

'So you *do* sell, then?'

'Counsel, dear boy, counsel. As we refer to it at "See Thru-Windows".'

'How's that going?'

'I think people are beginning to see through us. Har, har, har.'

'That must be a right pain in the glass,' chips in Wullie.

'Very drole, William, very drole. Har. Har.'

'Don't want to interrupt your jocularity lads but...' I apologetically interrupt.

'Frightfully sorry old boy, do continue.'

'Thank you. Right then, Nigel, I'm looking for someone to take over my town showroom. He must have, as the French say, a certain savoir faire. Like wot you have.'

'Mais certainement, monsieur Samuel.'

'Sammy, he speaks French. You could sell Renaults and Citroens and.....'

'Wullie, shut it. I'm trying to have an intelligent conversation with Nigel. O.K?'

'Unfortunately, I know nothing about automobiles, dear boy,' replies Nigel.

'You don't have to. Eck, my salesman, is a walking encyclopaedia on motors. But he needs a real good dose of that savoir faire of yours.'

'Sammy, Sammy, this is what I was telling you. Nigel can teach Eck that savvy thing and Eck can teach Nigel - aboot motors.'

'Yes, Wullie.Yes,' I reply rattily, getting pissed off with his inane claptrap.

'So in effect I would be performing the role of "Professor Higgins" in "My Fair Lady" on dear, what's his name – Eck. That's Alec. Sounds a challenge. Eh, what.'

'Believe me, "The Prof." had it easy. Wait till you meet Eck. So you'd be interested?'

'Well, with the window game losing its sparkle, Har, har, har, it looks like you have yourself a general manager, old chap.'

'There's my card, Nigel. Could you be in the showroom at three o'clock tomorrow to meet the wife and discuss salary and the like?'

'Certainly Samuel. Till tomorrow. Look forward to seeing you then. Pip, pip,' said shaking hands with all and then departing.

'Typical Nigel, promotes himself from posh salesman tae general manager and then doesn't buy a round tae celebrate,' laments Wullie, adding, 'What did you make of him?'

'A posh tosser. His jokes are worse than yours....but, Wullie, with all his savoir faire Ella will go a bundle on him. And that my dear old chap is all that matters. Eh! what. Pip, pip. Old boy. Har, har, har.'

'Sammy, what *is* this savvy thing?'

Putting a comforting arm around his shoulders I confide in him, 'Nothing you ever have to worry about, Wullie.'

The following day finds me hanging around the showroom door. At just before three the tall elegant figure of Nigel approaches. I open the door explaining as I do,

'She's due any minute now, Nigel. Please take a seat.'

'Jolly good, Samuel.'

We have no sooner sat down than Ella screeches into one of our two permanently "Out of Order" reserved parking meters, as arranged for me by the now still ever attentive Victor Fenwick.

I open the door to her. 'Good afternoon my dear, I'd like you to meet Nigel. Nigel, my wife, Ella.'

'Enchante, my dear lady,' he says suavely taking her hand and kissing it.

'Nothing personal Nigel. I'm running late for my friends at Chez Maison, I'll need tae, er, to dash,' she replies in a fluster. He's hooked her. Now reel her in Nige boy.

'I understand fully, my dear lady. One must never be late for Pierre's, to die for, afternoon teas. He *does* get so upset.'

I can tell from her body language she's been reeled in. 'Perhaps a *few* minutes late won't matter. Now Nigel what brings you here? You don't exactly fit in with Sammy's usual assho....er, asshociates.'

'Your charming husband has offered me the general manager's situation of this fine establishment.'

'Has he now. Sammy! Why have I not been informed of this?'

'Hot off the press, Ella. I thought it was time we had a manager of a stature in keeping with the prestige of the showroom.' I've been practising that speech all day.

'What a marvellous idea. Would you care to join me for afternoon tea Nigel?'

'Absolutely delighted my dear lady,' replies the old smoothie taking the offered hand to help her rise.

'Good idea Ella. I'm so hungry I could eat a scabby horse,' I enthuse.

'Regretfully Sammy, Chez Maison does *not* cater for such a delicacy. Come Nigel, we don't want to be too late. Sammy a taxi please, if you will.'

Resisting the urge to give her a touch of the forelock and the finger of satisfaction I order the taxi. As it disappears out the cul-de-sac, I find myself outside on the pavement jumping up in the air clicking my heels shouting, 'I'm free, free, free....'

'You'd be better aff back in your cage, pal,' growls Malky, the street cleaner.

A week later, with Nigel now in residence in town along with an unhappy Eck, finds me turning the Jag into my old parking spot at my Maryhill fiefdom. There to greet me at the office door is a very happy looking Vera. As I leave the car and walk towards her that beautiful radiant smile breaks across her face as she gives me a modest kiss on the cheek for the benefit of the cheering and whistling onlookers, Hughie and Rab. As she takes my hand, leading me towards my office a lump develops in my throat and a mixture of humility and pride wells up compounded further as I find myself looking at a banner pinned above my desk: WELCOME HOME SAMMY. Under it is a bottle of champagne in an ice bucket. As I turn to Vera to give her a thank you kiss I notice that Seamus is blindfolded and Maggie turned to the wall.

I then hear the soothing whisper in my ear, 'I've missed you Sammy.'

It's great to be back in the real world – sliding down the razor edge of life. Wa- he!

Having now spent a month back in my Maryhill fiefdom during which time I have employed a trainee salesman, Fraser, to take Eck's place, I decide to visit the town showroom to find out how Nigel and Eck are getting on. Having heard nothing untoward from Ella, who is still running conducted tours of the premises, I can only but assume all is well. However, contrary to this assumption, as I enter the showroom I'm met with a very glum looking Eck. This doesn't bode well.

'How's it going Eck?'

'Oh, all right, Mr.Samuel,' comes a less than exuberant reply from a now very refined and cultured voice.

'Not like you to be down in the dumps. What's the problem, Eck?'

'It's Nigel's enhancement programme.'

'Go on then show me some of it.'

Taking up his position along side a Merc he recites, 'The Mercedes C300, what an excellent choice of marque, if I may say so sir. The engine is of the finest precision German engineering, developing a thrust of……'

'Brilliant Eck, I wouldn't have recognised that, as the old you. What a transformation. Well done Nigel and especially well done you - Eck,' I applaud.

'If you don't mind Mr Samuel, my name now is Alec or Alexander if you prefer.'

'Aye. Alright Eck. So what's upsetting you son, you sound great.'

'Well Mr Samuel, it's not the talking I mind, in fact I enjoy that, as it's a major contributory part of selling these marvellous marques.' This has got to be a clone, it can't be the real Eck. Continuing in his new articulation, 'It's the balancing of the telephone directories on my head I don't care for. It's rather sore on the old noddle.'

'Directories on you head, sore noddles, what the hell's going on?'

'Deportment. Nigel says it helps you to glide. All part of my etiquette he says.'

'Where is Nigel by the way?'

'At the bookie's and if not there then in the ....' At this moment the showroom door opened and a head wearing the Gestapo cap of a traffic warden peers round the edge of the door and nasally says, 'Is Nigel in Alexander?'

'Afraid not Steven. He's in the "Wan Swally".'

'Ta Alexander. I'll pop roon an see him there then. See ya ra morra mornin for a cuppa.'

'Sorry about that Mr. Samuel. As you will have gathered Steven is the local traffic warden. He's a very good friend of Nigel's... I take it you did notice the four extra "Out of Order" meters outside our premises - compliments of Steven?'

'No I didnae. That's brilliant Eck... Now if I can offer you a bit of advice son. The next time Nigel wants you to dae that deportment wie the telephone directories I suggest you let the

"Yellow Pages" dae the walking. You'll find it easier on your heid.'

Nigel might be a posh tosser but he's ticking all the boxes for me. A reincarnated Eck, fit for presentation tae the Queen, and *four* extra parking meters. Now that's what I call class.

# CHAPTER SIXTEEN

## THE HONEYTRAP

I break the journey into work by stopping off at Ronnie's for one of his nourishing high cholesterol breakfasts. It's up to its usual gut busting, grease laden, standard that gives the stomach an ideal protective lining coat for the day's further abuse.

As I'm about to leave the premises, having washed down the mandatory dosage of indigestion tablets, now free with each meal, with tea made from a tenth time recycled tea bag (Ronnie's contribution towards helping global warming he tells all) he wheezes, 'Huvnae seen, Eck, in wie you of late, Sammy.'

'No, he's working in the town showroom. You wouldn't recognise him, Ronnie. Wears all the best of gear now, Armani suits, carnation in the lapel, Gucci shoes, Jermyn Street hand tailored shirts, real man about town and talks dead posh. Reminds me of me.'

'Dis he indeed? That's just whit I need in here – a classy heid waiter. Tell him if he ever needs a job…'

'Listen, Ronnie, even the old Eck was too classy for in here…. And that's saying something.'

'You being a food connoisseur an aw that, wid know like.'

With that I bid mine smart arse host the customary two finger farewell as I continue my journey. In the mirror I see him returning my goodwill gesture with one hand and scratching his unmentionables with the other.


Arriving back in the office I grab a beer from the fridge, loosen my tie and plonk myself, with beer in hand, in my favourite leather swivel chair awaiting the arrival of Wullie, who I've summoned for a "council of war" meeting regarding yet another crisis. I've no sooner taken my first gulp of beer when a screech of tyres, giggling in the general office as Vera is flirted with, announces the arrival of Wullie.

'Help yourself to a beer,' I say to his back as he is already heading for the fridge.

Opening the fridge door I hear, 'Ta, Sammy that's generous of you. There's nane left.'

'Only one thing for it then...Rileys.'


As we saunter up the road, Wullie is complaining about the rising unemployment while the Tories allow the bankers to pay themselves obscene bonuses. It's pointless informing him that the worse than useless New Labour party is in power since us Scots tend to blame all our ills on the hated English and by association the Tory party. As I'm about to expound my own theories on the corrupt thieving bastard bankers, we have turned the corner into Maryhill Road and there in the distance, outside Rileys, is "Holy Joe" our local fire and brimstone evangelist.

Wullie mutters to me out the side of his mouth as we slow our steps, 'Huvnae seen him for a while.'

'Nae wonder after that last time.'

'Remember it. He'd ventured intae Rileys and was ranting oot his usual "repent sinners" garbage when he came face tae face wie Agnes. He says tae her, "Dae ye have a message for

Satan". "Aye" says Agnes grabbing his lapels and sticking the heid on him.

He got the message right enough,' hoots Wullie with laughter.

By this time we've arrived at Joe standing on a milk crate shouting to all those passing by to "repent while there is yet time". Answered by the faithful with the customary "V" sign, or an "up yours" or worse retort.

'Received any messages for Satan of late, Joe?' enquires Wullie, as we turn in towards Rileys. This starts him off again, with finger pointing and in a wrath of God doomed voice, 'Sinners do not enter those dark satanic doors for they will lead you to evil.'

'Oh, no they won't,' we chorus in true pantomime tradition.

'To touch the amber nectar of Satan is but to follow the path to degradation.'

'Oh, no it's not,' we chorus back.

As he gears up for his next tirade, he loses our attention for tottering towards us in her high stiletto heels is Peaches, one of the "girls", nearly dressed in a black mini skirt with black fishnet stockings, showing just a hint of flesh above the giggly band. A red satin blouse revealing a plunging mountainous cleavage completes her work apparel.

"Holy Joe" starts again, his voice getting slower with each advancing step of Peaches, 'D..do. n..not..let..S..satan's lures turn..you..from..the..straight..and..narrow..my...' With bulging eyes he gives up his hectoring to watch Peache's ample frontage bob up and down towards him.

'Hi boys, how're you daen,' says Peaches, cheerfully to Wullie and me.

'Being preached tae, Peaches, on the virtues of ...'

'Don't listen tae Joe. He's a pussy cat. Aren't you, cuddles?' she pouts, 'Same time Thursday O.K for you, Joe?'

Clearing his throat Joe harrumps, 'You still daen your buy two get one free deal, Peaches?'

'Aye, but make sure you bring your loyalty card. It's double points week,' she replies with a wink, uplifting her boobs, and wiggles off down the road to the lecherous admiration of Joe's open-mouthed gawp.

'Now you make sure you remember your loyalty card, Joe, if you want to be taken to heaven,' is Wullie's departing remark.

As we make our way through the dark satanic doors I notice Joe's hand glide stealthly to an inside pocket and seruptitiously place a half bottle of Satan's amber nectar to his lips. Wullie, also noticing this remarks, 'Think it must be a Nectar loyalty card Sammy.'

To be fair to Joe he has a point regarding the satanic doors for as soon as we enter the Devil's agent on earth gives forth with, 'Aye, whit dae yous two want?' said in her usual broken glass aggro voice but with her Quasimodo's mother's wink at me.

'Two pints of heavy…,' starts Wullie, only to be finished by Agnes with, 'And a packet of nuts for, *Sammy*.' Wullie looks at me aghast. I shrug. What else can I do? Wullie lifts the drinks and I take the nuts off Agnes who whispers, 'You playing hard tae get or whit?' I shudder. Fortunately Wullie is now out of earshot. Twazzle, the bar drunk isn't. He gives me a wink and a rude punched arm gesture with a, 'Waheee Sammy boy,' then carries on talking to himself. Holy shit. What next?

Taking my seat Wullie looks quizzically at me, 'What have you been up tae wie Agnes?'

'Do's a favour Wullie. You don't think I'd do…' He would. So making him promise to tell nobody, I tell him the story. When I finish he roars with laughter. Arsehole.

'I wouldnae worry too much, Sammy, she's obviously just nuts about you. Sorry, Sammy, sorry.' Wiping tears from his eyes and enjoying every moment of my embarrassed unease he continues, 'It's just I keep getting this image of you and Agnes....' I give him one of my wilting stares. 'Right then. Your other problem is....'

'Ella.'

'She intae nuts as well?' As I make to get up towards him he hastily continues, 'Sorry, Sammy. Sorry.  What's up wie you and Ella then?'

'Well, I've got this feeling we're drifting apart.'

'Told you not to buy that water bed,' he hoots. I give him another of my wilting stares.

'Sorry, Sammy. Sorry. Couldnae resist it. I'm now all ears - promise,' he says doing his usual cupped hands routine pose behind his ears.

Calming down I start to tell him, 'Right. Well, Ella and me are sitting at home last Wednesday evening when the phone goes. I get up to answer it. When I get back she says anxiously to me, "Who was that?"'

'Wrong number,' I answer. Then it suddenly dawns on me. I'm not usually home on a Wednesday. I'm usually out playing cards with Georgie but he called it off with a dose of Delhi belly from a dodgy curry. Wullie, then sees this as an opportunity to do his impression of an Indian head and arm rhythm movement at the same time chanting, 'Georgie's got, Delhi belly from a dodgy curry. Georgie's got Delhi belly from a...'

Interrupting him, as you've got to, I carry on, 'So, why do you think Ella was anxious about the call?.......Because she thought I recognised the caller..... and I did.' Answering my own question.

'Who was it?'

'Posh, poncey, Nigel.'

'So what. Ella's not like that. Nor is Nigel.'

'Listen Wullie, with Ella's money, she's fair game for every chancer in the universe. Especially the likes of Nigel. He's skint. The bookies have his money. *And* she still goes to Chez Maison with him.'

'But from what you've told me its all circumferences anyway.'

'Circumstances Wullie. C-i-r-c-u-m-s-t-a-n-c-e-s.'

'That's what I've been trying to tell you. Ella's just a wee bit taken wie yon savvy fair thing that Nigel's got. And that's about all.'

'Savoir faire, Wullie.'

'That's what I said. What *is* wrong with your hearing?'

'Well, what am I going to do about it?'

'I hear some of those digital hearing aids are……'

'It's not my hearing, it's my predicament I'm talking about.'

'Ah! Right. Well, what do *you* think you should do?'

'Get shot of the lecherous posh git.'

'Now I'm getting the picture but I don't think it would be a good idea to get rid of, Nigel.'

'And why not?'

'Because without Nigel in the town showroom, Ella will have you back in town tooty de sweetie. You know she's looking for an excuse to get you out of Maryhill.

'A fair summing up, Wullie. But I've been doing a bit of thinking myself,' I explain tapping my head with my forefinger. 'To give Nigel his due, he's done a grand job on Eck. He's taught him proper etiquette and how tae talk proper. Top man is Eck now.'

'He's a good boy is Eck, but to run a showroom I have my doubts.'

'You haven't seen him lately. You wouldn't recognise him. Trust me he's Nigel's natural successor.'

'Aye, that's as maybe, but it still leaves you a man down if you get rid of Nigel.'

'Covered. I've got young Fraser just itching to get into town amongst the birds. Eck can do his, "Professor Higgins", on him. Not that he'll have to do a lot. Fraser has built in class just like *myself*. So don't worry about *me* getting shot of poncey Nigel.'

'Look, Sammy. Instead of all this palaver, why don't you just go into town and ask Nigel if he's knocking off Ella.'

'Hold it right there, Wullie,' I retort indignantly.'There's no need for vulgarity. I know it's him. He's for the chop and that's that. Final.'

'I still think you're over reacting. It's still all circum…..'

'Listen you. I wouldnae be in this predicament but for you.'

'Me?'

'Aye, you. It was you that introduced me to him so just you get those leetle grey cells working tae figure out how tae get shot of him – *without* Ella knowing. O.K?'

'O.K, Sammy. But as I've said before and I'll say again, it's all circum…'

'No it's not, Wullie. I'm right - you'll see.'

'You'll need tae give me a little time for zee leetle grey cells to work, Sammy.

'Aye, O.K Clouseau. See you in the morning.'

The following morning having just parked up in the forecourt I am met by Wullie just leaving his close whistling tunelessly away to himself. Seeing me he heads towards me and with an open arm gesture to the sky gushes, 'Think I've cracked it Sammy.'

'Great. Let's hear it,' I say as we head for my office.

He starts explaining to me, 'When I got home last night I put on a DVD.' With a shrug of his shoulders and his usual swagger he then does an impression. 'Now, not a lot of people know this.' I haven't a clue who, so I venture, 'Jimmy Cagney?'

'No Sammy. It was Michael Caine,' comes the hurt reply, '….It was about spies during the cold war with Russia.'

'Well it would be cold if it was Russia'

'Funny you should say that, Sammy. Did I tell you the one about the guy's house that was right in the middle of…..'

'The boundary between Russia and Poland,' I continue for him.

'….and he was asked what country he wanted to live in, Russia or Poland.'

'And he said Poland, because he'd heard Russia was freezing,' I finish for him.

'What you call a borderline case. Boom- Boom,' he finishes with an exaggerated right leg stomp and extended arm gesture, palm up, standard of the old stand-up comedians. 'Right, enough of this jocularity,' he continues. 'Back tae business. Well, in the film the Russians used a thing called a honey trap tae get people to do things they don't want tae do. Following?

'Yeah. But what's a honey trap?'

'Well, what they do is use a good looking bird tae trap a man in a compromising position and then take photos of him. Know what I mean, Sammy?'

'Yeah. And how do you propose we do that, then?'

'We get a bird tae trap Nigel and take photos of them, then let Ella see them. Simple.'

'Sounds good. But where do we get this bird?' At this, Wullie points towards Vera's office.

'No way, Wullie. Vera's a sweet innocent ……'

'Sammy. It's me you're talking to. Look nothing will *actually* happen. Just a pretend compromising position. O.K?'

'All right. Supposing I get Vera to agree?'

'Well, I've got a mate in the closed circuit TV game who owes me a favour. So we can install the cameras in one of the cars and…………' He outlined his plan.

A couple of days later, Vera, dressed in black shoulder length wig, short tight skirt, plunging neck blouse, mink stole, and black seamed stockings all perched on top of three inch stiletto heels slides into the Jag. We then set off for town. When we reach town I park at the entrance of the cul-de-sac leading to the Barrington-Bell showroom. I then get out to release, from its cage in the boot, a French poodle named Phoebe borrowed from a neighbour. I then open Vera's door to watch the elegant way she slips herself from the passenger seat. The DNA globules start their samba rhythm and with a supreme effort I ignore them and sorrowfully hand her the dog's lead and watch, as a very poor substitute, her shimmy her way along the cul-de-sac towards the showroom and stop at the window. After a minute's perusal she continues towards the door. I see the door open as she arrives at it. Opened by Nigel. This I know, without looking, because it's Eck's day off.

I then get back in the car and wait. Phase one of "Operation Honey Trap" has started.

The following, is based on Vera's account of what happened next.

Nigel on opening the door greets Vera in his usual courteous manner, 'Good afternoon madam. Can I be of assistance to you?

'I do hope so,' Vera replies in a sultry tone looking at him with hand on hip.

'Anything in particular that has taken madam's attention?'

'The Rolls-Royce,' she purrs in the same sultry voice.

'Oh! I do say, madam has the most exquisite taste. An excellent choice. The finest example of precision engineering and reliability available. Would madam care to see the magnificent engine? A true work of art.'

'No, thank you. I leave that to my chauffeur. I'm only interested in the interior, particularly the back seat if you know what I mean,' she intones with a wink.

'Certainly, madam,' replies Nigel opening the rear door to expose the sumptuous interior of real leather upholstery, plush carpeting and real wood veneer trim.

'To madam's liking?'

Vera, brushes past Nigel, fakes a trip over the dog lead, and sprawls towards the interior. As she does so she grabs Nigel's lapels and skilfully pulls him on top of her as they land on the plush carpeting. As they land Vera's skirt rides up her thighs showing her shapely leg clad in black seamed stockings and suspenders with a goodly hint of flesh above the giggly band.

Vera grapples with Nigel, holding him close shouting, 'HELP, SOMEONE HELP... RAPE!.... RAPE!'

Nigel, untangling himself from the melee, stands up, adjusts his rumpled attire and offers his hand to the still legs apart Vera. 'My hand, madam. I can assure you I had no such intention.'

As Nigel pulls Vera to her feet, she retorts, 'Don't you "madam me" you, you, sex fiend.'

'I can absolutely assure madam that I most certainly am not.'

'I've heard of men like you taking advantage of defenceless women like me. Come, Phoebe, away from this horrid man,' said as Phoebe is marking its territory with a leg cock, against the wheels of the Rolls.

As Vera strides towards the door a distraught Nigel calls after her, 'I could always knock something off for......cash.......madam.'

As Vera takes her leave from the showroom she turns towards me and from a distance gives me the thumbs up sign. Phase one of "Operation Honey Trap" complete.

The following day, Wullie enters the office whistling tunelessly and excitedly gabbles, 'Deserving of an Oscar quotes the *Hollywood Star*. In breathtaking colour and super cinema-scope,' he continues, as he crosses to the video and inserts a tape.

'The hidden cameras in the Roller worked O.K, then?'

'A treat. It's like a Hollywood blockbuster,' he declares picking up the remote control and sets the tape in motion. It's over in two minutes but is exactly as we wanted.

'The Russians couldnae do any better. Eh! Sammy.'

'Vera's missed her vocation. She should have been an actress,' I say with pride.

'Aye. She certainly seems a natural…. at it,' he replies. I eye him suspiciously not caring for his hidden innuendo. No response, just that annoying smirk of his playing at the corners of his mouth.

'What happens now?' I enquire.

'My mate will pick out the best bits and make stills of them.'

'Now remember you, one copy only.' I warn him. 'We don't want the whole of Glasgow seeing this,'

'Bit late telling me that, Sammy. They're already on "You Tube".' As I advance on him he beats a hasty retreat out the door, laughing his head off. He does like his little joke. At least I think it's a joke. With him you never know.

That evening, as I'm leaving for home, Wullie pulls into the forecourt signalling me to stop. Getting out he hands me a plain brown A4 envelope.

'Glad I caught you Sammy. There's the photos. They should do the trick.'

'Thanks pal. Fancy a beer? Maybe go to Kennys instead of Rileys for a change.'

'Trying tae body swerve Agnes?' he answers with that supercilious smirk of his.

'Shush, Wullie. Walls have ice cream,' I reply, looking around in panic.

'Vera still here then?' he queries, still with *that* smirk. 'Anyway, I cannae tonight, Sammy. Busy.' As I look past him, in the gloom, towards his van I see a female shadow flit from the van into his close entrance.

The following morning on leaving the house, knowing that Ella is not as yet up and about, I leave the plain brown A4 envelope behind the door.

Phase two of "Operation Honey Trap" has started. As I drive into work my mobile goes. Without looking at caller I.D, I know who it is. Ella on cue. I ignore it and head for Ronnies. With my stomach revolting at the thought of a "Greasy Spoon" high cholesterol breakfast two days in a row I settle for a coffee of rotten sock flavour, on the menu as "Columbian Nectar", and a croissant which you could use to hammer in six inch nails. Checking my mobile's messages; it was who I thought - Ella. She wants me to return home immediately. No rush there then. Time to do my bit for Global warming. I order a cracked mug of Ronnie's "Eco-Green" recycled tea to finish off my cigar. I should point out that Ronnie has opted out of the no-smoking ban. Not that anyone would notice the difference in his perma-smoke, grease filled, establishment. I bid him farewell with the customary two finger salute which he returns with his one hand while the other wipes his nose on his sleeve. Pure class...... I about turn the Jag and head home.

Arriving home, I'm hardly out the car when the front door is wrenched open.

The Victorian, lead stained-glass panel in the front door, shows signs of distress as it bounces off the hall wall. What is it with her and doors?

Ella hollers, all signs of her demure posh accent gone, 'You - In - Now!'

She then turns and heads inside. She gets the finger. I follow her into the kitchen with the usual precaution prevailing, door left open.

With a face like thunder and in a voice to match she growls, 'Look what I found behind the door this morning, just after you left for work.'

Ella by this time is standing at the kitchen table which brings back a flood of memories.

'What did you find, my dear?'

'Don't start any of your snash wie me.'

On the table lies the photographs from the brown envelope showing the whole sordid episode in glorious colour. I pretend to be engrossed in them, possibly over doing it because she snatches them from my view and stuffs them back in the envelope.

'Doesn't leave much to the imagination, does it?' I comment.

'Took you long enough to discover that. There's a note with it from your pal Dougie, of the *Sunday Informer*, asking you to give him a ring right away.'

'Not the *Informer* again. I thought I'd sorted them out that last time.'

'Wie you, the last time's always the first time again.' Ella logic. Don't ask.

'It says to phone him *right* away. So do it!'

'No time like the present then, is there my dear?'

'Grrrrr.'

Knowing what to expect following that growl I hastily lift the phone and punch in the numbers for Wullie who I have, regretfully, forgotten to warn of the call. It answers,

*'Hello Wullie Leckie speaking how....'*

'That you Dougie?

*'I've already told you it's me, Wullie Leckie.'*

'Yeah Ella got them this morning.'

*'Oh! It's you Sammy. Ella got what?'*

'So what's it all about?'

*'That's what I'd like tae know Sammy.'*

'Sorry, I was busy all day yesterday.'

*'I know. I was with you for most of it.'*

'You're what?'

*'Your mate, Wullie. As I keep telling you.'*

'You cannae use a headline like that.'

*'Fine. Fine wie me Sammy. You've gone. Flipped.'*

'Now look Dougie I don't want to remind you of that little incident on the golf course that might be construed as cheating.'

*'Sammy, you know I don't play golf.'*

'I don't think the golf club would like to hear about it.'

*'I couldnae care less if they do.'*

'Right, I knew you'd understand.'

*'Not a single word Sammy.'*

'See you later Dougie.'

*'It's not Dougie you want to see Sammy it's a heid doctor. And you say I've got a problem with vinegar on my chips. You've lost it. Talking to yourself now.'*

I put the phone down thinking, what a muppet. Why didn't he hang up?

'Well…what did Dougie say.'

'He says, he couldn't get hold of me so he dropped the photos off with the note.'

'Yes, yes, we know that. Get on with it,' in her best exasperated tone.

'So I ask him, what's it all about.'

'Yes, yes. I heard that. What was that about a headline?'

'He says he *was* going to use the headline, SEX FIEND USES UPMARKET SHOWROOM AS SEX LAIR'

'The dirty swine. Wait till I lay ma hands on him. Barrington- Bell will be ruined. The shame of it all. What will I tell my "Chez Maison" girls? I'll never be able tae show ma face in public again. It's all your….'

'Ella! Stop. What I said was, if you'd just bother to listen for once, was that Dougie *was* going to use the headline.'

'*Was* going to?'

'Yes. I had to remind him of a little indiscretion he committed on the golf course. If word got out he'd be flung out his club. You know what *they're* like.

With the usual Ella instant personality change she gives me a hug and a kiss, 'Sammy, you rascal, imagine using blackmail on your pal.'

'Well, when needs must, Ella. Only when needs must.'

'Now, get that Nigel out of my showroom - now! How could I have been had so easy.'

'Had, so *easy*, Ella?'

'You!' she laughs as she takes a playful swipe at me. Just like her old self. A wonderful infectious laugh and glowing smile. Could there be salvation for us yet, I wonder.

I pull the Jag into one of the permanently suspended meters outside Barrington-Bell. Nigel on seeing me arrive has the showroom door open, 'A very good day, Mr.Samuel.'

'It certainly is but unfortunately not for you Nigel.'

'How so, Mr.Samuel?'

'Possibly because of these, Nigel,' I smugly reply, handing him the photographs.

He studies them and then splutters, 'Where did you get these malicious fabrications, Samuel? I can fully explain them.'

'I got them off the *Sunday Informer.*'

'No. Not them,' exclaims Nigel, in distress, 'For the sake of my family I do not want to go through what they do to you. Can you please help me, Samuel?'

I'm knocked off my guard by his family revelations. However, on gaining control of my surprise, 'Tell you what, Nigel. You check in your P45 now, and I'll square it with my contacts in the *Informer.* How does that grab you?'

'Absolutely marvellous. I am eternally grateful to you Samuel for your kindness and please extend my humblest apologies to Mrs. Robb. Whatever, must she think of me. It was a set-up you know.'

'The *Informer's* like that Nigel. No one knows, as you know, better than me.'

'I bid you good day, Samuel. Thank you for everything. I am ever so sorry to be leaving your employ under these circumstances. Regards also to, *Alexander.* You have a good capable lad there. He'll handle the showroom with consummate ease for you, Samuel.'

'Er, er, eh, thanks, Nigel. Just before you go Nigel - a question.'

'By all means, my dear chap.'

'Did you,' nodding over my shoulder, '....you know with Ella?'

'*Certainly not*, Samuel. You should be ashamed of yourself thinking such thoughts of a fine lady like Mrs.Robb. I wish you and Mrs. Robb every happiness for the future. It's been my great pleasure to meet you both.'

With that he turns on his heel, and with that elegant graceful movement of his was gone.

Funny, he never mentioned family before. I should be elated at the outcome but an invasive feeling of gloom is haunting me – I *have* condemned an innocent man.

The following day finds me in my office trying to clear up the events of yesterday with a very confused Wullie, who is doing the talking, 'Now, let's see if I've got this right, Sammy. You left the photos, I gave you, for Ella to find?'

'Correct.'

'Then you phone me, pretending to Ella you're phoning Dougie.'

'Correct.'

'Then you tell Ella you've done a deal with Dougie, because he cheated at golf.'

'Correct.'

'And Ella? *Was,* er, Nigel….. giving her one?'

'Certainly not, Wullie. What sort of person do you think Ella is?' I answer indignantly. 'For the sake of his family he didn't want the scandal exposed.'

'But Sammy, there was *no* scandal to expose, we - made - it - up. The whole charade was totally unnecessary. Don't you understand? It was all in your imagination. Why didn't you ask him if he was having it off with Ella, when I asked you to?'

'What does it matter? I'm still at Maryhill, Nigel's gone. Eck's in place and Ella hasn't a clue how it happened. Result,' I reply, feeling vindicated. A feeling I was later to regret.

'Well, I wish I didn't know what happened. All I know is, that I was part responsible for an innocent man losing his job,' Wullie states angrily, pushing himself up from his chair and leaving without a farewell. I've never seen him that upset.

That invasive feeling of gloom has turned to full depression. Not helped as it transpires by the incoming phone call, 'Sammy. Ella for you,' purrs Vera.

'That you, Sammy?'

'Yes!' I answer sharply.

'Mrs. Watson, you know the old biddy from across the road?'

'Aye.'

'Well her new dog's gone missing. It's a French poodle called Phoebe.'

'So. What's it to do wie me?'

'Well the last time she saw it was two days ago when she says she saw you clapping it's head and talking to it.'

'It wasn't me. I don't talk to Froggies.'

With that I slam the phone down thinking how bad can this day get when I suddenly remember - Fuck! The bloody thing's still in the Jag's boot.

In the wee small hours of the morning I sneak across the road to Mrs Watson's and lob a rigid Phoebe by the tail over her hedge. At least it deserves a decent funeral.

All told, not one of the more memorable episodes of my life.

# CHAPTER SEVENTEEN

## THE BUMMER BEAMER

Y ou find me in my "den" at home. The fact that it is an "Ella free" zone has not lifted my spirits in any way. The dismissal of Nigel was a bad mistake and that together with Wullie's avoidance of me, for several days now, has left me on a real downer. Neither Wullie nor Nigel are answering their phones. One more try. Lifting my phone I dab in the numbers. Surprise, surprise, an answer.

Obviously recognising my ID, he answers, 'Hi, Sammy. How's you?'

'Better, now I've got hold of you. Where've you been?'

'I'm at Invertattie Castle, in deepest Perthshire.'

'What are you doing away out there? You know you don't travel well.'

'Fishing. Wie Nigel.'

'Wie Nigel! I've been trying to get hold of Nigel to apologise.'

'Aye, we know. We ignored them. After you bulleted him he did a runner tae his family's ancestral pile – Invertattie Castle. He's the Laird.'

'If he's the Laird, what's he doing selling double glazing….and motors in Glasgow?'

'Boredom, Sammy, plain and simple boredom. I'll tell you all about it when I get back.'

'Tell me, how'd you know where to find him?'

'Did you think tae ask, Eck?'

'Eck?'

'Eck's, Nigel's bosom buddy, don't cher know. Eh what! Har, har.'

'No kiddin – Nigel's buddy. Would you believe that?'

Just then the airwaves are shattered with the dulcet tones of Ella, blasting their way through the solid "den" door, 'SAMMY! IN THE KITCHEN - NOW.'

'Got tae go, Wullie. It's Ella, on the warpath.'

'I know. Me and the whole of Perthshire heard her. See you tomorrow, Sammy.'


As I enter the kitchen, and in time honoured tradition leave the door in the open escape position I enquire, 'Yes, Ella, dear. How may I be of assistance to your humble self?'

'Are you working today?' she enquires, unusually ignoring my sarcasm.

'Later, once I've fixed the Jag's exhaust. It's loose.'

'Well, don't forget tonight's my Conservative Club's cheese and wine do. It's my big night. I'm being elected treasurer, so no excuses this time. You're going understand?'

'Ella it's this tooth…..'

'Ah! You want it removed dae you' she threatens on her advance towards me.

'No. No. It seems to be O.K now,' I reply running my tongue round the inside of my cheek.

'Good. That's it sorted then. I'm off. Looks a bit like rain; I better take my umbrella.'

'Yes, Ella, dearest.'

'Listen you, just because I let you off wie your sarcasm once doesn't mean I'm……'

With her Kung Foo finger moving into strike mode, I'm off through the open door.

Later in the day Ella turns her Ferrari into the driveway and parks alongside Sammy's Jaguar. Getting out of her car with handbag slung over her shoulder and brolly in hand she notices a pair of boiler suit clad legs projecting from under the Jaguar.

Taking the brolly she bends, with an elegant knees together flex, and prods the brolly between the unsuspecting legs. With a girlish giggle she opens the house door and still giggling enters the lounge, coming sharply to an abrupt halt, her face changing to a mask of horror. There sitting in his chair reading the paper is....Sammy.

With a voice between shock and panic she explodes, 'It's you! What the hell are you doing here?'

'Don't you remember, Ella - I live here.'

'Why aren't you under it? Who's under it?'

'Under what?'

'The Jag, you nyaff.'

'It's Hughie. The screws were rusted solid so I had to send for him.'

'Oh my God!' she wails, hands to head, 'I've brollied poor Hughie. It's all your fault.'

'My fault? How's that?'

'You should be under the car not sitting here reading the paper.' Ella logic. Don't ask.

With that she about turns and runs outside. I follow and when I reach Hughie bend down and slide him out from under the car by his legs. As he emerges his semi-conscious eyes are glazed and an enormous lump on his forehead is turning from yellow to a dark shade of purple.

'How do you like your leg being pulled, Hughie?' I enquire, of the concussed Hughie.

'This isn't the time for your inane remarks, dickhead. Is he alright?'

'Well, provided you ignore the fact he's concussed, has a lump the size of an Easter egg and severe trauma to his manhood, I'd say he's in good shape.'

'That's just typical of you. A man's at death's door and all you can offer is sarcasm.'

Fortunately for me at that moment Hughie shows signs of coming round. With a low groan he sits up with one hand holding his head, the other his manhood.

Ella bends down to face him, 'Let Ella kiss it better, Hughie.' A look of stark horror comes into his already spinning eyes. 'Your forehead Hughie, your forehead. I didnae mean your.....'

With that he's up and running as fast as his crab like gait will allow. Passing me he moans, 'The bloody woman's off her trolley.'

The running Ella being now right behind me wheezes, 'What, what did he say about my trolley?'

'It wasn't your trolley, it was your brolly. He never wants to see another one in his life. Can you blame him?'

By this time Hughie has made his escape. The smell of burning rubber being proof.

I wonder if he managed to fix the exhaust.

Finding no way of escape, I attended the Conservative Club's cheese and wine party with the treasurer elect, Ella, and much to my surprise I thoroughly enjoyed it. Contrary to Wullie's point of view that they're all "posh poofs" I have to disagree - they're not all posh. Sorry, just my little anti-politically correct joke. In fact there is a wide cross section of members from all walks of life all with one common aim - the removal of this inept, warmongering, arrogant, corrupt, Islington ruled government. I delight when I hear that. However, as I worked the room my Euro-sceptic views were not met with the one hundred per cent enthusiasm I expected so you can take it as read they won't be getting my vote. With Ella being the main attraction of the night, it allowed me un-chaperoned scope to circulate among the various attractive ladies. Very pleasant and informative that was too. As the excellent night drew to an end I vaguely remember my one last thought before I was led away to our taxi - that vintage port carries a wallop.

The following day finds me in the town showroom doing cover for Eck's day off, suffering from a first ever vintage port hangover. Pamela, a grumpy old bat out of the Ella mould, who has recently been put in place by, Ella, to keep the town accounts due to the hasty departure of Nigel, has to her credit, been plying me with cups of sweet black coffee, paracetamol and Irn-Bru. As I stand at the showroom door, coffee in hand, gulping in much needed fresh air I spy a person of recent acquaintance making his way towards me. It is the Chairman of the Conservative Club - a right smarmy bastard rejoicing in the title of The Right Honourable Everard Fortune-Smyth with whom I vaguely recall having a conversation last night.

As I open the door I greet him with a grovelling, 'Mr.Chairman, a pleasure to see you again, I trust I find you well.'

'Never better, Samuel. The name's Everard, by the way. I'm down to conclude our unfinished business from last night. If you remember, you mentioned a Bentley coupe due in sometime today.' Did I? That vintage port's got a lot to answer for. Looking quickly around the showroom he spots it and after circling and stroking it lovingly he soothingly murmurs, 'What an absolute beauty, Samuel. Are you certain it's pre-owned? It looks absolutely brand new.'

'May well you ask, Everard. A stunning example of the marque. The previous owner was a Lord.' Not a total untruth – it was Jimmy Lord the bookmaker. Now on hard times after yet another divorce and a series of uncooperative nags.

'Mm. An impressive provenance indeed. I must admit, it's me,' he purrs still stroking it. 'And the price,' he continues, looking at our discreet windscreen price, '…No need to haggle over that, Samuel.'

'Priced to go as we say in the trade.'

'Now did I mention I have a six month old BMW. Would it be possible to discuss the possibility of a trade-in?'

'Certainly Everard. Step this way I'm sure we can do a deal to our mutual advantage.'

After negotiations I venture, 'Now Everard, for the additional *cash* sum of two hundred pounds I can register you as a member of the Barrington-Bell Bentley Club. The advantages of being a member are too numerous to mention so I won't since I can tell you are anxious to join.'

'Sounds cheap at the price old chap,' replies Everard opening his wallet.

Later that day, during our evening meal and in one of the few lulls in Ella's never ending gabble on her associations and charities, I manage, 'That chairman of yours, Everard what's - his - name, came into the showroom this morning and bought the Bentley, no haggling. No haggling – what about that then? Traded in his Beamer. Turned out to be a nice little earner for us.'

'See I told you, you'd meet all the right people at our do's. And you refusing to go to them. Shame on you Sammy. He's one of Scotland's top insurance brokers, you know.'

'Oh, I know that. I didn't waste my time last night.'

This draws a suspicious look from Ella.

The following morning finds me looking for Hughie to see how he's keeping after his traumatic encounter with Ella and her brolly from a couple of days ago.

'How's the cripple?'

'On the mend, Sammy. That's more than can be said for the Beamer.'

'Eh! I'm not following, Hughie.'

'It's a bitsa,......'

'Never! The paperwork says it's only six months old,' I reply, shocked.

Hughie continues, 'That's true. Some bits are. Some bits aren't. Surprised you didn't spot it as one. It's been an insurance write off. Not as good a job as we'd dae but still a very high standard of pochling.'

'Thanks Hughie. Glad one of us is on the ball,' I reply, feeling ashamed of myself for not noticing the sham.

'Here take a look for yerself,' says Hughie, slipping under the hoisted Beamer.

Joining him, I cringe with further shame when he points out the obvious.

No way I'm going to disagree with Hughie's judgement. The two of us have re-built too many insurance write-offs over the years for him to make a mistake. A lesser man than Hughie would never have noticed it. My fault. I've allowed myself to be suckered by Everard's smooth talk. How could I have been so gullible. The guy doesn't haggle over the price, instantly agrees the trade-in *and* joins my Bentley club. I want my head examined. When you think about it, who better to carry out insurance write-off scams than an insurance insider. But who did the actual work on the car? There was a something I heard at Ella's Con (a very apt name given the circumstances) Club's recent do but I can't quite put my finger on it. Now who was it?

Racking my brain trying to remember who it was, as I walk back to the office from the workshop, I am brought out of my deep thoughts abruptly by a horn blaring car entering the forecourt behind me. As it comes to a skidding halt, out hops the bold boy himself. Bidding me, "the top of the morning, sur" in what I assume to be his new found Highland accent, but sounding decidedly Irish, he follows me into the office. Helping himself to a beer and taking a seat he commences, 'You've no doubt been wondering what happened at Invertattie Castle.'

'Yep.'

'Well, I wisnae happy about whit *we* did tae Nigel, so I tried tae contact him tae tell him but with nae luck. Then I remembered Eck. He tells me Nigel goes home on his weekends off tae this Invertattie place. Does Nigel have a phone number I ask him.

'"Yes Mr Leckie", he replies, all posh like he'd lived in Kelvinside all his days.'

'That's the new Eck, I was telling you about, Wullie.'

'Well anyway, I get the number and phone Nigel. He invites me up. And Sammy, you ought to see this place. It's like Buckingham Palace, wie a mile long tree lined drive, massive lawns, fountains, waterfalls and his own river wie real fish in it.'

'Real fish, indeed. My that's impressive. But tell me this, if it's that good why does he leave it? Especially if he's the Laird. That's like minor royalty up in the Highlands.'

'As I told you, he gets bored. How he can get bored wie all that I'll never know but he tells me he's a townie at heart. Cannae get enough of Glesca. Loves it. Stems from when he went tae Glesca Uni. His wife and two sons run the estate when he's away. Sarah, his wife, hates him doing his "wanderlust" thing. Nigel knows this but says he cannae help it – until now.

He got the fright of his life when you showed him those photos. And the thought of the *Informer's* scam scared him tae death even though there wisnae any *Informer* scam.

'Did you tell him there was no real scam?'

'No. I figure the scare's done him good. He'll stay at home now wie his lovely family.'

'That's good. I wouldn't have liked the *Informer* tae get their claws intae him.'

'Sammy, there you go again, you're still *believing* our story. Once and for all there's no story. We made it all up. O.K?'

'Oh, aye, so we did.'

'Now, you widnae believe this. Nigel says, wait for it…."He's for ever in your debt for calling off the *Informer's* bloodhounds". That's choice isn't it. Makes me feel a right heel, I don't know about you.'

'Wullie, nobody feels more rotten about it than me. I tried all ways tae contact Nigel, tae apologise, for getting rid of him.'

'But not tae give him his job back.'

'Couldnae, Wullie. Think about it. I was caught in a cleft stick. Ella had seen the photos so I couldn't very well tell her we had them posed, could I?'

'Well, it disnae matter now. As you say, it all ended for the best. Ella knows nothing but remember, Sammy, for the future…*facts only,* none of those circumferences.'

'Circumstances. C-i-r-c-u…..'

'Aye whateva. I'm just happy that Nigel's back where he belongs but most of all I'm delighted wie you, Sammy, for making the effort tae apologise tae a decent man.

Rising to shake my hand he continues, 'There's a good guy in you somewhere, trying to get out.'

'Tell me, Wullie, what condition's Nigel's car in? He wouldnae be looking for…'

'Sammy! After all you've done tae the bloke. You widnae....Aye, you would too.'

'Wullie, it's just the good guy in me trying tae escape.' Suddenly my depression's lifted.

As he leaves I mention to him I've another crisis looming. 'So what's new' he asks, as we arrange a "brain storming" for later in the day.

The "brain storming" meeting nearly finished, I am just finishing off my sad tale-of-woe, 'So there you are Wullie. I've been well and truly stitched up by the Right Hon. Everard Fortune-Smyth.'

'Well, from what you tell me it sounds like your own fault. Imagine allowing yourself to be conned by a posh git like Ever-Hard. You should know by now Sammy, that you, me, and the whole of us proletariat are only on this earth tae do the likes of his bidding.'

'No need tae rub it in, Wullie. I haven't always been a Tory you know. In fact with their leanings towards Europe, I'm not sure I'm even one now. Now if Maggie...'

'Don't start that again. I'm not in the mood tae hear aboot Maggie, *yet* again.'

'Well you started it, with all your New Labour proletariat claptrap.'

'O.K. O.K. Keys.' Thumbs held up for a truce. 'Let's get down tae business, Sammy. I'm going to really enjoy sorting this posh tosser Ever-hard out. Any ideas?'

'Well, firstly I'm going to cancel his membership to my Bentley club....with no refund.'

'Good. Good. That'll really rattle his cage, won't it? Listen are you sure he knows it was a bummer?'

'Trust me Wullie. I just know, he knows.'

'Well, it takes *one* to know *one,* as they say. What about the polis?'

'The polis! Wullie. The polis! When have we ever stooped as low as tae use them?'

'Sorry, Sammy, sorry. A mental aberration. My leetle grey cells need ze lubrication. Fancy one in Rileys?'

'Can't. Got to get home. Ella's forced me to go to her Ballet Society's opening night.' Adding lamely by way of an excuse, 'She's the treasurer of that as well.'

'See you, Sammy. You're losing the plot. Off tae see them toffy nosed poofters prancing aboot in in their tights and cod pieces.' That surprised me, the only cod pieces I thought he knew about was "Birds Eye". 'I'm really beginning to worry about you,' he bemoans shaking his head, 'Remember if you drop your programme tonight - don't bend down,' he chortles, as he takes himself off in the direction of Rileys.

He's right, I am being drawn out of my social environment. I need to have a good, long look at myself. I'll do it right after tonight's buffet…… of champers and caviar.

The following morning we continue the "brain storming". Wullie opens the proceedings with, 'After you left home last night I met Toni in Rileys doing his Al Capone impersonation.'

'Lucky you. Did you win a pyramid?'

'No.You widnae believe it, Sammy, after I bought ma square there was only wan square left so Toni bought it and it won. Isn't that amazing?'

'Truly amazing, Wullie.' Remember what I said about a mug being born every minute.

'Well, in any case his Capone impersonation gave me an idea. You know the one?' he queries as with hunched, swaggering, shoulders he drawls in a crap American accent, "You, ya dirty yellow rat".'

'That wasn't Capone. It was either Cagney or Bogart.'

'Well it disnae matter who it was. It gave me an idea,' he huffily replies as he outlines his plan. Finishing with, 'That should screw Ever-hard the Unfortunate-Smyth nicely.'

'Sounds good to me, Wullie. Do you know where to find Toni?'

'Yeah. He told me last night. He's doon at the Plaza Hotel flogging time share. I'll go and find him. Sooner we get started the better.'

Wullie heads off to the Plaza Hotel, in the town centre, and entering finds Toni in the entrance lobby of the hotel behind a sales booth littered with advertising brochures and an overhead banner bearing the slogan, "Tenerife Co-OwenR-Ship"

He's giving an old dear with a zimmer frame his sales pitch.

'No madam itsa no a time share.'

'What is it, well?'

'Iva already telt ye. Itsa co-ownership.'

'Whit's the difference?'

'Aye, whit's the difference?' adds a walking stick wielding pensioner beside the old dear.

'Well, one you donta own, the other we dae.'

'That's as clear as mud,' says the zimmer frame.

'Where's the photies of them then?' queries the walking stick.

'There's nane. Itsa visual concept.'

'Whit's that?'

'Ita no built yet. You huva tae visualisa them .'

'Can I ask you a question, son?' queries the pensioner brandishing his walking stick.

'Si senor.'

'Where's your mask, you robbing bastard?' the pensioner snarls taking a wild swipe at Toni who on turning to flee confronts a zimmer frame aimed at his head. Ducking and diving he disappears up a corridor. Five minutes later I see his head pop out of the "ladies" toilet in the corridor.

'Ita all clear, Wullie?'

'Ita all clear, Toni.'

'Cannae go mucha more ova this, Wullie. Ita getting very dangerous. Them pensioners geta violent wie me – every day they trya tae knocka ma brains oot.'

'Think I've got the solution. Sammy needs your talents. Paid of course.'

'Ama your man, Wullie. Grassy mila, ma mate.'

Wullie, looking closely at the sales booth's sign, starts wondering: "*Tenerife?* Co – *Owen* - R - Ship". Cannae be. Can it? Curiosity getting the better of him he asks, 'Tell me Toni, how'd you get this job?'

'The classifieds ina World Trade Review.'

'*You*. World Trade Review?'

'Aye. Itsa gospel for us yins ina the import, export game.'

'Who'd you speak tae?'

'Some Spanish bird called Rosaro.'

'She the boss?'

'Naw. He wis oot. She says they're going global. Using Glesca tae testa the water.'

Knowing he'll get no more sense out of Toni he bids him a, 'A very detchi. Toni.'

Operation "Ever-Hard" swings into action today. I've borrowed a tinted window black Merc from the town showroom. As a safeguard I had the number plates changed in Maryhill. The "gang", Wullie, aka "The Boss," and Toni, aka "Scarface Toni", the result of Wullie's deft work with a red perma ink pen, are dressed in Wullie's Bonnie and Clyde gangster costumes complete with dark glasses and *the* tommy-gun and are raring for action. I drive the Merc along a tree lined West End avenue until I come to a stone built end of terraced villa bearing the brass nameplate Everard Fortune-Smyth - Insurance Broker and stop directly outside. From an earlier drive-by I know that the Bentley is parked round the back.

As I bring the car to a stop Wullie is complaining to Toni, 'I cannae see a thing oot these shades, Toni.'

'Well, I donta know why. Them ma topa de range, genuine simulated reflectolites.'

'Disnae matter, I still cannae see a thing oot of them.'

'You no usa them right, Wullie.'

'Boss, tae you, right? How's it possible, Toni, to no usa them right. Eh?'

'Shut it both of you. "Operation Ever-Hard" is go. Go get him,' I order my troops.

As they get out, I crack the window open and can hear them as they approach the door.

'Look tough Toni baby.'

'How's this?'

'You're no oot for your Hallowe'en, you know.'

I watch mesmerised as Toni guides Wullie, who is still complaining about not being able to see, up the steps to the impressive front door. I shake my head in despair. I've got a bad feeling about this.

Out of my earshot the argument continues, 'I still cannae see a thing out of these,' moans Wullie.

'Once you getta inside you be O.K. They good inside.'

'Inside sunglasses? Who dae you think you're kidding?' By this time Toni has opened the front door and they enter straight into a sumptuous reception area. Sitting behind a massive desk is a thin, gaunt, hawk-faced, severe-looking middle aged witch with rimless glasses and hair tied into a bun. The spitting image of my grumpy old English teacher, Miss, nae teeth, Nesbit, thinks Wullie.

'Good morning gentlemen. Do you have an appointment?' she warbles, in a high pitched screech.

'Show her our appointment, Toni.'

Toni, on the command produces the tommy-gun from inside his velvet collared overcoat pointing it directly at her, 'No screaming lady. Ita be bad for a your health. Savvy?'

'Now, Mr.Everard, pleasa,' says Wullie, as Toni ushers her with the tommy-gun from behind her desk, in the direction of a door signed, *Mr.Everard Senior.* The matron, being unable to take her eyes off the tommy - gun opens the door to a prod from the gun, in her ribs.

'Efter you lady,' Toni growls.

As the door opens it reveals Everard, head down writing. Suddenly being aware of our presence he looks up startled and on gaining his composure demands, 'Who the hell are you and what do you want? In fact get out of my office immediately.'

'Toni!' At this Toni moves forward to cover Everard. 'To answer youra question Mister Insurance man, this man he Scarface Toni. He no get that face kissing babies. O.K? - Me, I'ma the boss. We botha your worst nightmare ifa you no cooperate. O.K?

Everard, very bravely goes for the phone on his desk only to be brought up abruptly by finding the tommy-gun up his nose, 'O.K O.K, no violence please,' bleats Everard, with raised hands.

'Easy Toni baby. Easy. No shoota him - just yet. Now Mr Insurance man, you listening?'

'Yes.Yes.You have my attention.'

'Right then Everhard,' Wullie having already got fed up calling him Mr Insurance man continues, '...The Bentley, round the back. Yes?'

'Yes, it's mine. Why?'

'Itsa not yours. It buya by a Mr. Robb by a mistake. He sella it tae you, yes?'

'Yes.'

'Bigga mistake. Ita belong tae *The Firm*. You understaund whata mean by *The Firm?*

'Yes,yes. Do geta er, get to the point will you please. I'm a very busy man.'

'I no lika his attitude Boss. I shoota him now?' And the dame as well?' At that the hawk-like receptionist who had been watching the happening in a trance faints. They leave her sprawled on the floor.

'Right Everhard, here's the deal. We take backa the Bentley. Yes?'

'Yes. Yes. Whatever you say...... And I get back my BMW.'

'Itsa no as easy asa that.'

'Somehow, I didn't think it would be.'

'Mr. Robb, he no a robba like you. You give him a bummer beamer. We no lika that but we lika Mr. Robb. Comprendi?'

'Yes. Yes. But what the blazes is a bummer beamer?'

'You no aska the questions, the boss he dae. Understaund?' snarls Toni as he brandishes the tommy-gun threateningly at Everard.

'A bummer beamer isa your BMW. An insurance write off - a phoney re-build. No usa tae nobody, so Mr. Robb he keepa it and your trade-in money as a good will gesture.'

'Over my dead body,' cries an indignant Everard.

'That's upa tae you. Toni he no lika you.'

'I shoota him now, boss.'

The receptionist who had just come round and was sitting upright on the floor, on hearing this, collapses into a faint again.

'Maybe, Toni. But first I hava tae ask him a question. How's Mr. Nutter?

'I've no idea who you're talking about. Who the hell is Nutter?' blusters Everard.

'You hava very bad memory Everhard, he your partner. Nutter the scrappy. Nutter the cutter. He cuta and welda your cars. We knowa this. He talka tae us, *voluntarily*. You knowa what I mean, by voluntary? A confirmation nod from Everard. 'He tella us you supply the motors.' Silence.

'Mr. Robb, he keepa the Beemer. Yes?'

'Yes,' replies a disgruntled, Everard, 'But can I at least get a refund on my Barrington-Bell, Bentley, membership?'

'You huvtae be kiddin, pal. *The Firm* disnae do refunds.'

'Well, what happens now?'

'The Costa crime, it very nice this time a year but remember the polis are nae use tae both our interests. You comprendi?'

'Yes. I comprendi,' sighs Everard, in a totally deflated tone.

'Then the keysa pleasa,' says Wullie holding out his hand. On receiving and checking the documentation he bids Everard, 'A very dechi.'

As they leave, Toni growls at the receptionist who has recovered again. She goes down for the third time. Out cold.

Puffing on the last of my Havana, I notice the Bentley appearing from out of the lane at the side of Everard's office. A hand gives me the thumbs up. Operation "Ever-Hard" is now complete and successful. Meanwhile out of my hearing a heated conversation is taking place inside the Bentley, as it heads for Maryhill.

'Know your trouble, Toni? You're trigger happy. Wanting tae blow their heids aff every two minutes.'

'I no lika him for whata he dae tae ma pal, Sammy.'

'And another thing, you - how dae you manage tae see oot of *your* glasses?'

'Me? I buy mine from Boots.'


As they pull into the forecourt I am right behind them. We head for my office where we break out the whisky to celebrate our success.

As Wullie and Toni recount their escapade I feel envious wishing I'd been there to personally witness the demise of smarmy Everard. Raising my glass I toast, 'To Glasgow's most wanted. Thanks guys. You've done great.' Much to my utter amazement.

'Do you think Everard will go to the polis, Sammy?'

'No way. Not with what we know about him and Nutter. They're yesterday's men.'

'Well, will you anon…anonmon….,'

'Anonymously.'

'Aye. That's whit I was about tae say, if you'd just let me finish…..let the polis know about him?' Wullie continued.

'Use the, er, nutter Wullie. With a bent broker and screwed scrappy in my pocket what would you do? They're now part of life's necessities.'

'Well, what are you going to do about his Beamer? It's still a bitsa.'

'Not my problem anymore, Wullie. It's the guy who bought it, that's got the problem.'

'You've sold it already!'

'Is there ice in Iceland?'

'Who to?'

'Dugald. He didn't have a car after wrapping the Beetle round the traffic lights.'

'See you, Sammy, you are *something else,* you know that.'

'Nice to know my talent's appreciated,' I answer, taking a bow.

'What if Everard says something tae Ella.'

'Good point Wullie. I think it's time tommy-gun Toni had a wee word with Everard.'

At this Toni takes his leave and heads for the phone.

'By the way how *did* you know Nutter was his partner?

'Let's just say Everard's ex-wife, Olive, doesn't like him very much.'

'Where did you meet her?'

'You know those Tory cheese and wine thingies that Ella keeps wanting me to go to?'

'Aye.'

'Well they're a hotbed of gossip. Wall to wall scandal. Had a nice wee chat with Olive and she told me.'

'Told you, just like that?'

'Er. Mmm. Let's not go there. Eh?'

'Sammy, you didn't?'

'When needs must Wullie. *Only* when needs must.'

'Sammy!'

'What?'

'Can I come tae the next one wie you?'

'What you! Amongst all them Tory poofters you don't like. *I couldnae* do that to you.'

In the background I can hear Toni speaking, 'Toni here, Mr Insurance man. I hear you're still chairman of the Conservative Club. Oh! Youva retired. Thata good decision fora your health.'

A good day's work.

I am quietly sitting at the kitchen table enjoying my coffee, awaiting a phone call from Wullie which is has been planned to coincide with Ella having breakfast with me, when suddenly the kitchen door swings violently open, the Victorian hinges registering their usual protest. Ella barges in, any form of her ladylike elegance missing, to stand directly in front of me, both hands on hips, and a snarl on her lips, 'Right you. What've you done wie our chairman?'

'Don't know what you're talking about Ella.'

'Don't come the bag wie me. You meet him. You sell him a car. Suddenly he's gone. Retired.'

'So what's that got to do with me?'

'It's got your shenanigans written all over it.'

'My shenanigans? Nothing to do with me. Honest.'

'Sammy. Every time I hear you say honest I know you're lying.'

I sneak a look at my watch. Wullie's call is due. My last words to him last night were – remember, no later than nine o'clock. With that my mobile rings.

I answer, 'Sammy Robb speaking…..'

*'Sammy, It's me. I know you don't want tae speak to me really so I'll hang up now.'* At least he's had the sense to hang up this time.

'…Yes Inspector.' *Pause.* 'I canny believe that.' *After a long pause.* 'She'll be devastated to hear that, Inspector.' *Looking suspiciously at Ella. After another long pause.* 'Thank you Inspector.'

'What was that all about?' asks, an anxious Ella.

'Well Ella, I'm sorry to tell you this but that BMW your chairman, Everard, traded in to me - was a bitsa.' Ella having been in the trade knows what I'm on about.

'Don't be daft Sammy. If it was, he obviously didn't know it was.'

'Sorry Ella, he knew all right. That was Inspector Carr, motor division, confirming to me that they've suspected Everard of being "Mr Big" for some time but had no evidence. Until now - me.'

'You've got to be joking Sammy.'

'No Ella, the police are out searching for him right now - *and* his girlfriend,' I add for devilment on remembering something Olive, Everard's ex, told me. This brings an embarrassed flush to Ella's cheeks. Why, I wonder? So I add, 'Her description could fit *you*.' To which she blushes an even deeper red. Blushing. Not like Ella.

'Sammy you tease. What was that about someone being devastated?' I note the expert change of subject and elect to let it go.

'That someone was - *you* Ella.'

'Me. Why?'

'Well being the secretary, I knew you'd be devastated by the further news.'

'What further news, Sammy?' An edge of panic creeping into her voice.

'The police suspect your treasurer of being an accomplice. Whoever *he* is.'

'It's not a *he* - it's a *me*,' wails Ella in total panic.

'I thought you were secretary?'

'You know I'm the *treasurer*. You attended my inauguration do,' screeches a now panic-striken Ella.

'Oh! My God, it is *you* then. Your'e his accomplice. I'm *shocked,* Ella, truly shocked. How could you?

'Sammy, I don't know a thing about it, honest.'

'You know Ella every time I hear you say honest I know you're lying.'

'Stop it, Sammy. Please stop it. What will I do?' she cries near to tears.

'I suppose you could flee the country before the plods catch up with you or, maybe…'

'Yes, yes, Sammy. Anything, anything,' she pleads.

'Or maybe…. I could drop the case but it would depend on……'

'Depend on what, Sammy? Just tell me….. *anything*,' she pleads as I advance towards her and the table edge.

Before falling asleep that night, I drift into an abyss of jumbled thoughts:

Ella's blushing embarrassments. Never seen that happen before. Never ever. Ella and Everard an item? Why not? He's a good looking suave city gentleman. Just her type. Chairman – treasurer. A close contact relationship. Ella's wealth. Remembering Nigel, I can't afford to make anymore wrong circumstantial errors…..Zzzzzzzzzzzz.

# CHAPTER EIGHTEEN

## THE MASTER PLAN

As Wullie and myself, having arranged to meet after work for a drink, are walking up the road to Rileys, I'm just finishing off one of my politicals on the evils of the European Union, of which there are many, but on this occasion I'm venting my wrath on bananas, 'Can you credit it Wullie, them *unelected* nutters in Brussels telling us tae straighten out our bananas. I ask you – straight bananas! Next the Polo mint will have tae fill in the hole in case someone gets their tongue stuck in it.'

'Talking of nutters, look who's outside Rileys – Zeke.'

'That's a bit harsh, Wullie. He's only a wee bit dolly dimple.'

'Starting a queue Zeke,' I query, on arriving outside Rileys.

'N-n-no. Sammy, I've j-just been p-put out t-t-temporar..ily, for swearing.'

'Out temporarily?'

'I-I-I've been put out wie exten-nu-tat-tat-ing c-c-ircumst…'

'Extenuating circumstances,' I finish for him. Now that's a first. Agnes allowing "extenuating circumstances" on swearing. Mind you they must have been really extenuating because she's given him a bar-stool to sit on.

'Thanks S-Sammy.'

'What were they?'

'I h-h-havnae sp-spent all ma f-fruit m-m-m-machine winnings – yet.'

'You actually won on *that* machine. Now there's a first.'

'Aye, S..Sammy. I've got a s..s.system. It's a s..s..secret. I c..c..annae even tell y..you.'

He better enjoy it while he can, she'll have the machine "fixed" again by tomorrow.

The conniving harridan at her best.

Clapping Zeke on the shoulder and shaking our heads in disgust we enter through those magnificent swing doors that used to welcome the weary but now seem only for the abused since the arrival of, Agnes, the ignoramus.

'Lesson to be learned there Wullie. Never show Agnes your plums,' I voice.

'It would take a brave man to do that. Wouldn't it now, Sammy?' He says with *that* knowing smirk. Don't worry I'll get my own back on him – eventually.

By this time we are at the bar. Agnes bears down on us, 'I hope him outside's no been putting queer notions intae your heids. He needed the fresh air.'

'Like a fart needs a *light*,' Wullie angrily retorts, still fuming at the way Zeke's been treated as he by-passes the bar and heads for a seat.

'Whit did he say?'

'He said you're quite *right,* Agnes,' I reply, trying to diffuse the situation.

She then gives me the Quasimodo's mother's moronic grin, asking, 'Will it be the usual then Sammy?'

'Aye.'

'I hope you havnae forgotten you know what Sammy,' lifting a tattooed muscle bound arm to her ear, simulating a phone, as she pulls the pints with the other.

With the arrival of the drinks I grab them and beat a hasty retreat towards Wullie's table. I've forgotten to lift the nuts. Sod them they can stay where they are. They've caused enough trouble.

Joining Wullie, I fume, 'She'll need tae go, Wullie. I've had enough tae last me…'

'Listen, Sammy, you could dae us all a favour if you'd just shag her and get it done wie. You know you won't get any peace till ye dae.'

'Grrrrrr.'

With that a passing Geeza interrupts, 'Whit are you up tae Sammy, growlin like a lion?'

'Trying to figure out a way to get rid of *her*,' I reply, with thumb gesture towards bar.

'Listen, Sammy, think aboot this. Naebody's ever *actually* stood up to her. Maybe if wan of us did it would strike terror intae her heart,' remarks the brain dead, Geeza.

'Whit heart, and who in their right mind would want tae commit harry - carry in any case?' queries Wullie.

'Well we could do a raffle, to see who,' wheezes Geeza not letting the matter drop.

'She doesn't allow raffles,' I have to remind him.

'A secret ballot then.'

'The last time we had one of those, Masonic Mick organised it and wouldn't tell us the result.'

'Well, I'll leave yous two brainboxes tae sort it oot,' whines Geeza.

'You know Sammy, I don't know who's the worst, him or Agnes,' Wullie comments to Geeza's departing back. 'But you're right aboot Agnes, she'll have tae go and the sooner the better. Little were we to know how soon.

With Geeza's departure we are now being entertained by a gleeful, Spike, who has just been released from jail after a slight misunderstanding with weights and measures on his fruit barrow. He says "he cannae get his heid roon this metric shit". I don't blame him. Yet another example of European interference in our affairs. Mind you, now that I think of it, he was done a few times by the Weights and Measures before metrication. In full voice he is rendering. 'Oh! Rose Marie I love ye, I'm always…'

Agnes's voice penetrating the rabble shouts, 'SHUT-IT! Or you're oot on your ear.'

'What did she say, Wullie?' queries Spike.

'She says, it's one of her favourites but she cannae hear. You've tae sing up.'

'OH! ROSE MARIE I LOV….' Now at full volume, his tonsorial effort is brought to a stuttering halt with a sodden beer cloth hurtling across the room and wedging in his open mouth.

'YOU - OOT - NOW!'

'I'd be better aff back in jail,' says a disgruntled Spike, flying through the air on his way outside to join Zeke.


The pub's suddenly mobbed. Thistle have a home game tonight against Auchentoshan Geriatrics, an over fifty amateur side, in the Glasgow Cup. The bookies have it at evens.

'Ready for another, Wullie.'

'Ma shout, Sammy but wid you go. I still cannae trust maself tae face up tae her.'

Taking the offered money, I wedge myself into a gap at the bar, hoping to be served by Jock. I'm out of luck, he's busy down the other end. Unfortunately the evil eye of Agnes settles on me.

'Yes, Sammy *dear*, the usual?' she asks in her gentlest crushed glass voice. Looking around in panic in case any one heard "dear", I am comforted to find no one paying any attention except Twazzle, the bar drunk. After a couple of belches he gives me a wink and the thumbs up accompanied by a, 'Wa-heeee, Sammy, boy,' as he gesticulates with a rude punch on the arm upward gesture. Throughout this encounter I was aware of Jock moving behind Agnes and suddenly disappearing from view.

As she finishes pulling the pints she says, 'Just get your nuts, now, Sammy,' as she takes a blind backward step to the gantry. Suddenly with a nerve jangling, 'Aaaargh', she disappears from view. Looking over the bartop, I notice the hatch to the cellar is open. Seconds later Jock appears from the cellar with a smirk twitching at the corner of his mouth. 'I think she's fallen for me.' Take what you like out of that remark. 'Suppose, I better phone for an ambulance for the auld bitch.'

The pub babble, which had fallen silent at Agnes's agonising wail, on realising what has happened starts up its cacophonous chorus again. No further interest being shown.

Least of all Jock, who enquires of me, 'Did Agnes finish serving you, Sammy?'

'No. Two pints of heavy and a packet of…..'

'Dry roast nuts,' finishes Jock.

'There you go, Sammy,' he says delivering the drinks and nuts. 'Suppose I'd better phone for that ambulance now,' he continues, as I hear howls of pain from down below in between foul mouthed abuse being hurled at Jock about his parentage. Tut-tut Agnes you'll need to bar yourself for that type of language.

Heading back to Wullie, it suddenly dawns on me - Jock knows I always get nuts with my pint. Did he deliberately open the hatch…no…not Jock. He wouldn't, would he? Mind you the way she treats the old soul. Facts, Sammy, facts, not circumstances......my lips are sealed – remember Nigel.

When I reach the table, Wullie enquires, 'Did I hear a bit of a noise at the bar.'

'Aye, but it was nothing to worry about. Just Agnes - she's fallen into the cellar.'

'Oh, is that all, told you she'd taken a tumble to you,' is Wullie's final comment.

The eventual outcome of Agnes's near brush with death was that with her having compound fractures of everything, that was the last we were ever to see of her.

Not a dry eye in the house.


In the harsh fluorescent glow of "Giovanni's Fish n' Chip" shop Wullie waits his turn to be served. At his turn he is served by a very attractive brunette who asks him, 'The usual, Wullie?' said as she wraps his fish supper, '.....and extra vinegar?'

'Suppose so, Tina.'

'Not like you to be down. Not feeling too well?'

'No, I'm fine. Just got something on my mind and I don't know what to do about it.'

'Would you like to tell me about it tonight. I finish at eight.'

'Suppose so.'

'Right, go on then invite me out.'

'Listen you two, when you've finished any chance of a black pudding supper wie chips and curry sauce.' This from the guy behind Wullie in the queue.

'Look pal, this is ma love life you're interfering in.'

'In a chip shop? You want tae get a life pal.'

'See you at eight, Tina,' says Wullie as he leaves, giving the black pudding-man a hard stare.

'See you at eight then, Willie,' chuckles Tina, at the exchange of handbag hostilities.

At eight o'clock Wullie, freshly shaved, teeth brushed, mouth washed, after shaved, hair combed and in his new denims, soft leather blouson, smart sports shirt and casual slip-ons is sitting anxiously awaiting Tina outside the chip shop. Out she comes having changed out of her work clothes.

On stepping into the car she says, 'Something smells nice and looks good too.'

'Thanks. But aren't I suppose to say that?..... How's about a run out into the country?'

'Sounds good, but I stink of chips. I need a shower and a change then we'll go. O.K?'

'Great. Where to?' asks Wullie, feeling highly elated.

'Head for Kirky.' The radio is playing romantic mood music.

When they arrive at Tina's neat semi-detached she invites him in. Wullie, giving the lounge a quick once over voices his opinion, 'You've got it looking lovely, Tina.'

'Well thank you kind sir,' she replies curtseying, '.....For that you can help yourself to a drink.'

'What's your pleasure, Tina?'

'Surely you haven't forgotten already,' she chides as she turns to go up the stairs. 'A Bailey's with ice. Nothing's changed Willie. Believe me nothing at all.'

Wullie suspects a hidden meaning behind that exchange but is not sure it is as he thinks. Why can't women say what they mean? Putting the thought to the side he heads to the drinks cabinet and pours Tina's Baileys and a large Grouse for himself then turns on the stereo. The system springs to life with the crooning voice of "Ole Blue Eyes" himself - Frankie Sinatra. Always her favourite. Happy memories. Frankie is bringing the haunting "Laura" to a close as Tina glides down the stairs looking stunningly beautiful in tight designer jeans and an open neck blouse showing ample cleavage.

A dumbstruck Wullie does his gawping act. 'Cat got your tongue, Wullie?' laughs Tina showing a lovely smile as she strokes his face.

'You look absolutely ravaging Tina.'

'Even ravishing, Wullie?'

'Aye, both,' stammers a tongue-tied Wullie.

'Hope for us yet then,' coos Tina in his ear just as Frankie is warbling, "I've got you under my skin." Remember that one, Willie?'

'How could I ever forget. What a night that was, I never wanted it to finish.'

'You could have fooled me. That was the last I saw of you.'

'Not entirely my fault, Tina.'

'I know. I left to go to Uni in Liverpool. You never contacted me. I didn't think you cared and the rest as they say is history. But that's not the reason you haven't asked me out since I got back is it?'

'No.'

'It's runaway Rita isn't it?'

'You know?'

'Of course. Made it my job to know. What I don't know is - do you still love her?'

'No Tina. I've always loved you. Always have. Always will.'

'Oh! Willie,' cries Tina launching herself at him, and with her arms around his neck and tears streaming down her face, she sobs, 'Me too. I've never stopped loving you throughout all those wasted years. And I'm never leaving you ever again.'

A long, lingering embrace is broken with Tina questioning Wullie, 'So what's the score with Rita now?'

'Nothing. I've done nothing about it Tina.'

'But you're going to.' Not a question. An emphatic statement.

'Yes Tina.'

Tina runs her fingers through Wullie's hair whispering in his ear, 'Do we have to go out. This is nice and comfy isn't it?'

'Mmmm.'

I'm sitting in my office thinking about nothing in particular other than hoping that Vera doesn't break her nails, her pride and joys, helping Hughie to change the engine on a recent insurance write-off I have acquired from my new source, Everard, when suddenly there's a knock on the door.

'Come.' The door opens and in wanders the bold boy himself, 'What's with all the knocking?'

'Well Vera's not at her desk…..' The unfinished innuendo left hanging.

'What can I do you for?'

'Well, you know when you left Rileys last night - well after a couple of pints with Geeza, I ended up in the chippy.'

'Mmm.'

'Well, a complete stranger tells me tae get a life. Sammy, my life's in a total crisis.'

'So what's new? Anyone actually *wanting* tae drink with Geeza's bound tae end wie his life in a crisis.'

'No Sammy, you don't understand. The crisis is ma *marriage.*'

'What's brought this on. The rutting season started early or what? Or is that lassie in the chippy still putting extra vinegar on your chips?'

'Sammy, would you please just listen to me. I've renewed my relationship with Tina……'

'Didnae know there was one to renew…….'

'There you go again interrupting. Could you not just listen for once.' I nod confirmation. 'So as I was saying, she's told me to sort out my marriage first……..'

'Is that first before you get the leg.....'

'Sammy! *Please,* let me finish…..... So we can get married.'

'Married! Married! I knew she was putting extra vinegar on your chips. But that's taking it a bit too far, is it not?'

'Aye, married. This is ma big chance tae be happy and I don't want tae blow it.'

'Wullie, listen tae me…you *are* happy. You're the *happiest* guy I know…you're *not* married. How happy do you want to be?'

'No. You listen, Sammy. There's something I've been meaning tae say tae you for years…I'm envious of you and Ella. You're so together. Know what I mean?'

That's it, the vinegar's finally addled his brain, what there is of it. 'What! Me and Ella, so together? You've got tae be kidding. Every day's like doing fifteen rounds wie Mike Tyson. I'm left punch drunk.'

'No you're not. It suits you to make out you're hard done by. She's good tae you and you don't appreciate it.'

'You don't know what you're talking about. You want tae try living wie her.'

'Listen, Sammy. I've never interfered before, right?'

I nod my head, 'Mmmm.'

'Well, things between you and Ella werenae always the way they are now. Sure, she's got a quick temper but only when provoked. And boy, dae you know how tae do that to her - big time. So, she's a serial social climber but only ever for the good of Karen and you. Nae humour? Of course she has…she married you. And, and,' holding his hand up to stop me interrupting. '…she's a good, decent, person under it all.'

'Whose side are you on?'

'Naebodys. Just let me finish. She loves you. If you cannae see that you're blind. She just gets frustrated wie all your dalliances.'

'My dalliances, as you call them, didn't start until she started her nonsense.'

'Bollocks. You've always been at it. However, that *nonsense*, is what I'm coming tae. Have you ever given any thought tae whit it is?'

'Yep. Chuck. It started when she found out he was coming home and got worse when he snuffed it.'

'I thought you thought that. Let me ask you this. Ever heard of a "womans change of life"? And all the things it does tae their hormones and brains and things.' Silence. Broken by, 'Sorry, Sammy. I'm oot of order. It's none of ma business.'

'That's all right, Wullie. You've given me food for thought. Food - for - thought. Thanks, pal....Now tae you. Any ideas what you're going to do with Rita?'

'I'm going tae Tenerife, tae sort oot Rita, and get her to agree a divorce.'

'Waste of time. She'll flash her boobs at you, you'll go all thon queer way. End of story.'

'Not anymore Sammy. No more "Mr Nice Guy".'

At this I have to turn away to stop me bursting out laughing. Pulling myself together I reply in the most serious voice I can muster, 'Right that does it. You couldn't find your own flies never mind fly on you own. I'm going with you and we'll sort your divorce out together.'

'Sammy, you dancer, that's grrreaat,' he replies, punching the air, 'But - Ella won't let you go with me after that last time.'

He has a point. She won't either, not after it took us two weeks to get back from a week end stag party in Dublin. Long story. It'll need to keep.

'Ella will want to go with you.'

'No problemo there. She cannae. She's non-persona gratis in Spain.'

'How come?'

'A few years back, we were out together in Las Americas, that's in Tenerife, and got separated as you do after a few bevvies. She flags down what she thought was a taxi. It turns out to be a police vice car. So they do her for soliciting. Well you know what she's like. One of them ended up crawling on all fours, the other pensioned off with his nerves. Outcome of all this, after the British Consul's intervention, was that she was deported. It was that or be jailed. Personally I think the authorities made a wrong decision.'

'Well, would you believe that. Ella, never,' chortles Wullie.

'So, no worry there then, with Ella. All you've got to do is get them leetle grey cells working and figure out how we're going to get to Tenerife together.'

'I'm on the master plan now, Sammy. "Operation Rita" is at go,' as he snaps a salute.


The following morning over one of our rare together "in harmony" breakfasts I decide to test the water, 'I was speaking to Wullie, yesterday…..'

'That must have been an intellectual challenge for you,' she interrupts from behind her Financial Times.

'Says he intends tae go tae Tenerife tae see Rita tae get a divorce.'

'And about time too.'

'He wants tae marry, Tina. You remember Tina? This brings a nod of the head as she lowers the paper to eye level. 'Well she's back in Glasgow, working in her uncle's chippy. You know Giovannis?'

'What is this, twenty questions?'

'Well, he's asked me….'

She puts the paper down, very carefully. Gives me one of her lingering death glowers and in that penetrating voice of hers accompanied with a Kung Foo finger stab at me threatens,

'Look you. Dae you think I came up the Clyde on a banana boat? You're no going tae Tenerife wie him. Understood? Dae you honestly think I've forgotten that Dublin debacle. End of…O.K?'

I must have been sitting with my mouth open for she finishes, 'Shut the gob, Sammy. It makes you look more gormless than you are. If that's humanly possible.'

Well, that's that. A pathetic attempt. We'll just have to go with Wullie's "Operation Rita" master plan - whatever that is.

I was soon to find out what Wullie's master plan, "Operation Rita" was. Having received a phone call from him suggesting, yet another, "brain storming" session in my office, I sit here awaiting his arrival. No sooner said than I hear a screech of brakes then giggling from the general office, as he flirts with Vera. Finally as the door opens.

'Hi! Sammy boy. Our problems are over. Ze leetle grey cells av come up wie a stoater.'

'Fire away Closeau.'

Ignoring my jibe, he continues in an affected posh voice, 'Well, you being the proprietor of Barrington-Bell, high class motors to the gentry, will get an invite from Lamborghini to the launch of their new model at the "Tenerife Motor Show".'

'Hold it right there, Wullie. Tenerife disnae have a motor show. Paris - yes. Milan - yes. London – yes. But Tenerife – no, no, no.'

'Ella's no tae know that, is she?'

'Mmm. O.K, say she doesn't twig, how do I get an invite?'

'From non other than, Toni Lamborghini.'

'Toni Lamborghini! Give's peace, Wullie. We don't know any Toni Lamborghini.'

'Aye, we do…. Our Toni…. Toni de Pyramid.'

'You've *got* tae be joking.'

'Don't worry, I'll teach him what tae say.' My whole body trembles at this.

'Teach him to say what and tae who?'

'The invite, tae Ella.'

'No. Wullie. No. You *can not* do this to me.'

'You got a better idea?'

'No,' comes my defeated reply.

'Right then. When she gets the invite, that's you sorted.'

'And what about, you?'

'I'll catch an earlier flight.'

'Wullie, as I've said before you're not capable of going on your own. You'll end up in Timbuctu. We're going together and that's final.'

'If you say so. That only leaves one trivial detail tae sort oot, Sammy.'

'Which is?'

'Remember and book a flight wie inside toilets.'

As I rise from my chair, he throws his arms in the air, 'Just joking, Sammy. Just, joking. What I was going tae say was, Ella cannae see us both at the airport together otherwise the game's over. But don't you worry your heid aboot that, this is where my master disguise will come in.'

Words fail me. Having witnessed his previous attempts at disguises - disaster awaits.


The following evening Ella can't contain herself with excitement as she relates to me that Lamborghini have been in touch with her by phone.

'Sammy, just listen to this. You wouldn't believe it. I've had this most charming phone call from the most romantic of Italian gentlemen,' she sighs.'It was only, Toni Lamborghini *himself*. He sounded just like Dean Martin.'

'Dean Martin, indeed, now that's clever wie him being dead as well,' I reply. 'Did you use a medium?'

'No. The phone. I already told you so.'

Her blank look reminds me she doesn't do humour, 'So what did Deano want?'

'He's only invited you and me to the "Tenerife Motor Show" for the grand launch of the new Lamborghini Special Edition. Can you imagine it, Sammy, a Lambo in *my* showroom. It'll be the only one in Glasgow, if not the country.'

'Only if we get selected. We're not even a main distributor.'

'Listen you, you make sure we get selected - O.K. It's just a pity I can't go myself due to that minor bit of bother you got me into over there.'

Not rising to the bait I sympathetically reply, 'Well, if you don't go neither will, I.'

'Have you no been listening tae - a - word - I - say,' spoken in her old vernacular, all traces of Bearsden posh gone. 'I want that Lambo, in *ma* showroom. You're going and that's final. In fact I'm taking you to the airport maself tae make sure you go, ya scunner.'

Well, that's it I'm going. Ella's accepted there's a "Tenerife Motor Show". Regretfully, however, she's insisting on taking me to the airport. That I didn't need since I have no confidence in the "master of disguises" disguise. However "Operation Rita" is now set to roll. This minor set back apart, all is going well. How wrong could I be.

# CHAPTER NINETEEN

## *DEPARTURE*

Well it's finally arrived. Today's the day "Operation Rita" rolls. Wullie and me, after much nerve jangling trauma with Ella, are off to Tenerife to the lively holiday resort of Los Cristianos, to meet Wullie's wife Rita in the hope of securing an amicable divorce settlement. Runaway Rita's been gone for nearly two years now and unbelievably neither of them have been in touch with each other during this period. I'm not even sure that he'd noticed she was gone until Tina, the love of his life, showed up recently in Glasgow.

So why am I getting myself involved in his personal problems? Well, as you've no doubt gathered, he's been my pal from way back; to the days when we played football in the street together with a tanner ball and jackets down for goal posts and got chased by the local bobby through the back courts, got skint knees and had "jeely pieces" flung out the window to us. Now that's, real blood brother bonding. Since those carefree days we have been through thick and thin together and are still united in our unwavering quest not to be ground down by life's little obstacles. With a background like ours I just can't stand back and let him go downhill any longer. He goes out and comes home whenever he pleases, cracks jokes, laughs, drinks, womanises constantly and never stops enjoying himself. Keeping this up he could die of happiness, a thought which doesn't bear thinking about. You might think this all jealously but I can assure you I have his welfare at heart. Re-marriage is what he needs to bring him back into the world of reality. And re-marriage is what he's getting.

To reiterate, for my own benefit. Ella is giving me a lift to the airport. This means that for the success of our master plan, she mustn't recognise Wullie. We are now totally dependent on his master disguise which he refuses to disclose to me, confiding that if he does I'll keep looking at him and give him away. It's a racing certainty that a blind man will be able to recognise him at fifty paces. We then fly to Tenerife, settle his divorce and fly home, then tell Ella she's been entered in the raffle for the Lambo. We'll dream up some excuse for this when the time comes. Sounds simple except for the first hurdle; his disguise. Bound to be a disaster.

However, before Ella and me leave for the airport, I'm going to have another attempt at persuading her otherwise. If I could crack her, the master plan would have a reasonable chance of success. Let's see what happens. Entering the kitchen, leaving the door open in the escape position as usual, I open the sparring with, 'Good morning Ella, dear,'

'It will be when you're on that plane,' she counters.

Having now dispensed with the morning pleasantries, I continue, 'Listen Ella, I've been thinking about that. You've no doubt got your usual busy day ahead. Why don't I get Eck to give me a lift…'

'You were just thinking. Now that's unique. As a matter of a fact, I *am* busy ……..'

'There you are then, *problemo* solved. I'll phone Eck to take us.'

'But not *too* busy to take you, Sammy. I know you're up to something. Can't put my finger on it, as yet, but there's a something. What time's your flight again?

'Two o'clock.'

'That means check-in opens twelve midday. We'll have you checked in by twelve thirty. That fits in nicely, since I have an unmissable appointment at two.

Nice try, Sammy. And......'

'Yes Ella?'

'Bugger up the Lambo deal and you'd better not come home. Understand? My car twenty minutes O.K?'

'Yes, Ella, dear.' Back turned to her on exiting of kitchen she gets the middle digit.

I know what you're thinking - another pathetic attempt at asserting my authority. Correct.

As we're leaving the house, Ella's mobile rings. Recognising the caller ID she excuses herself to take the call inside, explaining that it is very important. Everything Ella does now is important. Thirty minutes later we depart.

My personage having being inspected for foreign bodies is found fit to travel in Ella's pride and joy – her Ferrari coupe. I fasten myself well into the passenger seat. The "Traumatizer" at Blackpool will have nothing on this ride due to our late departure. And so it proved. I must mention to her sometime that the hard-shoulders on motorways are not the overtaking lanes not that it really matters to someone who treats the seventy speed limit as a purely arbitrary guide.

Finally, arriving at the airport with my nerves twanging and with knuckles drained of blood I find I am still clutching the safety belt - deeply, deeply in love with it. As I sit there in a state of shock, Ella calmly says, 'You're not looking yourself Sammy. You're not worried about flying again, are you?'

"Flying? A doddle, compared with that ordeal I've just been through", I'm dying to tell her but the power of speech seems to have deserted me, so I just nod weakly.

'Are we parking in our usual executive slot, Sammy?'

An attempt at speech produces, 'H-h-head f-f-for the p-p-parking meters.'

Sure enough Callum's there, leaning against his second income, a parking meter, having a smoke.

'Callum. How's it going?' I squeak.

'Smashing Sammy. Oh! Hello….. Mrs. Robb,' says a very shocked, Callum, recognising Ella from a previously unhappy encounter with her in the terminal.

'Still front line security then, Callum?' I query, with voice returning to near normal.

'Aye Sammy. Promoted since I last saw you, tae principal security officer - second class. I'm just out for a smoke before I go on duty.'

'Are there any of those fascist armed police thugs still about, Callum?' enquires Ella . Obviously her last encounter with them still fresh in her memory.

'Yes Mrs. Robb. The airport's still on terrorist alert.'

'Good,' replies a bridling Ella.

'Are you off on your hols then, Sammy?'

'No Callum. Business in Tenerife.'

'Tenerife. That's the two o'clock flight with Scotfly. Sammy. I'm on duty for that one,' replies Callum, as he stubs out his fag. Looking at his watch he continues, 'Due on shift now as a matter of fact. Come on round tae our compound and I'll get a pass for you and Mrs. Robb.'

Parking up and retrieving my bags from the Ferrari, I try yet another attempt to bid farewell to Ella. 'Thanks for the lift Ella. See you in a few days time.'

'No way, *Sammay*. I'm sticking to you like glue until I see you on that plane. I know you're up to something,' was her reply to my generous offer.

We then proceed to the terminal building. I can tell from Ella's body language she is ready for round two with the police. As we enter the terminal there are unfortunately no police in evidence for her to assault. Pity that. One little brawl could have solved my immediate problem. Pressing on to the departures screen we discover the flight to be delayed by one hour due to the usual French air traffic control go slow.

On the subject of the French and their reason for trying to constantly bugger us up; I would suggest giving them a taste of their own medicine. My recommendation would be that it should be mandatory for all planes, over-flying France, to jettison their toilet effluent on it. I don't want to panic anyone travelling to France but I would in future pay due attention to the skies. The purchase of an umbrella might be a sound investment. Apologies for this digression but a day without learning about the devious tricks of our E.U neighbours is, in my opinion, a day lost.

Ella is not happy about this delay. This means the check-in will not now be until one o'clock. Her meeting at two o'clock will be running tight. Due to Ella's prolonged phone call prior to our departure for the airport, coupled with the Froggies going in the huff, the check-in queue is a mile long. After a good look around she throws her hands up in despair, excuses herself and goes to the "ladies".

I am now in the heart of the danger zone of our master plan. This gives me a chance to study my fellow travellers. I can't initially see Wullie, but my attention can't help but be drawn to an Arab gent two in front of me. He is dressed in a turban made out of what looks like a red gingham dish towel. A purple tunic looking to all purposes like a lady's sleeveless night gown is being worn over a white collarless grandfather shirt. Denims and trainers complete the ensemble. Facially he is of dark brown complexion with a lop-sided orange moustache and dark glasses. I've located the "master of disguise".

Can you imagine anyone, with even half a brain, disguising themselves as an *Arab* during a terrorist alert. My nerves, which by this time are in free fall, are not helped when he turns round and gives me a conspiratorial wink. I then don't believe what I am now looking at. Due to the heat of the terminal, whatever he's coloured his face with is running down in rivulets and dripping off his chin onto his tunic. His winking eye is now stuck shut with the running gunge. In panic, I turn round to see if Ella has seen this unfurling shambles. Fortunately she has not returned from the "ladies". Turning back to Wullie, I endeavour to signal, by virtue of covert hand movements, to the brown stain accumulating below his chin. He nods his understanding, looks down, licks his finger and dabs it into the brown accumulated mass and….tastes it.

He then, unbelievably, gives me a thumbs-up mouthing silently - "lovely".

A quick backward glance establishes the imminent arrival of Ella. With a further furtive overhead warning hand signal towards Ella, Numbnuts has the good sense to face towards check-in. The antics of Wullie have not gone unnoticed by the queue. There is a ground swell of low mutterings and gestures towards him. He's either unaware of this or is concentrating on eating his face, which I now suspect is chocolate. Either way my nerves are now totally shot. I need my "calm-me-down" pills. Had it not been for the arrival of Ella, I was for the off.

On her arrival at the queue, she immediately starts on me, 'No movement in the queue then,' said aggressively, as if I'm responsible.

I reply, still traumatised, in what appears to me to be a croak, 'Not my fault. They haven't even opened the check-in yet. Looks like it'll be at ….least another hour before they do.'

Ella replies looking at her watch, 'Sorry, Sammy. Can't wait any longer. I'm going to be late for my appointment. I'll need to dash.'

Goody, is my first thought, but instead of leaving it like that I foolishly reply, 'Not with Everard, is it?' The blushing appears again as it did when I mischievously mentioned to her the possibility of Everard having a girlfriend that looked like her. Interesting or what?

'Certainly not,' she bridles. 'How could you say that *after* what happened to him.'

'It's the *before,* I'm interested in Ella.' Giving her my best penetrating stare. She wilts under it, as in all modesty most women do.

Her blush now turns into a scarlet radiant hue as she replies, 'Oh! Sammy, Sammy, it was a nothingness. Just a mild infatuation. Nothing, *and I mean nothing* happened, honest.'

'You know Ella, every time I hear you saying honest I know you're lying…….'

She moves fast throwing her arms round my neck and on kissing me brings forth a loud cheer from the waiting queue.

This brings her blush back and lowering her voice to a whisper she says, 'Sammy, there's only ever been one man in my life - you. I love you to bits. It's just you're so infuriating. So…so…'

'Loveable,' I add, feeling slightly euphoric.

'Yes. Loveable, even with your devious ways, your sarcasm, your…….. I just love you, but I know you don't love me anymore and I fully understand why. I've behaved terrible towards you.'

'That - is - true, Ella, you have. But believe it or not, I do - love - you.'

'That's what I wanted to hear. Look Sammy, I've got a lot to tell you,' she says checking her watch. 'But if I don't go now I'm going to be late for my meeting. It's very important to me *and you*, believe me, otherwise I wouldn't go. I'll tell you all about it when you get back. But before I go, tell William he looks stupid dressed as an Arab. And remember and make sure he gets that divorce. Tina's lovely. She'll be good for him.'

I just numbly nod being totally gobsmacked. She knows. All the planning for nothing.

'H..how d..did you know?' I stutter, stupidly.

'You told me. Tina, Giovannis, chippy. Ring a bell? Took a run into to see her. Somebody, forgot to tell her not to tell me anything. Didn't they? Incidentally you can tell Toni he does a good Dean Martin.'

'You know about him, as well?'

'As soon as he tried to flog me a pyramid,' she laughs, in that catching adorable way of hers she can turn on when she wants to.

'But why all the pretence?'

'Well, I wouldn't have, had I known what I know now….that you still love me….,' This elicits a cheer from the bored waiting queue. Lowering her voice she continues, 'I just didn't think you did any more….,' and with tears, yes real tears, welling in her eyes, '…..because of the way I've treated you. I'm so very, very, sorry and ashamed, Sammy.' With that the tears flow to cries of, 'Shame on you, Sammy,' from the weary queue.

'Ella, my love,' I reply theatrically, reaching for her as she turns away from me in a scene reminiscent of "Brief encounter".

Over her shoulder she tearfully sobs, 'I've got to go, Sammy. It's so important for both of us.' Then turning to face me, 'I love you, Sammy. Always will.' With a blown kiss she is off to further loud cheering from the queue.

I wonder who her important meeting's with. Important for both of us? Ah! Well, one problem at a time. I better tell Wullie not to bother with his disguise anymore. As I turn towards him….

WHAM! There's a crash of doors opening, a thunder of feet running and a task force of armed police storm into the hall screaming at Wullie to hit the floor with face down, arms and legs open.

He looks towards me - too late. I've taken shelter behind an extremely obese woman. As I peep around her ample girth I see Wullie spreadeagled on the floor pinned there by an armed officer with his foot between his shoulder blades and a gun at his head.

I should feel sorry for him as he lies there, but I don't. What I'm feeling must be closer to murder for the "master of disguises". An Arab disguise - unbelievable. Saner loonies are locked up. They frisk him and man-handle him upright and at gunpoint march him towards a security door. I recognise the door. It's the same one Ella was hauled through not so long ago, whilst practising her free kicks on the same gang of fascist thugs. Ella's words not mine. Personally, I think they do a grand job in keeping us safe from the likes of Ella and now, Numbnuts.

I hear, above the bedlam that has erupted around me, Wullie's, panicking voice tailing off, 'Sammy.. dae.. something... they.... think….. I'm …..a…… terrorist.' Gone.

I've a feeling I've been here before. The first thing I'm going to do is go outside for a cigar - to calm down. Then when I've calmed down, I'm going to think of some way of disembowelling him - slowly. Irrespective of Ella knowing of our little subterfuge, can you imagine if she had witnessed this utter shambles. A tremor runs down my spine. Too terrible to contemplate.

I knew he'd blow it, bigtime. I just knew.

# CHAPTER TWENTY

## THE ARRIVAL

Sitting outside, puffing my cigar and happily deliberating upon the demise of Wullie, I am awakened from my deep reverie by Callum, who has also come outside for a smoke.

'Sammy. What're you doing here? You should be boarding.'

With a deep sigh I reply, 'You're not going to believe this. Wullie's only gone and done an Ella. He's been arrested by the police as a suspected terrorist.'

'Never Sammy. Not Wullie. Just goes to show you. You drink wie a guy an you never suspect. All I can say is I'm shocked. Shock......'

'Callum - get a grip of your knickers. Wullie's not a suspect. Him and me are....'

I had to take Callum into my confidence. Nothing to lose. He is now part of the abandoned master plan.

'Sammy, you go and join your check-in queue but I don't think you should try to find Wullie.......,'

'Nor - do - I,' agreed through gritted teeth.

'....You don't want the polis to recognise you after that problem wie Ella. They might lift you too.'

'Good thinking, Callum.' There's maybe more to him than I've given him credit for.

'As a principal security officer - second-class, I'll see what I can do, Sammy. If I get it sorted, I'll send Wullie to you in departures.'

'You're some tea-pot-lid Callum. I'll see you O.K when I get back,' I tell him, rubbing fingers and thumb together in the universal money language.

Well, you've got to look after principal security officers - second-class, for you never know when they're likely to become first-class principal security officers, second-class.

At Callum's suggestion, I re-join the check-in queue. Checking in, I then negotiate passport control without incident only to fall foul of the now intolerable security delays.

Shoes off - toes peeking out of holey socks. Belts off; guys wandering around holding up their trousers with one hand. Security buzzers wailing - guys getting frisked for - for what? Invariably a bunch of malevolent keys. What a shambles, in an alleged civilised society. This I'm thinking, as I re-thread my belt through its loops and hop about on one leg trying to re-shoe myself as I head for the departures lounge.

How did this ignominy happen to us? Who allowed terrorists into our country? Non other than the usual suspects; our weak, E.U grovelling, brain excused, arrogant, never had a proper job in their lives - and I use the next word tentatively for fear of offending those of a sensitive nature - "parliamentarians".

We never seem to have been out "The Theatre of War" since the arrival of New Labour. For, I suspect, as long as we allow our illustrious leader to have a "Stars and Stripes" flag, a bugle, and a photographer, he'll be there, leading the charge into, Bosnia, Serbia, Kosovo, Iraq, Afghanistan or where ever there's a photo opportunity. Unfortunately, had it not been for the premature death of John Smith, a *proper* leader of the *proper* Labour party, I'm sure this once great party would never have reduced us to our present status of an "al-Qaeda" training camp as has New Labour. Sorry about the digression. Well, at least it's stopped me thinking about another total disaster – Wullie. Now where was I?

Reaching the departures lounge and being aware of the usual long and tedious wait ahead I decide to ease the pain with several large medicinal brandies. These brandies truth be known, are to steady my nerves for take-off. Not that I would ever admit that to anyone preferring, in this instance, to blame it on Wullie's pre-boarding antics.   After a period of ever increasing suspense awaiting the arrival of Wullie, I finally hear the flight boarding being announced over the terminal inter-com. Still no sign of Wullie. Playing for time I allow all my fellow travellers to go before me until I'm the only one left. Still no Wullie. Callum's obviously failed. Decision time. With Wullie, obviously on his way to Guantanamo Bay, can I survive for four days, on my own, without Ella or Wullie? It's ya-hoo time, a no-brainer, as I set off to join the stragglers at the end of the queue.

Awaiting me at the entrance to the plane is an absolute drop - dead - stunner of a flight attendant. Pinned to her tunic, above an ample bosom, showing a healthy cleavage, is a badge proclaiming her to be Penny.

'Mr. Robb I presume? I've been waiting for you.'

'Lucky you, babe. I'm available.'

'You old smoothie. Your pal told me you'd say something like that.'

'My pal? My pal?'

'Yes. William,' proclaims Penny, leading me into the cabin and pointing to the front row. There, sitting at the window seat is the bold boy himself, freshly scrubbed of his dark tinge facial and dressed in fresh white shirt and denims. He grins and signals his welcome by patting the empty seat next to him. Taking the vacant seat I manage, with great self control, to stop myself from strangling him there and then. The gentleman in the aisle seat next to me, after the usual introductions, informs me his name is Norrie and the woman in the aisle seat next to him is his wife Netty.

The flight, now being over an hour delayed, wastes no time. Seat belts click, in rapid fire, and with cabin safety instructions over, comes the captain's order over the inter-com, "Cabin crew prepare for take-off". At this, Penny, after checking the cabin door, takes up her crew seat opposite us. I hear the sexy hiss of nylon on nylon friction as she crosses her shapely legs. The old DNA dots begin their war dance. Looking towards Wullie, expecting him to be goggled-eyed, I discover him otherwise engaged, being totally engrossed in the airline's in-flight magazine – at the kiddies puzzle section. That's him at his intellectual best. Struggling to find the inner adult within and losing.

The plane, an Airbus 319, with its mighty jet engines roaring, thunders down the runway at speed. At each advancing yard of runway I screw my eyes tighter until at last, with an audible sigh throughout the cabin announcing a successful take-off, I open them only to discover the beautiful apparition sitting opposite me has vanished.

The trolleys are at go, ready for their daily fleecing of the passengers. As the Airbus continues its gentle curving ascent heading south to warmer climes floating above the marshmallow clouds I get my first opportunity for a nice genteel chat with Wullie.

With great self control I manage to stop my hands which are trembling in front of me from forming a strangle hold round his neck, 'Right Numbnuts, what's been going on? And it better be good.'

Wullie counters in a pseudo American accent, 'Nuttin much buddy. When I leaves yuh, I gets taken to dah interrogation cell where dah CIA attach electrodes tae my.....'

'Just get on with it, will you?' I manage through gritted teeth.

'See you, Sammy, you've lost your sense of humour.'

'Nae wonder.'

'O.K den. As he throws dah switch ma goolies begin to fry.....'

'Wullie!'

'Oh, all right then - spoilsport. If ya must know, Callum manages to get a word with me before I get dragged before the boss man. Callum, tells me not to mention, under any circumstances, my connection with Ella as she's caused a wee bit of trouble in here before. Knowing Ella doesn't do trouble in wee bits - it gives me an idea. They take me in to be interrogated by the chief fascist. He asks me why the disguise? I tell him I'm fleeing from a mad woman called Ella....'

'You - did - what?'

'Calm down, Sammy. Calm down.' I hold my hands up in submission. Wullie, then continues, 'Right. Well, a glazed petrified look comes over the boss man's face. He then rises unsteadily to his feet and enquires in a trembling voice, "Is that an Ella Robb of "Campsie Vista", Bearsden?" Correct. That's the very one - I reply. He's gone ashen by this time as he yells, "Callum. *She's back!* The mad woman's back. Put the airport on red alert." He then rises, shakes my hand and wishes me all the luck in the world, then disappears out the door. Callum then leads me out the back way into the plane - et voila,'.... said with an open arm, palm upwards, gesture....'and that's it. You couldnae make it up could you?' concludes Wullie.

'How long ago was this?'

'A wee while ago.'

'A wee while? And what have you been doing in that time while I've been out there chewing my finger nails up to my elbows with worry?'

'Just sitting here, with Penny and the gals having tea and biscuits - don't cher know,' answers the man of many crap disguises and lousy accents.

'Well, thanks a bloody million, there's me getting all, all .......'

'Agimitated?'

'Agitated.'

'See you, Sammy, learn tae calm doon, we're on our hols after all.'

'Oh, no we're not. You're going to....'

With that, our conversation ceases. The first of the trolleys pulls into the aisle. Penny opens a trolley drawer and comes out with a brandy, mixer and plastic cup handing it to Wullie. As she leans across me, I smell her sweet perfumed cleavage inches from my nose and as my DNA dots go into un-controllable cha-cha-cha rhythm she sexily murmurs to Wullie, 'There's a wee brandy to help steady your nerves after all you've been through, Willie.'

I don't believe my ears. "After all *he's* been through". With that remark, being a real pisser, not to mention his *free* brandy, I can't help showing my frustration at the pair of them with a peevish, 'A colouring-in book would be more appropriate.'

Penny turns, looks and chortles, 'Certainly sir. For yourself is it? Nothing too complex then, just the one colour do?'

Wullie and Norrie find this attempt at her child-like humour side splittingly hilarious.

When the trolley moves off Wullie nudges my arm and still guffawing asks, 'What's the in-flight movie, Sammy?'

'Nothing for you to worry about.'

'Don't think I've seen it. Who's in it, Sammy?'

'It's not a movie title, Numbnuts. It's me telling you not to……' I give up. It can get very, very frustrating talking to him at times. If only he'd go for that brain scan. Something simple required, 'You're - not - watching - the - movie - O.K'

'How not?'

'Right. Tell me why we're going to, Tenerife?'

'Don't tell me you've forgotten already.' Here we go again.

'Listen you. I know why. It's you. Do you know *why*?'

'O.K. O.K. Grumpy. For me tae sort out my marriage.'

'Now we're getting there, but we need to talk about it before we land. Like now.'

'See you, Sammy, you're getting tae be a real bore.'

'Look Wullie, it's for your own good. If you want tae be married we cannae have you wandering about aimlessly in life can we?'

'Married! Take my advice and keep wandering aimlessly, Wullie,' says Norrie, leaning across me to give his uninvited point of view to Wullie.

'Do *you* mind, Norrie. This is crucial to his future.' Pointing at Wullie, who has returned to his dotto puzzle in the in-flight magazine.

'O.K. Have it your own way but it sounded tae me like you were trying to marry him off.'

'I am. But I've got tae get him divorced first of all. That all right wie you?'

'You mean he's getting divorced tae get married again? He must be away wie the fairies. And you, you should be ashamed of yourself letting him dae it.'

'Look you…….' I give up. What's the point. He's as bad as Wullie.

As I turn to continue my conversation with Wullie I catch a snippet of what Norrie is whispering to Netty, 'Wullie…married…divorce,' hangs in the air.

'Sorry about that interruption, Wullie,'

'That's O.K Sammy. Did you sell him a motor?'

'Don't try to change the subject. Tell me about Tina, from the chippy.'

'Well, I've known her for years. Fancied her big time when I was young.'

'Was she the swot from Queen Margaret….?'

'Aye. I met her when I was on the milk.'

'Don't let's get on to when you were on the milk. That's censored.'

'Happy days. Remember when……….'

'Wullie!'

'See you, Sammy, you're no exactly a bundle of fun anymair now, are you? Right then - Tina. She went to Uni in Liverpool tae study law. She got married tae a Scouser and I lost contact wie her. Havnae clapped eyes on her in years until now and I still fancy her rotten.'

Out the corner of my eye I'm aware of Norrie leaning over to Netty and whispering,

'Wullie's childhood sweetheart left him tae marry someone else. He never stops thinking about her.' I wonder if Norrie works as an agony aunt courier?

Netty, in turn repeats this to the woman sitting behind her husband who in turns tells it to…… and so forth up the cabin.

I return to Wullie and query him, 'So what happened then?'

'She was unhappily married. She tells me it was all her fault as she couldnae stop thinking of me. She knew she'd made a mistake. It ended in divorce.' Wullie stops. Emotions, theatrically welling up he continues, 'Tina couldn't settle in the marital home and returned tae Glasgow….. Sammy, I need that divorce badly.'

I hear the cabin whispering-network behind me starting up. 'Poor Wullie. He's all choked up with emotion. Tina's divorced her husband but because Wullie's wife Rita's won't give him a divorce Tina won't have him until he gets one. Poor soul. Shame. He looks so yummy.' Yummy? This must be a plane load of female desperadoes.

Continuing my inquest on Wullie, I say to him, 'So, when she returned to Glasgow she went to work in… a *chippy?*'

'Yep. Giovanni's her uncle. She only works there evenings tae help pay her tuition. She's back at Uni finishing her law degree.'

'And that's where you met her again. In the chippy?'

'Aye. Sammy.'

'And that's where she's been putting loads of vinegar on your chips and turning you into a sex bomb.'

The whispering desperadoes, having had the magic word "sex" relayed to them, rise to the occasion with their heads craning above the seat headrests staring intently towards Wullie. Even Wullie, in his sublime ignorance notices this disturbance and asks me, 'What's going on Sammy?'

'Just doing their exercises.'

'The ones to stop you getting DVD?'

'Try DVT.'

'Aw. Right then,' Answered in his usual glaikit manner when he's distracted. The kids dotto puzzle must be proving tough. Continuing, 'So there you are then, Sammy.'

'So there I am, what? We've got, she went tae Liverpool, married, got divorced then returned to Glasgow. Then what?'

'Well we've been…….. you know what.'

'You do, you - know - what - to - you - know - who, all the time so what's the difference?'

'Not since I met Tina again. That's, *the difference*. Honest Sammy.'

I hear a lone female voice from the whispering desperadoes tell the cabin in a stage whisper, "Wullie's the stable jockey. What was that you asked, Mavis? Is he still in the saddle? Hold on I'll find out. If he is do you want me to give him you phone number? Was that a - yes - please, I heard, Mavis?"

This brings about howls of manic female laughter from the desperadoes.

'Right then. Back to business, Wullie. So you're telling me that you and Tina are an item.'

'Yep. That's correct Sammy.'

'A serious item?'

'Obviously. That's the reason we're going tae Tenerife, isn't it? If we can get this divorce thing settled we're going tae....tae get married.'

'So you *are* serious about marriage.'

'Of course. Why'd you think I'm here.'

'That's all I wanted to hear, Wullie. Let me be the first tae congratulate you.'

The whispering gang have moved up a gear to crescendo volume, "Wullie's getting married. Wullie's getting married," is the chant. Getting hold of Wullie's arm, I pull him to his feet turning him to face the chanting female chorus. Frighteningly scary.

There before our eyes is the whole cabin standing, drinks aloft, with Norrie conducting them in singing Cliff's, "Congratulations and celebrations ...." A real tear-jerking moment. No wonder the tears start flowing, from Wullie, as he returns their good wishes with a hand blown kiss and a sobbed, 'I love you all – ya hear.' What a milker.

Wullie, is then woman-handled from his seat to be exhibited to all the female desperadoes throughout the cabin. As he is being dragged into the melee he shouts to me, 'Sammy, I love Tina. Please, please, sort it out for me.'

'Make sure you do big man,' says Norrie beside me.

'You've changed your tune. The last I heard from you, you didnae want him married.'

'That was then. Now's now.' Another one from the Ella school of logic. I knew he was a weirdo when I met him. Now confirmed.

The carnival atmosphere gains momentum developing into a full scale party for the remainder of the flight being only brought to a halt with the Captain's order for all to return to their seats and fasten their seatbelts for landing. Wullie, when he returns to his seat is a mess in more senses than one. He is reeking of drink and his eyes, which have given up all hope of seeing straight, are having a staring-out contest with each another.

He is shirtless with every available area of naked skin covered in lipstick. A bra round his neck and frilly panties set at a jaunty angle on his head round off his inglorious escapade. A photo opportunity exists. I take it. One for the "Honey trap" album. Wait till he sees this. Sweet revenge for his piss-taking of me during my traumatic Agnes saga.

The plane lands to a great cheer but with no one showing any signs of getting off. It takes much cajoling from the Captain, flight attendants and ground staff to slowly disembark the partygoers. Exiting I bid my farewell to a very smug and contented looking Penny. My brain goes into overtime. Has the Penny dropped….them. Was that her triumphal headwear Wullie was wearing? The mile high club. Surely not. He didn't - did he? The hypocrite. I've got to know.

I catch up with him at baggage reclaim. 'Still sporting your triumphant headwear then?'

'Eh!'he retorts. I point to his head. On reaching up he removes the offending garment.

'Bloody Hell, Sammy. Have I been walking around wie these on my....?' I nod. 'Who dae you think they belong to?'

'You're - asking - me? Last time I saw Penny she had a very smug and contented look on her face,' I retort looking accusingly at him.

Holding his hand up, 'Naw, naw, Sammy I know where you're going with this. Not me pal. I told you. Tina's the one for me and I meant that. I'd try asking the Captain if your nose is bothering you.'

'The Captain?'

'Yup. He was the one dancing and cavorting wie Penny.'

'Well, who was driving then while he was cavorting?'

'Auto.'

'Otto who?'

'Automatic pilot,' hoots Wullie and Norrie, who has just joined us, together.

'See.... see you two,' I splutter.

'Never mind Sammy,' says Norrie putting his arm round my shoulder. 'Just came to tell you, me and the wife think that that low mileage (of course) minted Focus you told us about, sounds a good deal tae us. We'll come and see you when we get back.'

'Only trouble is Norrie, I cannae guarantee it'll be there when you get back. But I tell you what, if you could see your way to a wee cash deposit, a phone call.... Thanks Norrie,' I say to him as I tuck the two hundred euros into my hip. Looking over at Wullie I see him shaking his head. I shrug. Being a captain of industry, twenty-four hour days are my business norm. He wouldn't understand.

As we depart the baggage hall a motley guard of honour assembles either side of Wullie to usher him out chanting,

'There's only oneeeee Wullie Leckie - only oneeeee Wullie Leckie – only oneeee….'

As Wullie enters from his triumphant strut through the guard of honour he is once again covered in lipstick. The once pristine white shirt now worn outside his trousers bears lipstick written names and phone numbers all over it. As he passes me I notice along the bottom of the shirt, 'Staying at The Arona. Room 520 - Penny.' As I've said before the truth being a stranger to Wullie, I start wondering again. Did he?

Touch down.

# CHAPTER TWENTY ONE

## HOME

Exiting into the arrivals hall we are greeted with with a booming voice cutting through the cacophony of airport noise.

'Hi zer amigos. Senors Sammy y Wullie. Zees way.'

The massive frame of Owen awaits us. We shake hands and clap backs, all round.

'Long time no see, the baith of yous.' He hasn't lost it. Articulate as ever, 'I wuz going tae ask you if you'd had a good flight but I can tell by the look of you, yous both have. Especially you Wullie. What have you been up tae?'

'We've been celebrating my forthcoming marriage. Rhino.'

Wullie, is the only person I know who can get off with calling him Rhino without having his head pulverised into ash. It stems from his days as a builder in Glasgow, where as "Rhino", he was known as being "thick-skinned and charging like fuck". Having used him - I know.

'Congrats, Wullie, but don't you think you should get divorced first?' observes Owen.

'That's, why we're here. I take it you know where Rita lives? I reply.

'Nae probs there, Sammy boy. All the ex-pats know each other here.'

'Good. What's the next move then?'

'Over tae there…,' says Owen pointing at one of the terminal bars, 'then back tae ma place. It'll be too late tae see Rita by the time yous settle in.'

Summoning the barman, Owen asks for, 'Tres cervezzas, senor. Pour for four.' And on arrival of the beers, 'Grassy ass, senor.'

Wullie, mouth hanging open, being totally dumfounded at Owen's linguistic skills remarks, 'Didnae take you long tae crack the lingo. Rhino.'

'Being a natural linguist helps.' Pity English wasn't one of them.

'Nae doubt this is our starter for ten,' comments Wullie downing his beer in a oner.

Owen replies, 'Well yous arenae seeing Rita till tae morrow. So what's the hurry? We'll finish this and head for town.' And oblivion. Well as Wullie would say - you're on your holidays. Enjoy yourself. And so ended the long day.

I'd like to say we were up bright and early to attend to our business but unfortunately that is not the case. On rising at the crack of midday nursing a ferocious headache and a bout of nausea, I dress appropriate to the temperature which has to be in the eighties, in tee-shirt, shorts and trainers. As I pass Wullie's bedroom he's giving out the full symphonic snoring rendition of the Warshaw concerto. At the bottom of the stairs I head for an open patio door. Owen is climbing out of the swimming pool.

Seeing me, he hollers, 'Hi! Sammy hold on a sec and I'll make you some breakfast.'

At the thought of this my stomach does a good impersonation of a volcanic eruption and coupled with a returning fit of nausea, I shakily answer, 'Two paracetemol and a can of Irn-Bru will do fine if you've got them, Owen.'

'Never without. You no feelin so good then, Sammy. Must be a wee bit of jet leg. What about, Wullie?'

'Let him sleep. He's a big day ahead of him.'

'You know the score wie Reet, don't you?'

'No, not really,' I reply.

'Well, I'll let you find out for yourself,' says Owen with a conspiratorial wink.

'Go on give's a clue at least.'

'Naw. It'll spoil the fun. Honest it will, Sammy.'

'Well, if you say so Owen, but I think you're rotting.'

Off he goes into his kitchen chortling away to himself. I hate that when someone starts something and won't finish it. Don't you?

However, his departure gives me an opportunity to look around. The villa is a large two - storey hacienda stepped into the hillside overlooking the clear blue sparkling waters of the Atlantic. The vista is stunning; looking down on Los Cristianos and Las Americas far below. The tiled patio I am lounging on leads to a double garage, outside which sits yesterday's run-around, one of these massively hideous petrol guzzling Chelsea tractors which I generally hate but given this mountain location seems somehow appropriate.

I'm enjoying the pervading smell of the bougainvillea when Owen returns with his breakfast plate overflowing with bacon, sausages, eggs, black pudding, tomatoes….. I make another hasty dash for the toilet. Returning I am happy to see that Owen has cleared away all evidence of his light snack. He is drinking coffee which he offers to me. Two black coffees later with heaps of sugar, an Irn-Bru chaser and two paracetemol and I'm beginning to feel reasonably human again.

'Nice pad you've got here, Owen.'

'No bad eh! Bit better than I had in Glesca.'

'Still in the building trade?'

'Loosely.'

'How loose is loose?'

'Space visuals.'

'That sounds out of this world. What is it?'

'Well you take a plot of land and have tae visualise a building on it…'

'Just like this?' I query.

'Aye. Just like this. Then I sell it tae you.'

'So it doesn't actually exist?'

'Aye and no. It doesn't actually exist now. That's where the visuality comes in.'

'The stronger the imagination the better the visual the better the house.'

'Brilliant Sammy. You're a natural. Couldnae describe it better maself. If you ever want a job….'

'No thanks Owen. It sounds awfully like visual time share tae me.'

'Sh! Sammy….,' whispers Owen aghast with his finger to lips. '… You cannae use the "T" word over here anymore or you'll get me the jail.'

At this point Wullie breezes in large as life; shaved, scrubbed, polished and in his new holiday gear. Back to front baseball cap, singlet, Bermuda shorts and flip-flops.

A psychedelic mismatch of orange, green, yellow and purple. My stomach heaves again.

'What's for brunch, Owen?'

'What about some bacon, sausages, eggs, black pudding, fried bread…' replies Owen.

'Just the biz, Rhino,' replies Wullie.

At that my stomach erupts yet again and I head for the toilet at a high rate of knots.

By the time we pull ourselves together it's mid afternoon before we set off for Los Cristianos. Starting as a gentle drive down through the glorious pinewood foothills of Mount Teide, with the smell of the pinewoods drifting in through the open windows and the warm wind ruffling our hair, all seemed peaceful and tranquil. Then, without warning, as we approach a series of hairpin bends with their sheer vertical drops, Owen increases our speed resulting in our tranquil drive suddenly becoming a terrifying white knuckle ride.   Taking a blind hairpin on two wheels, Wullie jokes, 'Did you see that sign back there, Owen?'

'Whit sign was that, Wullie?'

'The one that said – that was a dangerous bend back there.'

'Widnae worry about it, Wullie, the Irish get everywhere.' Replied without rancour, bearing in mind his Irish ancestry.

We finish the nerve-wracking journey by pulling into the harbour car park in Los Cristianos. Exiting the car park I look at Wullie and nod towards the port kiosk. He nods back. Veering off, from Owen, we head for the port kiosk and order two large brandies to steady our shattered nerves.

Owen, realising we are no longer in his company, about turns and joins us. 'There yous are. Nothing like a brandy tae cure a hangover, is there?' opines Owen, little realising that any last vestige of our hangovers disappeared after the first hairpin bend of the wild descent of the mountain. Finishing our steadiers, we take a short walk past the fish stalls and outdoor cafes to an apartment block overlooking the beach.

'Here we are guys. Reet's on the top flair. She's expecting yous. I phoned before we left.'

As I look towards Wullie he pre-empts my thoughts, 'Sammy, I cannae do it. You promised me on the plane you'd sort it oot for me.'

'I knew you'd bottle it – Chickenshit.'

'I'm sorry. Real sorry, Sammy. I just cannae…..'

'Aw, shut up and let me get on wie it.'

'Sammy.'

'What now!'

'Thanks, you're a *real* pal.'

'Wait tae you see what happens first…. Owen!'

'Yes Sammy?' queries Owen.

'Don't let Chickenshit move an inch until I get back.'

As Sammy disappears into the apartments Wullie and Owen sit down on the prom seats, looking out to sea where a flotilla of pleasure and fishing boats are at anchor. The hot, balmy air is broken with a ferry tooting its departure to the adjacent island of La Gomera as Wullie queries, 'Didnae see any signs of totty back in your house Owen. Gone celibate?'

'No way, Jose. Knowing yous were coming, I sent Rosaro back tae her parents in Barcelona tae give us peace.'

'She Spanish?'

'Aye, It's one of those mysteries, Wullie. There seems tae be a lot of them in Spain.'

'Er, eh, right,' answers Wullie, in a fluster, whilst trying to puzzle out where he's heard the name Rosaro before.

Just then a youngster on a skateboard comes whizzing along the prom. Standing the board on its nose opposite Owen, he says, 'Owen, the cops are in the square rounding up your touts.'

'Thanks kid,' replies Owen slipping him money and patting his head.

'What touts, Owen?'

'They're no touts in the sense of touts. They're ma mobile intelligence officers. My creme de la creme. My visual space executives.'

'I thought I heard you telling Sammy you were ligit.'

'I am. It's ma wee side-line that's causing a bit of bother.'

'Whit's that then?'

'It's ma special scratch cards that's causing a bit of hassle.'

'What's special about them?'

'Well wie the old cards you got nothing for nothing. With my specials you get nothing...'

'......For something,' finishes Wullie, adding, '....How much?'

'A euro a go. A real bargain for what's on offer.'

'Which is what?'

'A free week in one of the apartments. All expenses paid.'

'That seems fair enough. So why's the local council getting upset?'

'They cannae get their heads around my visual concept.'

'Why's that?'

'They seem tae want the houses built before I sell the cards. They've nae sense of...'

'Visuality.'

'Got it in one, Wullie.'

'How rotten is that? Not allowing you to sell cards for something that doesn't exist.' And never will if I know Rhino thinks Wullie.

Suddenly! Enlightenment - *Rosaro.* The name, which has been bugging him since Owen mentioned it, now registers, and sets Wullie thinking of Toni's recent escapade in a Glasgow hotel. Wullie, then enquires, 'Tell me something Rhino, are you trying tae flog this visual concept of yours in, Glesca?'

'Aye. Tenerife "Co – *Owen* - R – Ship" that's me. Dae you get it?'

'Aye. Clever stuff Owen.'

'Thought it up maself so ah did. I'm just tipping ma toe in the water, tae see how the market reacts before I go global. Should be aw right, I've got wan of ma top visual space executives lookin efter ma interest in Glesca. An Eyetie called Toni Lamborghini, used tae sell pyramids. Dae you know him?'

An emphatic, 'No,' from Wullie.

'Dead handy having an English speaking Eyetie on the payroll. I'll send him tae Italy when I go global.'

An Italian - speaking real Italian or even vaguely recognisable English would suit you better, Wullie is thinking, when out of the corner of his eye he catches movement.

As I emerge from the apartment entrance I catch their eye and signal them both over. Crossing the plaza they eagerly gather round me hoping for the good news which I reveal, 'All sorted Wullie. Divorce settlement agreed. You're h-ooome and dry pal.'

Owen then gives Wullie a lung deflating congratulatory slap on the back. Recovering painfully, he wheezes, 'S..s..see you Sammy, you're *the* man,' as he punches the air.

'Thanks Wullie. Tell me, did you ever meet the chef Rita ran away with?'

'No.'

'Didn't think so. Well you're about to - SCOTT!'

From the apartment entrance strides a good looking six foot athletically built black guy.

I say to him, 'Scott, this is Wullie. Reet's soon to be no - more - husband.'

'Pleased tae meet you, Wullie.' Spoken in a strong Glasgow dialect. 'Sorry if I caused you any hassle. It couldnae be helped, Wullie, me an Reet's madly in love. I always wanted tae come and tell you tae your face but I kept bottling it.'

'Nothing to be ashamed of Scott - bottling it. Not my style personally but I know that some people cannae hack reality,' replies an unabashed hypocritical Wullie.

'Come on up and meet Reet and…well you'll see…….' says Scott.

At this Owen looks across at me and winks. I wink back. I now know what's in store for Wullie but I'm not telling.

Leaving Owen organising his mobile intelligence units, Wullie, Scott and me take the lift up to the top floor. Pushing, a still reluctant, Wullie forward, we enter the apartment behind Scott who shouts, 'Rita love, Wullie's here.'

Out of a bedroom Rita appears looking much younger than her thirty eight years with her flaming red hair swaying luxuriantly on her shoulders.

'Hello, Wullie. Long time no see. Sorry I've not been in touch. It's just I've been pretty busy these past two years.' With that she about turns and re-enters the bedroom.

Manoeuvring Wullie into the bedroom behind Rita we are confronted with two white wicker cots side by side at the foot of a double bed. The room is large, cool and airy with a dazzling shaft of sunlight playing across the tiled floor. I lead Wullie to the cots. There, in the shadow of the sunshine, lie the two babies sound asleep. Wullie looks in, gasps, and wafting a limp hand with the other holding his head, pure theatre, he whimpers,

'Sammy. Sammy they're, they're……..'

'Black.'

'They're, they're………………………'

'Twins.'

'They've got, they've got…………'

'Red hair.'

'She's, she's,' pointing at Rita.

'Their mother.'

'He's, he's………………………….'

'Their father.'

'I'm, I'm…………………………….'

'Not their father.'

'No. I'm…I'm going tae faint.'

I point him towards the bed where he collapses.

'Will he be alright?' queries Scott, who had remained silent throughout Wullie's histrionics.

'Just get him a glass of water and two paracetemol. He'll wake up claiming to have one of his traumatised headaches.'

'Does he still get them? He used to say I was responsible for them,' says Rita as she follows Scott into the kitchen. Truth is he's been getting them ever since Jessie Kelly beat him at peever when he was a wee boy. Rita returns with the water. As I lift Wullie's head to administer the water he shows signs of coming round.

Sitting him up on the bed edge he groggily moans, 'Sammy, Sammy,' clutching at my arm theatrically. 'Black babies, two of them, twins, red hair. Have I been ……been dreaming?' He knows how to milk it.

'No Wullie. What you've had is a reality check. Reet and me's had a long chat. Here's the score. Are you listening?'

'All ears,' said cupping both hands behind his ears. He's recovered.

'Reet's happy to have a divorce. That so Reet?'

'Yes Sammy. The sooner the better so's Scott and me can get married for the sake of the twins,' agrees Rita holding and squeezing Scott's hand.

Pity she hadn't thought about that sooner. However, being diplomatic, I say nothing.

If I can keep Wullie in the permadaze he's already in everything should go as planned.

'All Reet wants is - could you pay the legal fees? I've told her that's alright with you.'

'Definitely,' confirms a still dazed Wullie.

'Good. That's a result for you both,' I affirm, anxious to get us out before he screws up my negotiations.

'Sammy. Thanks for everything,' coos Rita standing on her tiptoes to give me a kiss.

We take our leave. Divorce agreed. Everyone happy.

I oft think, in due modesty, that that's my purpose on earth - people's happiness.

'Right,' says Owen leaning on the bonnet of the Chelsea tractor, about to eat an ice cream. '…time to celebrate. Let's hit town.'

Another lost day looms on the horizon. Owen has been magnificent. Without him we were no-starters in our quest but he should carry, in all honesty, a Government Health Warning. He's a dangerous man to socialise with. Life to him is like dolly-mixtures to an elephant. One dollop and gone in an instant ready for the next. Time to move on. As the Russian saying goes, "After two days fish smell." I trust you are not thinking that I was insinuating that Owen smells for if he did it would only be of the milk of human kindness. Granted he's as rough as they come but is just as soft as the ice cream he's devoured in one gulp. Having said that I'm still glad, for my health's sake, to be heading for home to - Ella.

'Did I say glad? Help! Wullie. Help. I've got sunstroke.'

Shortly after Sammy and Wullie's plane had taken off from Glasgow Airport, Ella, after a detour to the town showroom, heads for her unmissable appointment. Slipping out of a humble Ford Mondeo, her Ferrari now being in the town showroom bearing a "for sale" sticker, she takes tentative footsteps up the well worn stone steps of an imposing town office. She hopes, fervently, that they will lead her to the rehabilitation of her former self. Reaching the top landing she presses the matching brass button of a name plate bearing the name Dr. Gavin Strangefellow, Psychiatrist.

A further few miles away Vera is leaving an envelope on Sammy's desk marked "Personal". Eck, being of a natural inquisitive disposition steams open the envelope to discover that Vera has met someone at her karate class who wants to marry her. Being as she's now pushing twenty two she feels the sands of time to be running out for her biological clock. She has accepted the proposal. Thanks for everything it's been a real education, I will love you always - Vera. The envelope is returned to Sammy's desk alongside the keys of the Vespa scooter.

On the way to the airport Wullie announces from the passenger seat, 'Rhino, That was some break. Nae offence but I'll be glad tae get back to work for a holiday.'

'Nae offence taken, Wullie. It must be terrible to be getting so decrepit, so young.'

'Well it was worth it, wasn't it? You're now free to divorce and marry Tina. And that was what this was all about,' I mumble, almost nodding off in the backseat. A few days with Owen can be very hard on your metabolism.

'I didn't tell you, Sammy. I phoned Tina this morning and she's over the moon. Sends her love tae all yous. She's asked me tae ask you if you'd be my best man?'

'Try and stop me.'

'And me as well,' chimes in Owen, '...Bags me a maid of honour.'

'No many of *them* aboot,' retorts Wullie to gales of laughter from us all, releasing the hidden tension we had all been feeling over the last few days.

As Owen drops us off outside departures and we bid him our fond and grateful goodbyes he says, 'Remember and drop intae see ma man in Glesca won't you, lads? Anywan that can sell pyramids is worth your while tae get tae know. He could dae you a lot of good. His name's Toni Lamborghini. Dae you think you'll remember that name?'

'That's one we'll *never* forget, Owen,' Wullie and me laughingly splutter in harmony, as we grab our bags and disappear into the terminal before Owen has time to think about the hilarity.

Standing in the check-in queue a sudden thought strikes me. 'Wullie, I've just been thinking. I suppose you could say we caught Rita *Red heided*.'

'Is that meant to be some sort of *Black humour,* Sammy?'

'Watch it, Wullie, there could be some of those politically correct loonies earwigging.'

A previous phone call to Ella, has ensured that we are picked up at Glasgow Airport. She confided in me, in a very friendly and loving tone, that she has missed me and that all was well and looks forward to telling me all about her important meetings, with...? She wouldn't tell me, but promises she will when I get home.

Could this be the emergence of a new Ella. - Me. What's there to change?

Meanwhile, inside the terminal Wullie asks, 'Are you sure Sammy I don't need a disguise to get past those fascist security thugs in Glesca? Could you just not let me wear ma moustache and walk wie a stutter.'

'Grr….rr'

'See you, Sammy. You've just nae sense of humour anymair.'

After clearing customs, miraculously without incident, considering the clinking contraband bottle noises emanating from Wullie's bags, we enter arrivals where I notice and return the wild hand-waving of a radiantly happy looking Ella. A feeling of ecstatic euphoria engulfs me – as I observe behind her the *Globe's* news-board: BLAIR RESIGNS Wa – hee, "Happy days – are – here – again, tra –la – la-la…."

# *Acknowledgements*

Being as I have researched nothing and have depended solely on my now rather aged and feeble memory I can only but accept full responsibility for errors relating to times, dates, locations and events. However, bearing in mind the story is a complete work of fiction and has no bearing to any living or dead persons, other than the obvious (Blair, Thatcher, Smith), does it really matter? The political opinions of Sammy and Wullie are not necessarily of my own persuasion but they are there purely for the benefit of the story. To those offend in any way I extend my apologies with the exception of the *New* Labour Party whom I hold totally responsible for the usurping and ruination of *The* Labour Party. Finally, I would like to extend my gratitude to my editor Pam for her unstinting guidance and tolerance without which I would have given up the project. Who just said I should have?

Norrie McKinlay
Tenerife
September 2010

.

Lightning Source UK Ltd.
Milton Keynes UK
23 October 2010

161808UK00001B/1/P